PRAISE FOR *THE FALL*

"The fast-paced but thoughtful second entry in Penn's divided-America dystopian Wall trilogy picks up ten years after the first....Readers looking for an action-packed story....big surprises, and an emotional punch will find themselves on the edge of their seats as twists and turns come their way."

—Publisher's Weekly BookLife Review

"The Fall - Book 2 in The Wall Trilogy, Brian Penn has exemplified excellence yet again with the second book in his dystopian trilogy. But this time, The Fall picks up with an even more stellar plot and higher stakes....making this a perfect novel for all types of readers who love the best in Dystopian and Science Fiction reads....Brian Penn's new book is perhaps even better than the first. With top-level writing, fantastically well-developed characters, and an incredible plot, The Fall is an exceptionally worthy read. With brilliant storytelling and an intriguing, most clever writing style, The Fall by Brian Penn comes highly recommended by Chick Lit Book Café."

—Micah Giordonela for CLBC

"The Fall by Brian Penn explores themes of identity, freedom, and resilience, set against a vividly depicted dystopian backdrop. With intricate character development and an immersive storyline, it draws readers into a wild journey filled with suspense and revelation. Penn's masterful storytelling and rich prose make this a compelling read for fans of complex, layered fiction."

—Kyle Eaton, Los Angeles Book Review

"The Fall, by Brian Penn, is a philosophical and introspective novel that explores themes of identity, morality, and the human condition....Penn writes with a lyrical intensity that often feels like reading a piece of music. It's thought-provoking without being preachy....The Fall is a richly textured, introspective novel that rewards patient readers who appreciate layered storytelling and philosophical musings....If you're looking for a book that challenges both the mind and the heart, this one is worth picking up."

– Literary Titan

THE

FALL

BOOK 2

The Fall

by Brian Penn

Published by

Ink Penn LLC

THE
FALL

BOOK 2

BRIAN PENN

Ink Penn
LLC

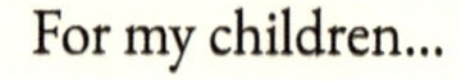

For my children...

"The best way to keep a prisoner from escaping is to make sure he never knows he's in prison."

—Fyodor Dostoevsky

Fan art
by
Jessalynn Adams

CHAPTER ONE

Asher

THE PAIN IS ACUTE. It starts subtly but quickly transforms into a violent stabbing. I feel like a fish trying to flop back into the water as the gutting knife makes its first incision. Even worse than the pain is the confusion. A moment ago, wasn't I fishing with Sarai? Taking in the aromas of jasmine and lavender? Her smile—a radiant glimmer of hope—oxygen for my soul. Now, I feel as if I'm suffocating. Perhaps I fell off the boat; maybe I'm drowning? Then I quickly remember that my time with Sarai is not real—not now anyway.

I can see. Well, a little, anyway. I am drifting in what seems like smoky lilac clouds. Soft and soothing. It contradicts the agony that I'm in. Translucent fish swim by me. I reach for them, but then they disappear. Am I hallucinating? Am I dead? I am thinking, so I must exist. I try to shout, but my mouth won't open.

When my LifeCell was harvested, it was relatively painless. On the other hand, I have heard receiving one is quite the opposite. Entering this world is painful and requires sacrifice. It's a prerequisite for creating new life. From the agony of a mother giving birth to the sore, calloused hands of a gardener. My father used to say, 'Pain is the ultimate artist. Suffering is the great sculptor of perseverance and character.' But why am I in such misery?

Then it hits me.

Protocol.

But who? Whose LifeCell have I reaped? Or, more accurately, who has sacrificed themselves for me? And how? Cephas was supposed to destroy this place, along with me in it. Was it him? Did he feel the need to atone for his past sins against me? My body convulses in anguish. My eyes slowly crack open. Through the blurry, translucent pink gel in which my body is suspended, I see who has culled their own life. I am momentarily relieved when I realize it isn't Sarai. Nor Cephas. My physical pain is replaced by heartbreak when I see who has died for me. And I should have expected it.

Floating lifelessly in the abominable pink womb across from me is my father.

Silas, the peacemaker.

He is now Silas the Lamb.

And now I'm Lazarus.

Asher

Cephas and Jude performed my resurrection at the behest of my father. They also monitored me for the two weeks it took for my body to recover in the rehabilitation chambers after they removed me from the *womb*, where I was resurrected. For the first ten days, I banged on the thick glass, begging them to let me out, to take me to Sarai. After Cephas mouthed the words: "buckethead" for the thirtieth time, I finally conceded. He couldn't hear anyway.

Finally, after day fourteen, Cephas opens the chamber. I yank the tangle of needles and tubes from my body.

"Good morning, nephew, how ya feeling?" Cephas says with a hint of sorrow. His voice seems softer, perhaps tired. The lines on his face are deeper and darker. His eyes droop closer to the tip of his nose, further from his unruly eyebrows.

I slump over, attempting to catch my breath.

"Easy there, nephew, just breathe and take it easy."

Take it easy? Two weeks ago, I was dead; the last fourteen days have been the longest in my life. Trapped inside a cage, wondering about Sarai. Alive, yet dead. But that's how I have always felt when I'm away from her.

I peer over at Jude and nod. He seems even skinnier.

"How long was I rotting in the *womb*?" I ask as I start to shake. All of a sudden, I feel bitterly cold. Cephas wraps a blanket around me.

"Long enough to be desperately in need of a shower," Jude sniffs. Good to see his sense of humor is still intact.

Cephas whacks him on the back of his sweaty head. "Nine months."

"What was that for?" Jude demands with false shock.

"You know what it was for, buckethead!"

"C'mon now, Asher has been out for a while. Everyone needs a little Jude when they first wake up!"

"Yeah, you're just like a cup of coffee," Cephas nods sarcastically.

I shake my head; those two are like an old married couple or long-lost brothers. "Where is my father? Where is his body?"

"Cremated."

"You had him cremated? Without me?" I say in a chafed tone.

Cephas sits. His knees creak, and his ankles groan. It's been nine months, but it seems he has aged nine years. "That was his request, nephew. He didn't want you to return the favor—sacrifice yourself for him, and round and round we go."

"There would be no Merry Go Round if you had just done what I told you. Why? Why did you let him?"

"I tried to stop him, Asher. He, your father, insisted. You know he is a peaceful man, but he is also stubborn."

Jude rolls his eyes. "Yeah, it's an epidemic around here."

"Of course, he would. That's why I told you to destroy this place. Why didn't you listen to me? Why!? Why, Uncle?" My anger is rising now that I have lost my father for the second time.

"I'll tell you why!" Jude snaps. "Because Cephas was going to do it himself. He asked me to manage it and give you his LifeCell, but your father had other plans, and you know how convincing Silas is. Heck, *I* would have done it if I thought my puny little LifeCell would work."

I shake my head; my breathing is still labored, and my lungs are still trying to find footing. "This isn't right. I shouldn't be here. This is a violation of the natural order of things. You once said, 'God has brought us home. Who are we to snatch them out of His hands.' I would have thought my father would have agreed with that. Don't you?"

"Yes, this may be unnatural, but so is a child dying before their parents. Silas knew you are the leader he could never be and that your work isn't finished here," barks Cephas.

My head is spinning. "This went against everything he believed."

Cephas places his hefty mitt on my shoulder. "Maybe his beliefs changed after he lost you. You did it for Sarai."

Sarai.

My heart begins to beat out of my chest. My lungs can't keep up. Is she here? Does she know? I try to summon saliva to my dry mouth. The anticipation of seeing her again is almost too much. But I need to deal with what is right before me first.

"This must stop. This place needs to be destroyed," I say firmly.

"That's the plan. We were just waiting on you," Jude informs me.

I take a deep breath of musty air and stand on my wobbly legs. Cephas hands me some water, and I guzzle it. The cold liquid snaking its way into my stomach causes my chest to shake. The indifferent lights above me reverberate off the frigid walls, causing me to shiver again. This entire place is a dereliction of morality. And I am one of its main beneficiaries. It's a strange feeling to know that anything I do from this point forward wasn't meant to be. Or was it? I shake my head and gag slightly as I start to smell my body odor; the rehabilitation chambers constantly work your atrophied muscles.

"And Sarai? Does she know?"

"She's outside."

Without hesitation, I sprint towards the door. I trip over my weak legs, but after a bit of a struggle, I pull myself back up. I fall again before finding the door.

"Take it easy, son," Cephas warns me. "There is something else you need to know!"

I ignore him. Whatever it is, it can wait. I must see Sarai.

"Perhaps a wash first?" Jude spits from the side of his mouth.

"At least put on some clothes." Cephas throws me a patched-up pair of pants and a torn shirt. For a moment, I forgot I was naked. I slide on the threadbare clothes.

Cephas clears his throat. "Nephew, I need to tell you something."

But I'm already out the door.

A whoosh of cold air chills my skin. The sun is blinding. My eyes struggle to adjust. Then I see her behind the Jeep. Her back is towards me. Her long hair whips violently in the wind, flogging her back. I can't tell if her hair is lighter or if it's the sun. Even her silhouette is stunning. My mouth is dry once more. I am more nervous than on our wedding day, or when we first kissed. This is a second chance I never thought I would have. And I do not deserve it.

I look horrible and ragged, my clothes frayed, my hair frazzled. Her beauty has multiplied. She makes the sunset look dull. My legs begin to flounder. I don't know if it's from atrophy or if I'm being leveled by the sight of her. I regain my composure. I take a step closer to her and stop. I am hesitant. Inherently, I should not be here; I should not exist. But I guess neither should she. Perhaps that is why fate has managed to keep us apart. Do I dare continue to tempt it? Or will the ground open and swallow me whole if I take another step?

She looks as if she is holding something, delicately rocking back and forth. Finally, she turns. I hear it first. A tiny wail penetrates the wind—a primal, guileless cry. Then I see something more beautiful than her, which I didn't think was possible—a baby.

My baby.

Sarai

Standing next to the Jeep, I watch the sun begin to set as I try to calm my son. At three months old, he is down to two feedings at night. Not that I have slept much since Asher gave himself for me. Cephas didn't tell me until this morning what Silas had done. He didn't want to raise my hopes if it didn't work. That explains why Asher's mother has been so sad of late. I hope he doesn't blame me for his death. My anxious arms rock our child back and forth. My jittery and restless legs bounce and shake in anticipation of seeing Asher again.

I turn. At first I don't recognize him. His gait is weak and wobbled. His eyes are flaccid and weary. I have never seen him look so frail. For some reason, I expected to see the old Asher, before he was sculpted to look like Amos. But, as he gets closer and more in focus, I see him for who he is: his strength, his sacrifice, his unparalleled love for me.

For the first time in months, I feel whole. He is now within feet of me. I'm afraid to speak. I don't want to wake myself in case I'm dreaming. The moment feels too fragile for words. A moment that shouldn't exist, yet here we are.

As usual, he reads my mind.

"Tell me we are not dreaming." Asher's voice is hoarse and scratchy.

"I'm sorry about Silas," is all I can manage to say.

"He did what he does best and on his terms."

"Much like his son."

Asher touches our baby's forehead. "Is it a—"

"A boy," I answer, delighted to finally tell him.

"What is his... what's his name?" Asher stutters. He looks utterly exhausted.

"Silas."

"Silas?" Asher looks back at The Mountain for a second. "Did you know what he was going to do? Did you know what my father was planning?"

"No. I named him today."

Asher holds out his hands. "May I?"

"Of course. He's yours."

Asher gently takes Silas from my tired arms. As his hands brush against me, I am overwhelmed with frenzied emotion—from heartbreaking love to bridled passion. I have goosebumps the size of peas. I shouldn't be surprised. With Asher, every touch is like the first touch. Now I know he is real and that this is not a dream.

Asher kisses our son on the forehead, and I can see that he notices the white blotches on Silas's skin. I wonder if he is thinking the same thing I am—whether our baby is wounded, like my brother was?

"He's beautiful," Asher says, almost as if reading my mind again.

"Yes, he is, like his father."

"I wish that upon no one," he jokes.

"So, what are you waiting for?"

"What, what do you mean?"

"I haven't seen you in months, and here you are in the flesh, and you still haven't kissed me."

He smiles. "That was the only thing on my mind until you handed me my son."

"So what? Now I'm chopped liver?"

"Sort of."

I punch him in the arm and then pull him close to me. "Don't think just because you will be changing a diaper tonight at three in the morning that you will be too tired to kiss me."

"'Too tired to kiss you?' I have not known you to utter such nonsense, Sultana."

I'm glad to see our banter is still intact. But something seems different about him; something is off. It's in his eyes. But then again, he just found out he had lost his father—yet gained a son—on the same day. Who wouldn't be changed? The irony is not lost on me. One Silas is gone, replaced by another. Asher in the middle. An unnatural circle of life.

But then, since my protocol, there is something different about me that I can't quite place either. It's not just the headaches and the sometimes unpleasant thoughts. Something else. First came the guilt. Then, a nagging feeling that every moment I now live is borrowed. This is true, but it is more in an undeserved kind of way. Like something I can never repay.

Which is also, in a way, true.

The one thing I do know is that, like his father before him, Asher will make a great father. How can he not? His first instinct has always been to sacrifice himself for others, at least in his later years. In fact, it's becoming his family legacy. I can tell by the way he holds Silas, by his look—a look my father never gave me. He sees Silas for the first time and instantly falls in love.

Just like us.

Facing the warm sun, my goosebumps finally retreat. Over Asher's shoulder, I see Cephas and Jude slink out of The Mountain and watch our reunion from a distance. I want to yell at them and tell them to mind their business. But that, too, would take away from the moment.

Cephas folds his burly arms and grins. Jude awkwardly looks at his hands and pretends he is looking at something else. I shake my head and smile.

Asher takes a deep breath. Why are we both so nervous? His fingers are intertwined with mine. He spreads out his arms, pulling me close towards him. His lips are now inches from mine, both quivering. Finally, we kiss. And, like everything else, it feels like the first kiss. Rarely does a moment live up to the hype. This does. I am lost in the present. Everything around me fades to dust. It is a rare moment when our being together is not at risk. When our love is not targeted. I am afraid if I open my eyes, he will vanish like the dying sun. But he doesn't. My husband has returned to me. Silas's father is here in the flesh.

After a few moments, he pulls away.

"What?" I ask, a tad disappointed.

"I... I didn't want to drop him," Asher responds with a sideways smile, referring to Silas, who begins to whine.

"Just as well. You need a bath."

Asher

"It's done," Jude informs me. Cephas and Jude spent the past two days rigging the inside of The Mountain with explosives. All the machinery, computers, data, and backups for performing protocol are inside. Cephas stands to my right, holding a detonator. To my left is my dazzling wife. She is even more magnificent since she has become a mother. It suits her, and she wears it well.

It has been two months since I came out of protocol. We tried to blow The Mountain six weeks ago but had technical issues with the explosives. It took a couple more weeks to procure enough to hopefully do the job correctly this time.

I am surprised at how much I have taken to being a father. No one can describe to you what it is to have that feeling. To love your offspring. I never knew how much God loved me until I had Silas. I get it now. Love is more powerful coming down than it is going up. We love our children more than our parents. God loves us more than we love Him. Even more than I love this treasure in my arms.

I hold Silas as he murmurs and coos. Sarai can't help but reach for him. "He's fine," I tell her.

A crisp wind blusters in. "Maybe he's cold?" she states.

"He's got two blankets on."

"Maybe he's hungry," she responds, knowing fully that he is not. We have gotten to know his hungry cries. Like an old couple fighting over a remote, we playfully fight over Silas.

Cephas shakes his head. He doesn't quite understand, not having children of his own. He only had me as a rebellious teenager. And that was only because my parents were gone. It wasn't something he asked for. He made sure I knew that every day. But he is a changed man now.

Maybe it's because I'm a new dad, or because I have been given a second chance, but I want to spend every minute with Silas. I sometimes argue with Sarai about who gets to change his diaper. Lack of sleep doesn't bother me; it's just time away from him. Time away from Sarai. I feel like

I'm missing something when I sleep. When I rock him to sleep at night, I realize I am holding a small piece of heaven in my arms. He is so innocent and precious. He is still unblemished. I don't want to expose him to the horrors of this world. All I have known is strife and war. For every blessing I have received, I have been doled out ten times that amount in suffering. But when I peer down at my son, I know it is worth it. But still, I don't want him to see what I have seen. Do the things that I have done. But I know it is inevitable. As we are all fallible humans.

I gently touch the white blots on his face and wonder if he will be like Sarai's brother, Eleazar. Will he be bullied because of it? Sarai says it will make him stronger, just like her brother was. I know I can't protect Silas from everything forever, but it breaks my heart to think about. Having a child has furthered my ability to differentiate between cruelty and virtue.

When exhausted, I sometimes second-guess my qualifications to be a father. How is this done? Does anybody really know? Who am I to raise another human being? But then I chalk it up to new parent jitters. I'm sure I'm not the only one with these doubts. For now, at least, I know what *not* to do.

Sarai, on the other hand, seems to have been born with the knowledge of how to do this. A mother's instinct. She watches me with a smile and gives me a look as if to say, "You got this."

I lean over and kiss her soft lips.

The past two months have probably been the best sixty days of our lives. We are at relative peace. Sarai and I can finally be together unfettered. God has blessed us with an amazing child. But I can't shake this nagging feeling that the other shoe will drop soon. I have come to expect it.

It has always dropped before.

She leans over and kisses me again, quickly lifting my dreary disposition.

Cephas clears his throat. "Shall we wait until you're finished, or should we get on with what we came here to do?"

Sarai and I share a laugh.

Jude elbows Cephas. "Geez, don't be such a mean uncle. You were in love once, weren't ya?"

"I'm pressing the button, bucketheads," Cephas informs us.

"Hang on," Sarai tells him. "We sure this is the right thing to do?"

I am surprised by her question.

Cephas stares at the mountain. "You mean destroying this abomination your father created? Yes, I am sure."

I know why she is asking. Without it, she wouldn't be here. Neither would I. And neither would our son.

"Doesn't it put us at a disadvantage?" she says, thinking out loud.

"What do you mean?" I ask.

"If my father reacquires the technology, he can have an invincible army."

I never thought of it in those terms. Renatus had always used protocol for himself and his cronies. I don't want to consider what he would do if he harvested at a massive scale.

Cephas brings our thinking back down to where it needs to be. "Yeah, but at what cost? Unless you have forgotten, someone must die for another to be reborn."

"Yeah, you're right. I don't know what I was thinking," she relents.

I understand. Letting go of this kind of absolute power is hard, even if it's the right thing to do. It's human nature. Ask any dictator. Or any politician, for that matter.

Sarai peers over at Cephas with a new resolve. "Do it."

"Here goes nothing." Cephas presses the detonator.

The Mountain rumbles and shakes as five tons of explosives combust within its belly. Small fires and explosions pierce out of the Mountain as it works hard to contain the eruptions. I hold Silas, and Sarai holds me as we watch the fireworks.

Unblinking, Cephas and Jude watch as if they are staring at the sun setting into the ocean. Silas will not remember this, but I am glad he is here to witness it. Another part of me wishes Renatus were also here to see this.

The spiteful part of me would relish in him watching his baby, his life's work, burn to the ground. Think about all the lives stolen by this place. All the families that were torn apart. All the undeserving who have stood on the dead shoulders of those they deemed inferior to them.

But if Cephas has taught me one thing, it's that I need to let go. Forgive.

The Mountain continues to belch small explosions as sections of it begin to implode. This calamity, this debauchery of science, has been destroyed. Let's hope it's once and for all. Let's hope we are the last generation to partake in such impure and immoral abuse of power. As embers and ash rain down around us, I feel hope rising. A solitary tear trickles down Sarai's cheek. She can also feel it: a change in the tides, a chance for us to finally be a family—something that seemed ridiculous mere months ago.

I look to the sky and close my eyes. Is peace finally within our grasp?

Cephas peers over at us as the Mountain burns. "Well, that's it, guys. No more second chances."

I can only hope we no longer need them.

CHAPTER TWO

Ten Years Later

Amos

THE CHECKPOINT BETWEEN ZION East and West is grossly under-staffed. The bus's squeaky brakes announces its stop. It is dark, just past 10:30 PM. Hundreds per day are migrating into Zion West, escaping the ever-growing fascist rule that Renatus has been implementing over the past decade.

A weary and spiritless soldier trudges onto the bus. One by one, he checks the passports of the reeking passengers, all in desperate need of a bath after their four-day journey.

Amos's passport and immigration paperwork are all fake, of course. His beard and hair are long and straggly. On the last stop, he carpeted himself with horse manure, hoping the soldier won't inspect him too closely.

It works.

The soldier peers at his paperwork. "State your business with Zion West."

"Asylum."

"Political, religious, or national?"

"All of them."

The soldier sniffs the stagnant air, ripe with Amos's foul stench, and steps back. He stamps his passport. "Approved. Welcome to Zion West. And take a wash."

Amos sighs in relief as the soldier departs. The bus's overtaxed engine starts up again, spewing smoke. He temporarily closes his window to give himself a break from the noxious, inky fumes. The electric buses stopped months ago, ever since Renatus ramped up the cadence of his Electro-Magnetic Pulse (EMP) drops.

Amos thinks about his childhood as he peers out the window, barely able to handle his own smell. His family was poor, even though his father was ambitious. But he wasn't ambitious for himself, as he was inherently lazy; he was ambitious for his son. He wanted Amos to become a Lazurite elite, not the simple patrolmen he turned out to be. As a young boy, his father was also timid and bullied, so he decided to live out his revenge through Amos. When Amos was seven, his father encouraged him to terrorize the other children. No way would he have his child endure being a sheep, as he had. His son would be a wolf. There weren't many other choices, growing up a Lazurite. You were a sheep or a wolf; there were no sheepdogs. And though he had brawn, as he got older, Amos just wasn't smart enough to be an elite. He could never see the big picture. Nor was he good at the political game. If he had come from the right family, then maybe.

But now it is his turn. His turn for power and fame. He can finally see the forest for the trees. Renatus called him a disgrace for being captured and bloodletted, allowing Asher to assume his identity and fool all of Zion. He even spent five years in jail as punishment. And after all of that, he is still out to prove himself to Renatus and his father. That he isn't just a simple patrolman. That he has the physical and mental capacity to achieve everything Asher has done, in his skin. If not more. He now sees his disadvantaged youth and lack of privilege as an asset. Many elites don't have to fight for their position. It is handed to them, based on their family line.

Of course, the weak are weeded out early, but at least they have a chance, thinks Amos.

A man pushing a drink cart wheels by. "Water?"

Amos raises his hand. "Here."

Amos pays him and guzzles the water so fast it slides onto his face, beads of fluid getting caught in his oily and musty beard.

"Another."

He should have resented Renatus for his treatment over the past five years, but he now considers it part of his penance. When you wrong Zion, you owe Zion. Or at least you owe Renatus.

This mission was Amos's idea. He came up with it on his own. It was daring. It had audacity. In fact, it was so good that when he told Renatus about it, he was floored that he hadn't come up with it on his own. Renatus also told him not to come back if he failed. This was it for him, all or nothing.

Amos hatched the idea at SeaPen. It took prison for him to become goal-oriented. There, he wrote down all the things he wanted to accomplish and how he would act on them—assuming he survived the SeaPen experience. He was beaten almost daily. It didn't help that he was constantly mistaken for Asher. Just looking the same as the *Traitor of Zion* was enough to spark a fight. But soon, he grew to like the dust-ups. In fact, he got rather good at them. It wasn't too long until he was taking on elites.

Two days later, still on the rumbling bus, Amos awakens from his slumber. The bus driver announces over the intercom, "Last stop, the Capitol. Please exit with all of your belongings."

Amos exits the bus and inhales the fresh, crisp air. To his left are the pacifying sounds of the Pacific Ocean. A sound he sorely missed. He spits in disgust at the sight of filthy Drecks walking the same streets that used to belong to the Lazurites. Some of them are even barefoot. The nipping Pacific breeze blows trash past his feet. *My homeland is littered with bloody*

Drecks! These streets used to be clean. A woman and her two children beg for food on the corner. *This must be their idea of freedom and prosperity.*

If he is successful in what he is setting out to do, he will have the power and recognition his father always wanted for him. He will have Renatus's approval. He will become a celebrity in Zion East. He will return to a hero's welcome, the one Asher stole from him years ago. His shame will be erased. His atonement complete. Maybe he will even be granted Second Life Rights. To people like him and Renatus, one life isn't enough to cement a legacy. There is so much more he wants to do. So much more power he needs to attain.

Just ten miles away is Pt. Reyes, Renatus's old compound.

Sarai and Asher's new home.

Now, he needs to shave.

Asher

In the last ten years, we have not had a full-scale battle with Renatus and his newly formed armies. They have mostly been border skirmishes and terrorist attacks. In fact, we are fighting one such skirmish now. I think he is testing us, gathering data on the size and strength of our army.

I have requested many times to march our armies into Zion East and end this thing once and for all. And even though my wife is the leader of the West, it has been to no avail. The newly formed senate, war-weary, is not keen on starting another war. They claim our supply of weapons and troops is insufficient to handle such a prolonged engagement. They aren't wrong, but when has it ever been enough? War is messy. I believe they don't have the courage, faith, or constitution for it. Evil and tyranny must be stomped out in its infancy. Let it fester, and it spreads to the entire body, killing the host.

The people have enjoyed relative peace for so long that they have forgotten how we attained it. Peace isn't a static state. Peace is fluid and requires constant effort and attention. The past ten years of relative prosperity have made our populace weak and complacent.

"Wait!" I tell my men, wiping my clammy hands on my pants. No matter how cold it is, I always sweat before a battle. I fear the day that I don't.

"But, sir, they are right below us. The timing is perfect," Kenan pleads with me.

"Patience." I am trying to teach Kenan the art of warfare. On how to become a general. However, more important than tactics and strategy is leadership.

My army stands on three different ridges, looking down into a valley. The Lazurites are slowly marching in between us.

I raise my hand. "Wait. Wait."

"But sir—"

I wait a few more seconds to ensure we maximize our advantage. "Now!"

My men on both sides push Rollers down the side of the hill. They are massive balls full of plasma and explosives. They barrel into the meaty part of the Lazurite regiment. The explosions send their men flying into the air. Some even land in the trees. We have caught them off guard. They immediately start firing their plasma weapons towards us.

I turn to Kenan. "Lesson one: always make the most of the element of surprise when you have it."

"What next?" Kenan asks as he watches the men stampede down the hill.

I retrieve my ricochet from my belt and throw a wink and an easy nod. "Why, we follow them, of course."

Kenan is hesitant. "But sir, you are a general, and I am training to become one."

I raise an eyebrow. "Are you saying we are too important to die?"

"It's not that. It's just who will lead these men if we die?"

I put my hand on his shoulder. "How long have you been fighting by my side?"

"Ten years."

"And in all those years, have you seen me once stay safely behind?"

"No. I haven't."

"You wanna lead men?" I ask him point blank.

"Yes, I think, I... yes, sir."

"Lesson two: men don't follow tactics or strategy. They don't even necessarily follow orders—not in the long run, anyhow. Men follow action. Men follow courage. Men follow truth and justice. Leading from behind is cowardly. Sure, this army will do what they are told. But you see those men down there. They would lay down their lives for me. Why? Because they know I would do the same for them. To be a great leader, you must become a great servant."

Kenan tugs at his bottom lip with a look of uncertainty. "But if we die now, who will lead them?"

"If we have done our job, they won't need us to tell them how to fight. Inspiration to fight for what is right will come from within. After a while, tactics and strategy become muscle memory. And eventually, so will courage. Look at them down there. Do you think any of them must be told that fighting for liberty is a just cause?"

Kenan squints his eyes. "I think I get it."

"Lesson three, you need to be sure."

"I... I am sure."

I reach out my hands and square his shoulders with mine. I can tell he is nervous. I don't know if this is his calling. But if he wants this, we will make a general out of him yet. He needs baptism by fire. No more standing on the sidelines. "Then show me."

I sprint down the hill, screaming a battle cry that Legion would be proud of. I smile every time I think of the giant. I wonder where he is and what he is doing now. I only hope he has found peace. I do miss Legion. My friend. Our savior. A Dreck Angel on my shoulder. I wish he would have come with me to help create this New America. What a general he would have made. A man of few words but much action. The world could use more like him.

I am pleased to see Kenan is right behind me. He fires his plasma rifle and swings his StunClub as we get into close-quarters fighting. I fling my ricochet until my wrist is sore. My men watch me. They are also watching Kenan. There is hope for him yet. It doesn't take long until the Lazurites are overwhelmed. Like I said before, a skirmish.

Unfortunately, none of them want to surrender. I'm sure Renatus has commanded them to fight till the death. For those who don't, something worse probably awaits them back home.

I try to plead with them. I try to spare their lives, telling them they don't have to return to Zion East. That they can join us and live free. That they can actually fight for something worth fighting for.

They refuse.

War is still a nasty business that I hate.

But.

It has become easier and easier to participate in. No longer do I see the faces of all the men I have killed. Now, it's just one big blur. What is worse, I can no longer count the bodies of the brave men who have died fighting for me. It is just a kaleidoscope of blood and tears. My soldier's blood. Their family's tears.

Fighting *for* me.

No.

Fighting *with* me.

Right?

Sometimes, I'm not so sure anymore. I wave my men over.

"Gather around troops." They circle me and Kenan. "Well done today. Once again, you have proven your courage. Your Dreckmanship."

"Dreckmanship?" one of my soldiers yells out with a laugh. "You just make that up, sir?"

"No, it's in your field manual," I lie. This elicits laughter and chuckles through my battalion. "And well done to Kenan!"

"Well done!" they bellow back.

I turn to Kenan and whisper, "Lesson four, inspire. Also, a little humor never hurt anything. And before you rib your men, be a little self-deprecating first."

"I think I get it, sir."

"No. Know you do. It's not only your enemies that can smell fear and uncertainty. If men are to follow you to their deaths, you better be damn sure."

A soldier in his fifties with a long black beard steps onto a tree stump. "I have a question. When is that wifey of yours going to let us march into Zion East and finish the job?"

A few hoots and hollers in agreement, but mostly silence in the face of his insolence.

Kenan steps up. "You don't speak to your general with such disrespect."

I place my hand on his shoulder and whisper, "It's okay, Kenan. Sometimes, you must let them speak their mind." I turn to Black Beard. "Once the Senate finds their audacity, that is exactly what we will do!"

Asher

Three years ago, the narcdrops started up again. I see one now landing in the distance. We try to shoot their drones down before they cross the border, but there are just too many of them. A group of addicts scuttles towards the pallet, teeming with demondust and God only knows what else. I recognize one of the addicts—a young soldier under my command. This is another reason we lack the number of troops we need. Cephas wants Sarai and I to re-instate a draft. I won't do it. If you have to force a soldier to fight for his or her freedom, then I don't want them in my army.

The soldier, who I think is named Timothy, eyes me, then quickly turns his head in shame.

I wave him over. "Timothy, come here, soldier."

Skittish and somewhat humiliated, he slinks his shoulders and marches over to me. "Asher, sir, how was the patrol?"

"You have a baby at home, don't you, soldier?"

"Yes, sir, ten months old. A boy."

I place my hand on his shoulder and nod toward the narcdrop. "What are you doing, soldier? You know better than this."

"Yes, sir. I am sorry, sir. I will do better in the future."

I hand him a card with an address on it. "Go see Cephas. He leads a group. I think it could help you."

"I will, sir. Thank you, sir."

"And go home, Timothy. Go see your wife and your son." Which is, ironically, where I want to be right now.

"Yes, sir." He turns and stops, "Sir, am I still enlisted in your army?"

I feign like I'm thinking about it. I want him to know how serious this is. I want him to turn away from it. "Yes, soldier. But next time I see you near a narcdrop, it better be because you are bringing it to one of our eradication centers."

"Of course, sir. Thank you, sir!"

Watching him, my soul feels heavy for a moment. I sometimes forget the burden my people have been through. I adopt a softer tone. "And Timothy,

I get it that things are rough right now. That rebuilding isn't easy. But it won't always be this way. Things will get better. We will make it better by being vigilant and making the hard choices. The right choices."

"That's why I'm in your army, sir."

He runs off. I receive a few salutes as I trudge through town. To my right, gleaming on a HoloTube is my wife, softly uttering her campaign slogan: "Re-elect Sarai for Prime Servant. Honesty, integrity, hope." Prime Servant. That was her idea. It sounds better than President or Sovereign. She wanted to convey the idea that we are meant to be servant leaders. For the people, of the people. Over the past hundred years, there is barely any evidence that we ever had a Constitution. The document has been shredded; our country is fractured. Sarai wants to change that, and I intend to help her.

To my left is another campaign ad from her primary opponent: "Vote Neriah for your Prime Servant. To end the corruption and bring back order. For peace and prosperity. We can do better. We must do better."

Corruption? It's just one of the many things we have been accused of. After doing this for ten years, I am convinced all politicians are liars. Or, at the very least, truth-benders. Except for my wife, of course. She understands that one cannot truly serve without sacrifice. She has also learned very quickly what a dirty game politics can be. When she first decided to run, I told her from the onset, *Don't be that politician who tries to please everyone. Don't be the one to look at polls.* People's views and wants change like the wind. Feelings are fickle. It's our steadfast principles that should never change. Emotions are like a wayward butterfly drifting in the breeze. Chasing votes is like trying to catch that butterfly with your teeth.

"Asher! Liberator of Zion!" Two twin boys, about ten, run up to me. "Can we get a picture?"

"Just Asher, boys." I hate the many surnames people keep coming up with for me. Liberator of Zion. Vanquisher of Legion. Savior of the

Drecks. Asher the Audacious. Yes, I did kill a shark once with nothing but a metal boomerang. But c'mon, these monikers are getting ridiculous.

I bend down next to them as their mother pulls out her camera. One of the boys peers at my ricochet.

"Wanna hold it?"

"Can I?" he asks with a toothy smile.

"Just don't throw it at your brother," I joke, handing it to him. He holds it up for the camera, partially covering his dirty face and grimy hair. During the pictures, I can hear both of their stomachs rumble. Their mother is skinny and dressed in oversized rags.

He returns my ricochet and peers up at me with wistful green eyes. "One day, when I'm your age, I will have a ricochet and fight the Lazurites!"

"I pray when you're my age, the war will be over." I pat him on the head. "Now run along and be good."

"Thank you," the mother says kindly.

"When is the last time they ate?" I ask her.

She also lowers her head in shame. "Yesterday. You see, I work when I can, but their father, my husband, he—" She nods in the direction of the narcdrop.

"We are doing what we can," I say empathetically and hand her all the spare money I have in my pockets.

"Thank you so much, Asher." She turns to leave and stops. "And I am voting for your wife."

I watch her children run and throw curved sticks at each other like ricochets and laugh. I long for their innocence and naiveté, their pure thoughts.

Since I went through protocol, a battle has been waging in my head to hold onto virtuous thoughts. I've noticed the changes more and more. I have even become callous to the horrors of war. Am I still the Asher my father envisioned? The one my uncle hoped for?

My headache has returned. I need to be home.

Sarai

I am no longer afraid of the ocean. Like tiny, coarse fingers, the sand massages my bare feet. I watch Silas build and destroy mini sand castles at the water's edge. Sunscreen and a large hat protect his hypo-pigmented skin and eyes. After the ceaseless bullying, he is now home-schooled. They made fun of his wide mouth and the large gaps between his teeth. Called him a ghost on account of his skin. They would mimic his shaking and call him a demonduster, who is itching for his next fix.

But as I did for my brother, Eleazar, I see nothing but deep and pure love. Silas's seizures have worsened over the last few months, and every time he shakes, my heart stops beating. It feels like the entire earth shakes with him. He is our own *wounded prince*. Now I know what my father felt. Silas's speech has improved, though. And even though it looks bad this close to the election, Asher has insisted on the best tutors and private in-house doctors.

"Hey mom, does Eden exist?" Silas asks me out of the blue, as he tends to do.

"Eden? Where did you hear about that?"

"Billy told me. Can we go sometime?"

"Why?" I ask.

"I hear it's full of gold!"

"It's a myth from the old world sweetie. Besides, gold isn't the most important thing, is it?"

"No."

"What is?"

"Family."

"And speaking of family." I point towards the hill.

Asher. I see him descend the rocky hillside and make his way onto the sand. The years have been hard on him. His hair is now completely gray. So is his thick stubble, thanks to his three-day patrol. He is lean, probably leaner than he should be. He still accompanies his men on the front lines. I fear for his safety, but he has told me on many occasions he will never lead from behind. That is why he still has their respect and their loyalty. Something I fear we will need greatly in the near future.

"Dad!" Silas yells, stumbling towards him.

"Slow down!" I tell him, knowing he won't.

"Do it, Dad, do it!" Silas requests, picking up a rock.

Asher, now about fifty yards away, nods. Silas throws the rock into the air just as Asher tosses his ricochet. It nails the rock, shattering it into dust.

"Yeah!" Silas yells, jumping up and down as fragments of rock rain down upon him. "Again!"

I shake my head at him and smile. *Show off*. Silas runs into his arms.

"Silly Silas! Have you been swimming yet today?" Asher asks him, his strong arms throwing him into the air.

"No, silly Daddy, I have been waiting for you!"

"I have something for you."

"What? What is it?" Silas dances in anticipation.

Asher pulls from his pocket a small necklace with a pelican, carved exquisitely from birch wood. Silas slides it on.

"I love it! Did you know a pelican can fit three times more fish in its mouth than in its stomach?"

"I did not know that, son."

"Your father can do the same," I joke.

"There's something else about the pelican," Asher tells him, kneeling down.

"What?"

"I'll save that one for your great uncle."

"Can we swim now? Please," Silas pleads.

"Gimme a minute to talk to your mom, then I'll change."

Asher lumbers over, sits next to me, and gives me a long kiss. His beard chaps my chin. He is weary; I can tell he hasn't slept much on this trip.

"How was he?"

"No seizures while you were gone."

Asher watches him skip and jump. "His motor skills seem to be improving."

"Yes." My tone turns somber. "There were two more bombings. Thirty dead."

"I heard."

"One was at the church downtown."

"I heard that too."

"How was the patrol?"

"A few Lazurites were causing trouble at the border; nothing major."

"What do you think he's up to?" I ask him, referring to my father.

"I don't know yet. I'm not sure what he's waiting for. My scouts tell me his army is big enough to mount a full-scale invasion. I don't understand the guerrilla warfare and the terror attacks. What is he trying to accomplish? What is his end game?"

"He is trying to install terror and fear. Wear us down slowly. I sometimes forget he has time on his side. Unlimited time. The narcdrops have doubled in the past six months. We can't find and burn the pallets fast enough. Our rehab centers are full. Our hospitals are overwhelmed with overdose victims. If the Senate had any sand, we could have finished this years ago." My blood pressure rises.

"I have a feeling he is up to something big, and soon it will be too late."

I squint at him. "Think we should make a unilateral move? Without Senate support?"

"Yes," he replies bluntly. "But not until after the election. I don't want to give them more ammunition against you than they already have. I hear the polls are almost even now."

"Neriah and her lies. I don't understand where she got all this money. Her ads are out-pacing mine four to one."

"We need to find out who's backing her. My guess is it's coming from the East." Asher pauses for a moment, then considers me. "You know she'll bring it up, right?"

"I know, she would be stupid not to," I blurt in frustration.

"And it's not a lie," he reminds me. "I am a liability now to you and this election. I should take a step back from the spotlight, stay in the shadows a bit until your campaign is over."

I wave him off. "Folly. Let's not forget you are the liberator of our people."

"That was a long time ago. The people forget easily."

I shake my head. "Being a politician has made me callous. I'm not sure I want this anymore."

His dry fingers grab my chin, and he pulls me close. "That is why you must do it."

He doesn't trust anyone who would actually want to do this job, not for a prolonged period of time, anyhow. Power corrupts, and the corrupted want power. It's a vicious circle. I pray I'm able to rise above it all. It's hard not to use that power to do what I believe is right. But then again, I'm sure every well-meaning dictator has thought that same thought.

The sun begins to descend into the ocean, and the sky radiates different hues of yellow, orange, and red. Silas stops for a moment and marvels at it. Sometimes, it takes being wounded to appreciate such beauty. What is the point of our struggles if we hardly notice a sunset anymore? Silas's virtue and wonder keep me from becoming too jaded.

"Dad?" Silas reminds him. "It's gonna be dark soon!"

"Okay, I'm coming," Asher tells him, getting up and heading towards the ocean.

"You're not going to change?" I ask him.

"Nope." He tosses me his ricochet, then strips down to his boxer shorts. "Last one in is a rotten OatBar!" he yells, running past Silas.

"Hey! You tricked me!" Silas runs after him into the ocean.

As the sun drowns behind them, I watch their shadows splash and jump up and down in the salty water. It makes me nervous every time they go in. This is the same cruel ocean that took my brother. Another headache sets in, and my animosity towards this election is becoming palpable. I don't understand. I never used to get this angry. I do my best to conceal it. Maybe it's the price of being a politician? Or maybe I have changed?

Or something has changed me?

Cephas

It's not a dark, dingy room like you see in the movies. It doesn't have bare walls, stale coffee, or uncomfortable chairs. Instead, it is warm, with bright colors. Three different types of coffee, always fresh. Cushy recliners in a circle facing each other.

Cephas was in those stone-cold, drab rooms many times before confessing his addictions. He put together this room himself. Including Cephas, there are ten total in this particular support group tonight.

"Anyone else like to share?" Cephas asks, voice gravelly. He folds his tree-stump forearms.

A gaunt and lanky man across from him fidgets in his chair. "I'm, I'm Bob. I... I have been on and off the Dust for almost twenty years now."

In unison, "Hi, Bob."

"Ya know, this last time, I quit for about nine months. Hadn't laid a finger on it! Then one of them damn narcdrops landed so close to me it almost hit my damn house. Sittin' there, right in front of me. Callin' to me. It was practically gift-wrapped with my name on it. It's them damn narcdrops. They won't stop. They just keep coming and coming and coming. It's everywhere I look, and it's free. I mean, how do ya get over somethin' that's always around you? I sometimes feel a guy like me doesn't stand a chance. How'd you do it, Ceph? How'd you get over it?"

Cephas clears his throat and leans in like a bear leaning into a honey jar. "Truth? I still haven't. Not sure you ever do. For me, it wasn't the Dust but the Tonic. It's something I struggle with on a daily basis, even after all these years. It's the first thing on my mind when I wake up and the last thing that enters my head when I go to bed."

"How do you do it?" a man with red eyes and a long mustache inquires. "How do you not let it control you?"

"Well, I have help."

"This group?"

"Well, yeah, this group, my friends, and—"

"God?" Bob cuts him off.

"Yes, that's right. God."

Bob scoffs, "Ya know how often I called out to God in my struggles, in my pain? I've lost my wife, my kids, my home, everything, and he was nowhere to be found!"

Cephas snorts. He is still getting used to being this personal and open. "Yeah, maybe so. Or maybe you are still alive because of Him. Maybe you are here because of Him. Listen, we have free will, and there will always be consequences to that free will. I mean, most of the time, our troubles come from the fact that we are just acting like a buckethead. Pure and simple.

And I don't pretend to know it all. I don't know why some suffer more than others. Why do good things happen to bad people, and the other way around? But what I can say is that your story isn't over, Bob. He's not through with you. He never will be. The good book says we can do all things through his Son, who strengthens us."

Bob sips his coffee. "Maybe. But why is there so much suffering?"

"Suffering that is not self-induced, you mean?"

"Yeah."

Cephas runs his stubby fingers down the lines in his face. "Again, I don't claim to have all the answers. But it is pain and suffering that forge character. Makes you stronger. But perhaps suffering is also a tough reminder that we are not in control. That we can't do it on our own."

"Maybe," Bob says with his own arms folded.

"You're right. Maybe. It's not a one-way street, Bob. It will require some effort on your side. Look, I'm not here to judge. I have been where you have been, all of you. God ain't here to judge, either. He's here to save for those willing to accept it. That part is free, my friends."

Cephas has been leading this group for over a year now. Without a Defiance to lead, it's been his new calling. He was never equipped to deal with his feelings, much less those of others. But he is getting there. Many of the men appreciate his gruff honesty.

Bob's face falls into his lengthy fingers. "I just don't know if I can do it."

"No one here pretends that it's easy. But you're here, aren't ya? That's one heck of a start."

Bob knocks his forehead with his fist. "You and God don't know half the things I have done. I… I am beyond saving, Ceph."

Cephas shakes his head. "If you knew everything I had done, you would probably be appalled. If I can be saved, anyone can. It's not about your past or what you have done. Are those things we need to deal with to help us move on? Why sure. But God is more concerned with your present and your future."

Who am I? Listen to me! Cephas thinks to himself. *For someone who doesn't like to talk, all of a sudden, I sound like a psychiatrist or preacher or something. If Jude could hear me now. I'm sure he would have something sarcastic to say.*

Cephas can see the wheels slowly grinding in Bob's head. *Just plant the seed; don't trample on it.* Cephas and the entire group are silent for three long minutes as they absorb Cephas's words. Cephas clears his throat again as if he is going to speak, but then something tells him not to. *Shut up for a minute and let them process.*

"Who brought snacks?" A twenty-something with red hair asks, breaking the silence.

"On the table, Red. Cookies." Cephas points his meaty finger.

Red grabs one and takes a bite, then immediately spits it out. "Oh, my nasty. Who made these, Ceph? Jude?"

This elicits snickers and laughs all around. *Jude isn't even here, and they are ribbing him.* Cephas smiles to himself.

Before the guffaws have a chance to die down, it happens. The oxygen is sucked out of the room. Acrid black smoke. Astringent heat. The noise is thundering. Like a jet engine right next to your eardrums.

Before Cephas can move, he is blown off his chair like the whites of a dandelion on a windy day. Debris, coffee, gross cookies, and ceiling fragments rain down upon him. He closes his eyes as a beam falls towards him in what feels like slow motion. He has become so used to tragedy he can slow it down and analyze it. Separate his feelings from it, then act upon it. Then he hears the one thing he cannot compartmentalize: the shrieks of agony from his friends. The beam speeds up and lands partially on his legs, followed by sheetrock, wires, and roofing tiles. The smoke thickens as his eyes close, his face covered in inky soot.

Then everything is quiet.

Jude

Jude watches the flames and embers from a distance. He wears a biohazard mask so the toxins from the burning demondust do not penetrate his lungs. *And people take this stuff willingly*, he thinks. He isn't necessarily tasked with this job, but it is sort of a hobby of his—destroying as many narcdrops as he can find. That, and making bad cookies for Cephas and his recovery group. This reminds him that he is supposed to meet Cephas for coffee in an hour.

He turns and heads back to his motorcycle as the evening chill descends upon him. He isn't as light-footed as he used to be—no longer just skin and bones. Post-Defiance has been pretty good to him. He even has a girlfriend named Ruth, who enjoys playing chess and doing puzzles. She also gets his sardonic sense of humor, or at least tolerates it. Perhaps he and Ruth will get married one day. Jude is ready; he already thought about popping the question. But it has only been six months, and he doesn't want to scare her off. But in today's world, six months can be a lifetime.

He keeps his grandma's ring in his sock drawer for such an occasion. It is a simple gold band with a diamond barely visible in the middle. Ruth isn't so concerned with material things, so Jude is sure it will be just fine. *Maybe I'll ask Asher for some proposal ideas. His fishing proposal went over well enough.*

He tosses on his cracked and battered helmet and turns around again to watch the demondust turn to ashes. It gives him great satisfaction watching what had enslaved so many of his people burn up and disappear into the crisp gray sky. By his math, every pallet torched is a family saved. Maybe even more.

He then notices something in the bushes to his left. *Is that a boot?* He rushes over to see two men lying frozen still on the ground, demondust powdered under their noses, paraphernalia littered by their feet. *Damn, they made it to the drop before I did. Overdose.* As he's about to leave, he notices the white particles take flight from one of their nostrils. *The wind?* Then, ever so faintly, he can see their chests lower and rise. They are alive. He bends down and checks their pulses just to be sure.

"Hey, hey! Wake up!" Jude yells, gently slapping one of their faces. He finds it odd that they are both alive, yet completely catatonic. There are no signs of an overdose. Pulse is normal. Skin color is good. They don't feel overly hot or cold.

Jude peers over at his motorcycle. There is no way to take them with him. He pulls out his cell phone, but there is no signal; it is still fried from the latest EMP Renatus dropped on them last month. He'll need to go and get help.

Then he hears it: the restrained whir of rotors. The massive drone appears from behind a giant pine tree. Jude draws his plasma rifle and scampers behind a set of pine trees. This is no ordinary HeliDrone. It is oval and much larger. What he sees next horrifies him. A massive tube extends from the bottom and sucks up the two men one at a time like a vacuum inhaling a couple of dead flies. Then, as fast as it arrived, it is gone.

A HarvestDrone.

The rumors must be true. Addicts have been disappearing into thin air for the past three weeks. One of his doctor friends who plays chess mentioned something about demondusters being brought in alive but comatose. They couldn't make sense of it.

Has Renatus changed the drug? And if so, for what purpose? Why is he harvesting again?

Before Jude can ponder further, he is shaken by a thundering bang in the distance. He knows exactly where the massive fireball and cloud of smoke came from.

Cephas.

He sprints to his motorcycle. After thirty minutes of dirt roads and shortcuts, he arrives. He is the first one there but can hear sirens in the distance. Lately, there have been too many of these types of attacks for fire and rescue to keep up.

He covers his face. The carnage is almost too much to take.

"Cephas!" he wails. "Cephas!"

He steps over a charred foot. Other body parts are strewn throughout the area as he climbs onto and through the wreckage.

"Cephas!"

He spots three fingers jutting out from the rubble.

"Cephas, is that you?"

He grabs the hand and pulls on it, but it's just a hand, attached to nothing. He studies it for a moment—too small to be Cephas's. He immediately drops it in horror and wonders how it got to this. How is this the new normal?

"Cephas! Where are you?"

He hears a faint murmur.

"Cephas! Is that you?"

"Here," replies a muffled voice.

Jude crawls to the noise and begins to pull burning debris from the location of the barely audible murmur, praying his friend is still alive.

"Cephas!"

"It's me," Cephas coughs. Covered in ash and debris, Jude can barely recognize his larger-than-life friend. He continues to dig, his long, wiry arms cut and burning, until he sees a blackened and sooty Cephas.

"I gotcha Cephas. I gotcha." Jude tries to pull him out from underneath the debris, but Cephas screams in agony.

"My leg, it's stuck," Cephas explains through gritted teeth.

Jude digs out the area and spots the sixteen-foot, six-by-ten beam under which his leg is trapped. His knuckles are now scraped to the bone, and his fingers are bleeding.

With strength he didn't know he had, he manages to lift it and set it aside.

"There."

He pulls Cephas out and helps him to his feet.

"You all right? Can you stand?"

"Yes, I think so," Cephas grunts.

Jude can't believe he is alive. "Someone is watching over you, my brother." He can't hide his relief that his best friend is standing. He embraces him and doesn't let go.

"Okay, okay. Come, help me find the others."

Limping and jarred, Cephas does what he can to dig through the rubble. With every dead body he finds, he becomes more and more nauseated.

"I should have known better. I should have searched the place before anyone else showed up," Cephas whispers, his words barely sliding through his cracked teeth and bleeding lips.

"You can't blame yourself for this, Cephas." Jude coughs at the smoke swirling into his face.

"They were my responsibility." Cephas fights back tears.

"Not everyone is your responsibility."

Cephas wipes blood from his sweaty brow. "I chose the place. I invited them here."

Jude hunches over, mirroring his body language in an attempt to be empathetic. "Don't do this to yourself, Cephas."

"It was me they were after."

"It was a random target, like the rest of them."

Cephas peers up at his friend with bloodshot eyes. "That's quite the coincidence then."

Jude attempts ill-timed humor: "You're not as important as you used to be."

Thirty minutes later, help arrives. Dejected, Jude and Cephas watch as the firemen and paramedics fill the body bags.

"They're all dead," Cephas groans, almost in shock. "How did... why am I... why am I still here?"

"Because you're Cephas," Jude says plainly.

"Red," Cephas blurts out coldly.

"What?"

"Red. The kid was only twenty." Cephas shakes his head and peers up to the sky. "I'm afraid this relative peace has made us complacent. The time for doing nothing is over. If the Senate won't do anything, I will convince Asher and Sarai to do it on their own!" He watches them zip the bag over what is left of Red's body and load him into a truck. "Poor kid, the last thing he had was one of your abominable baked goods."

Jude thinks nothing of his humorous remark. He doesn't think it is out of place or even paradoxical. They have seen so much tragedy in their lives; sometimes, humor is the only way they endure it all. Some situations can only be survived by contradicting them.

"This is not the worst of it," Jude tells him soberly.

"What can be worse than this?"

CHAPTER THREE

Asher

WE STROLL THE ROCKY hillside overlooking the vast Pacific. The winds have tempered as I watch Silas skip in front of me. Despite his condition, his seizures, and the bullying, he is always joyful. His eyes always sparkle, and his arms swing when he walks, like he is always about to arrive somewhere happy. His contentment is an inspiration to both Sarai and me.

I have taken to fatherhood. So much so that we have tried for another, with no luck yet. I chalk it up to stress. It isn't easy rebuilding a country during a civil war. My appreciation for Abraham Lincoln has risen tenfold. Sometimes, I feel that Sarai and I are alone in this battle. That we are the only ones who think the sacrifices are worth it.

Many have fallen back into their old ways. Living like they did when protocol was available to them—recklessly.

"There!" Silas yells, pointing at an old, dying branch hanging off a large oak tree.

I strap the retriever to my ricochet on his wrist and hand him my steel boomerang. I am told it's a symbol of hope and freedom for those in Zion East, under Renatus's dictatorship. People spray paint it on buildings and carve it into trees. He has promised his people the return of second-life protocol. He has promised them paradise. He is offering what no man can offer. There are too many people desperate enough to fall for it. Even after exposing him ten long years ago. Even after knowing what protocol costs, they still long for it. The human condition is self-serving. It makes me wonder sometimes if the fight is still worth it. If this is humanity, what are we trying to save?

I want to raise my son differently. But lately, he seems to be teaching me more than I'm teaching him.

"Dad?"

Silas brings me back into the moment. I pull his arm back behind him.

"Hold it like this—elbow up. Then, fling your wrist to the side. Picture in your mind's eye hitting the target."

"My mind has an eye?" he asks innocently. The wide gaps between his teeth cause him to speak with a partial lisp.

I smile at him. He always asks such great questions for a ten-year-old. "In a manner of speaking, yes. It's what you see when you close your eyes."

He shuts his eyes tight. "I see darkness."

I laugh. "Keep your eyes closed. Now, think about your target—the tree branch. Think about throwing it how I taught you. In your mind's eye, see it hit the branch. Actually, picture hitting the molecule inside the middle of the branch."

"Aim small, miss small," he tells me.

"Good, you remembered."

With his eyes still closed, he begins the motion of throwing the ricochet.

"Whoa, whoa! Not yet. Open your eyes first. Then throw it."

"But I can still see it in my mind," he argues.

"Trust me, it's better with your eyes open."

He pulls the ricochet behind his head and then tosses it towards the tree. It hits the dead branch perfectly, snapping it off the tree. He jumps in celebration and turns to me.

"I got it!"

I turn him back towards the tree. "Turn around, son. It's coming back."

"Oh yeah." He reaches out his hand with the retriever on it and catches the ricochet. "That was awesome!"

"Good job, son. Again?"

"Maybe later." He peers down at his feet.

"You okay, son?"

"Yeah."

I know when something is bothering him. "What is it?"

"I saw Grandfather on the HoloTube the other day. Why is he fighting us? I heard people say he is evil. Is it true? Is Mommy's daddy bad?"

I clear my throat and try to find the words. It's hard to tell someone with a pure heart about the wickedness of this world. Especially when they are family.

"Well, son, human nature is a selfish thing. You see, we are born that way, I think, and sometimes it's difficult to bring God into the equation when you are constantly surrounded by war and evil. You have to actively fight it."

"Why did he build The Wall?"

I was wondering when he would start asking these questions.

"They say he did it to separate us," I say. "To keep the good parts for himself and to use us for his benefit. But I think he did it out of fear."

"What do you mean?"

"Fear of freedom. What the people would do when they taste it. The people who want to control everyone always fear those who want to be free."

"And what happens if he wins? And builds The Wall again?"

I wrinkle my nose. "I don't think that will happen, son, but if it does, and we lose our freedom, there are other things more important that he can't take away. Ever."

"Like what?"

"Like hope. Things that are eternal."

"But why does he hate us?"

"I think it's because he hates who *he* is, even though he doesn't realize it. And because of that, he hates others."

"Even family?"

"Yes, even family, unfortunately."

He stares up at me for a long time. "What about you, Dad? You kill people, right?"

This is a tough one. I get down on one knee and square his shoulders to mine. "That is true, son. But only when I have to. And only to keep you and your mother safe. Only to keep our people free. Only to keep hope alive. And it pains me greatly every time I do."

"When I grow up, I want to be a great warrior like you."

"Then you should speak to your mother."

"But you're the one fighting."

"Physically, yes. But she is doing the harder part. She is trying to win the hearts and minds of the people. Of our enemies. They have lost faith; they no longer love."

Silas changes the subject. "Am I being punished?"

"Why would you say that, son?"

"For the way I look. For my seizures. For the way I talk. Because everyone makes fun of me."

My heart breaks.

"No, son. You are not being punished."

"Then why?"

"I don't have all the answers, but I will tell you this: those who go through difficult times come through it stronger than before."

"So my muscles will get bigger?"

I can't help but smile again. "No, son. Not your physical muscles, your mental ones."

"So, my brain? Like the mind's eye thing?"

"Sort of, yes. But not just your brain. Your soul, your spirit, your heart."

I can tell he is processing. "I think I get it. I didn't know I had so many things inside of me."

I get down on one knee and point to his face, then my face. "All this doesn't matter." I grab the muscles in his arm, then the ones in mine. "And these don't matter." I point to his heart. "This is all that matters. Look at me. My face has been rearranged to look like someone else, but I'm still the same inside. My heart hasn't changed."

My own words convict me. Am I still the same? How much has this war and protocol changed me? Can I continue to lead my men effectively? Will Sarai be re-elected Prime Servant? Will this country ever be united again? What if Renatus wins? My shoulders slump under the weight of it all.

"What did you look like before?"

I gaze at the vast ocean and slowly shake my head without realizing it.

"I don't remember."

Amos

Security opened the gates and let him walk right in. Why wouldn't they? Amos looks exactly like him. An hour ago, Amos studied a picture of Asher from one of his mini surveillance drones. He copied Asher's thin goatee almost perfectly. He also bought clothes similar to what Asher is wearing that day: gray cargo pants, black shin-high boots, and a tan long-sleeve shirt with two pockets. Although, his shirt only has one pocket, and is a slightly darker shade. Still, who will notice? He even has a counterfeit ricochet strapped to his side. *Remember, just be confident. You are Asher, not Amos. You are the Liberator of Zion. The vanquisher of Legion.* Just the thought of it makes him want to puke. It vexes him to no end that they look like twins and that The Traitor of Zion stole his identity. That he is called names and mistaken for Asher daily.

Now, it is time to use that to his advantage.

"Walked back, sir?" the security guard asks, a bit surprised.

"Needed the exercise," Amos responds. His drone also overheard that Asher was meeting with Kenan and a few of his generals this afternoon. He knows Asher won't be home for at least a few hours.

Amos approaches the palace's front door and peers at one of two armed guards standing near the door.

"Left my key card at the meeting. You mind?"

"Of course not, sir." One of the guards unlocks the door and lets him in.

And just like that, the wolf is inside. It is almost too easy.

Amos marvels at the grand entrance. The smell of sweet pea and hyacinth flowers assaults him as he gazes at the marble floors. For the past four days, he has smelled nothing but sweat and manure. The sweet aroma is almost overwhelming. *This place will soon belong to Renatus once again,* he thinks. *And I'll be seated to the right of his throne.*

As he turns the corner, he freezes for a moment. There is Sarai, with her campaign manager. Van Halen plays in the background. She is reading over flash cards. He can't help but notice her beauty and wonders if this was what his life could have been or still might be.

He clears his throat and steels himself.

"You're back early," Sarai says in a surprised tone.

"Meeting was canceled," Amos responds plainly.

"Oh. You wanna help me study for the debate?"

"Maybe later. I thought the little guy and I would do some fishing."

Sarai scrutinizes him. "You coming down with something? Your voice sounds hoarse."

This was the part Amos feared the most, getting by Sarai. He covers his mouth and coughs. "Maybe."

"You change your shirt?" She squints.

"Um, yeah, I spilled coffee on it."

She raises an eyebrow. "Thought you stopped drinking coffee?"

"It wasn't mine. Someone spilled it on me." He quickly changes the subject. "Where's the little guy?"

"In the living room, I think."

Amos starts to leave.

"Um, you forgetting something?" She perches her hands on her hips.

"Um."

"Hello? A kiss?"

"Right." Amos leans in, wondering if she'll know. Then he makes a show of coughing loudly.

"Actually, never mind. Not sure I want whatever it is you have."

Amos smiles and turns away from her.

"Oh, Asher, remind me what time we are meeting Cephas?"

Amos takes a deep breath before turning back to her. "Six."

"Okay. Wait, I thought it was five."

"Five. You're right. It's at five."

"You're losing it, hon."

Amos shrugs, then turns and wanders down the hallway, pretending to know where he is going. He spots the bathroom on his left, and he enters. He runs the faucet in the sink, splashing water on his face. *You can do this.* He checks his watch; it's almost time.

He exits the bathroom and passes by Asher's office. He can't help himself. He enters and sees an older ricochet in a glass display case. A label on the bottom reads, "Ricochet that defeated Legion in the 2099 Canonization." He spits in disgust. *It was luck,* he tells himself. He spies pictures of Asher before he was sculpted to look like him. *Why hasn't he been sculpted back? Maybe he likes looking like me?* He smiles, and the narcissist inside of him also thinks, *Maybe his wife prefers the way he looks now.*

He rifles through Asher's desk. He sees maps of different troop positions. He finds other pieces of paper with potential intelligence that could help Renatus. He folds them up and stuffs them into his pockets.

He then heads to the living room, where Silas is playing with an action figure of Asher, holding a small plastic ricochet. *He has an action figure now. Who does he think he is?* He then smiles to himself; *maybe I'll have an action figure one day.*

"Hey, buddy!" Amos feigns excitement.

"Daddy!" Silas jumps into his arms. "Thought you had a meeting?"

"Ended early. What do you say we take the boat out and catch some fish?"

"You sound different, Daddy."

"Have a little cold, is all, buddy. What do you think? Fishing?"

Silas nods his head with a wide grin. "Let's see if Mom wants to go with us this time. What do you think?"

"Mom is busy with election stuff, buddy, but we'll have fun, just you and me. What do you say?"

"Okay, bet I catch a bigger fish!"

"I bet you do. I... I forgot where I put the gear," Amos lies, rechecking his watch while nervously tapping his foot.

"In the boat!"

"And the keys?"

"I'll show you, silly Daddy."

Sarai

My campaign manager and I watch footage of my opponent, Neriah.

"She is very calming and unassuming. Her movements are natural and harmonious. She comes across as the mother everyone loves," My campaign manager says, putting on her glasses.

"That's because she was," I say solemnly.

"You know it will come up in the debate. We need an answer for it."

"How does she even know? I don't get where she is getting her intel. I mean, have you found out who's backing her?"

"My people are looking into it, but it's complex."

"It has to be my father."

"Probably, but we can't say anything unless we are sure. Besides, even if he is funding Neriah's campaign, it behooves us not to say anything."

"Why wouldn't we?" I counter, stunned. "I mean, if the enemy of our new republic is funding my opponent, wouldn't that automatically disqualify her?"

"In theory, yes. But this is more complicated than that. The mere fact that Renatus is your father and that he is meddling in this election would make you look bad as well. It could be seen as a conflict of interest."

I shake my head. "Seems I can't win."

"Yes, you can. We just have to walk a fine and narrow line, is all." She points to Neriah on the HoloTube. "And you can learn a thing or two from her."

I frown, almost offended. "Like what?"

"Demeanor mostly. Don't take this wrong, but as much as she looks natural and refined, you sometimes come off as the opposite."

I fidget and bite my bottom lip. "That's because this is not natural to me. None of it is."

"Then let's practice."

"Can't I just challenge her to a match with scourges?" I half-joke.

"Nope. The podium it will have to be."

I am not looking forward to this debate. As much as I enjoy serving and changing things for the better, I hate politics. But it is a necessary evil if you want a free country. I have spent hours preparing, answering mock questions, and controlling my tone and hand gestures. Trying not to sound too intelligent or superior without sounding stupid or dull. It's a delicate balance. Sharp, but not crafty. Humble, but not sheepish. How you say your words is almost as important as the words themselves. The eyes of the world will be upon me, the press critiquing my every word, my every move. It's like living in a glass house. No matter what I do or say, half of the population will hate me or, at the very least, adamantly disagree. But there is nothing I can do about that.

Then there is Asher; his past will surely come up. How will I respond when they attack him, me, and my family? We have sacrificed so much, yet we still need to prove ourselves daily. Asher does not envy me and has often told me he is glad that God chose me to take up this mantle and not him. It has been ten years since The Wall came down, and we have made little progress. It's hard to teach people how to be free again. For every new business that is started, two are destroyed by my father's bombs. For every addict that has overcome their addiction, three new ones sprout like weeds. The Dust is spreading like locusts through our communities. Every time there is a bombing, the schools close for a week. My father is fighting the long war and deteriorating our society by attacking our education system, and tearing apart the nuclear family via addiction.

We could have gone to Zion East and ended this years ago if the Senate weren't so split. If they had any guts at all. If they understood that freedom is not free. If I win, maybe we will go at this unilaterally and bypass the Senate. I have asked my lawyers to look into the legality of it. In our new Constitution, it's a bit of a gray area. I kind of suspect half our Senate is in bed with my father anyway.

"Let's go over this again." My campaign manager stands. "Prime Servant, can you explain your husband's actions?"

I grit my teeth and narrow my eyes. "He—"

"Wait. Stop," she interrupts me. "No good."

"What do you mean?"

"You can't be an open book, Sarai. I can tell from a mile away that you are agitated by the question."

"That's because I am." My heart is racing, and my headache is returning.

"Understandable, yes. But you can't let anyone else know that. You need to show tranquility, but don't be aloof."

"I hate this! It's like a big game," I say in frustration.

"That's because it is."

"I just want to do what's right, what's right for the people."

She takes off her glasses. "And unfortunately, to do that, you must play the game first."

"Let's finish this later."

I set down my index cards and talking points and pour another coffee. I peer out the window. In the distance, I can see the silhouettes of Asher and my son bobbing in the ocean. They are much farther out than usual. Fish must not be biting in close. I muse over what a great father Asher is and how lucky I am to have him—to have him and Silas. How we shouldn't even exist, and because of that, neither should our son. Yet here we are, miracles, though not by our choosing.

Then I hear his voice. The coffee cup slides from my hand and shatters on the marble floor. It's impossible. I turn, and my worst fear has been realized. How could I have been so stupid?

It's Asher.

Amos

His hands start to sweat. Amos peers around nervously for any other boats. He rechecks his watch. *They should have been here by now.* He rubs his hands on his pants. If they don't show up, this will have been for naught, and he will surely not survive this.

He ties a new bait onto Silas's line and casts his in. The winds pick up, slowly irritating the ocean. The swells are becoming increasingly larger. Amos begins to worry that the fishing boat might capsize if they stay here for too much longer.

"Haven't even gotten a bite yet," Silas whines.

"That's fishing," Amos tells him, his head on a swivel.

"Let's go to our normal spot. This spot sucks."

"Just a bit longer," Amos replies, his eyes becoming tight.

Amos studies the boy. His defects. He likes the kid and wonders if he, too, is bullied like Amos was as a child. But Amos grew up poor. Abused. This child resides in a mansion. His parents are the most powerful people on the planet right now. He lacks nothing. Wants for nothing. Soon, he will gift this spoiled child to Renatus, and finally get the recognition and treasure he believes he deserves. His legacy will be indelible. Asher had assumed his identity, and that became Amos's downfall. Now, that same identity, and Asher's offspring, will be his.

"Waves are getting big. Maybe we should go back?" Silas ponders out loud.

"We're okay, just a little while longer."

Something big tugs at his pole. "I caught a fish!" Silas yells.

So have I. "Keep reeling, keep the pressure on it! And keep that tip up! I told you, didn't I?"

Silas successfully reels in a large King Salmon. "Look at that, Dad! That's a trophy, isn't it?"

You sure are.

Amos nets the fish and pulls it into the boat. "That's a beauty." For a moment, and only a moment, Amos is proud of him, almost as if he were his own son. He thinks about his father and how he never took him fishing. Never did anything with him. But it's a fleeting moment, one that recedes into the deep recesses of his brain, where he doesn't dare go. At least not anymore. *Focus on the mission, Amos! This is your defining moment! It will be talked about for years.*

"That's my biggest by far!" Silas proudly stands next to it. "Take a picture, Dad."

Amos continues to scan the ocean. "We will, son, we will. Give me a bloody minute."

Bloody. I need to watch what I say. Silas didn't seem to notice.

He takes a deep breath, and the sulfuric smell of the sea clears his mind. Then, in the distance, Amos sees a boat speeding his way, crashing through the waves; inside are Asher and Sarai.

He rechecks his watch and curses to himself. He hands Silas a life jacket. "Put this on, son."

"Why? I can swim."

"Just put it on!"

Amos does the same. Asher's jet boat is only about a hundred yards away, slicing through the growing waves.

"Time for a swim." Amos yanks Silas up and tosses him into the ocean before following him in.

Silas yelps, "What are you doing? It's cold, Dad! It's so cold!"

He can hear his mother and father's screams just as Asher's boat approaches, bobbing in the water.

"I'm here, Silas!" Asher howls. "Dad is coming for you!"

A confused Silas peers to Amos, then Asher. Then he begins to bawl, not understanding what is happening.

As the jet boat slows, a massive wave pushes it towards Silas.

"Turn and shut the engine off!" Asher screams at Sarai.

Then, the ocean parts. What looks like a massive steel whale appears. It is a submarine. Amos can see the horror in Asher and Sarai's eyes, as a Lazurite elite pulls him and Silas into the open hatch.

"No!" Asher yells.

"Silas!" Sarai screams.

Before closing the hatch, Amos smiles back at them. "I win."

He only wishes his father could see him now. Bold and audacious. Successful in a plan of his own making. Soon he will be basking in the glory of his success, getting fat off of everything Zion has to offer. What he doesn't see is Asher jumping in after the submarine and fruitlessly trying to swim after it, clawing at the water.

Cephas

The bombing plays over and over in Cephas's head. He closes his eyes and can see the body bag being slowly zipped over Red's maimed body. Only twenty years old. Just a kid. The Dust destroyed half of his life. *Why is the sound of the zipper so loud?* Cephas places his giant paws over his ears, his eyes clenched shut. *How much more death can I stand to see? Will it never end?*

He is suddenly dizzy, his limbs weak. Cephas opens his eyes and stares at the bottle of Demon Tonic in front of him. As he slouches on the couch, it stands tall. One hundred proof. It stares back at him like an old friend.

But this friend you cannot trust! he tells himself. *This friend is a twisted temptress and a deceiver.*

What can one drink hurt? Counters another voice in his head.

He had swiped it from a fresh narcdrop on his way home after the bombing. His bloodshot eyes yearn for it. It beckons him. He twists off the top of the bottle and pours himself a shot. He lifts the shot glass until it is at eye level. Peering through it, he can see a blurry, distorted picture of his dead wife, hanging on what is otherwise his bare walls.

Her red curly hair made it look like her head was on fire. Her Irish temper sometimes followed suit. But, for the most part, she was even-keeled, even quiet. But, when she did speak, it usually behooved you to listen. Along with her red hair and pearly skin, she had two green thumbs. Her garden was always fruitful, and her flowers were immaculate. The only fruit the two of them could not bear were children. They tried for many years without success.

He sighs and tries to block her picture out with his thumb. He doesn't want her to see what he is about to do. He brings the drink to his nose and sniffs it. He has missed that earthy, peaty aroma. *Why wasn't I blessed with offspring? Maybe it was because I needed to be there for Asher? Maybe I didn't have the capacity for more, with my beloved being gone? Or maybe I didn't deserve it?* His wife used to tell him, "God knows what you need and what you can handle better than you do." It was his wife who helped him quit drinking. It was his wife who helped him find God. Helped him find himself.

Now she is gone. And what is left of their garden has been overtaken by weeds and dandelions. Their house is no longer carpeted with flowers. No longer can he smell the perfume of magnolias and lilies. No children of his own to convey his wisdom to. No grandchildren running around his house. The gloom that now infests his residence is palpable. When she died, a part of him did, also.

He grabs the photograph from the wall and holds it in one hand, the shot in the other. Her pine-green eyes were always so full of life. Brimming with joy. He pulls the picture to his dry, cracked lips and kisses it. It's not the first time. He closes his eyes and murmurs a quick prayer.

"Thank you for saving me again." He peers up to the heavens as if talking directly to her. "And I'm sure you're getting tired of it."

She is not. Grace and more grace were always her way. She was married to Cephas; it *had* to be her way.

He lumbers towards the kitchen and pours the Tonic from his glass. He then dumps the entire bottle down the drain. As the bottle empties, his spirit fills. Tears fall from his cheeks and join the life-sucking liquid spiraling down the drain. *At least there are fewer tears when pouring the Tonic down the drain than when pouring it down my throat.*

Cephas plunks back down on the couch and takes out his throwing knives. He throws them against the wall, hitting a hand-drawn target. They stick three inches into the sheetrock. He thinks about his parents and how his father was also hooked on the Tonic. He wonders if it would have been the same for his son or daughter if they had one, or if he would have broken the cycle in time. He knocks his forehead with his fist in disappointment. *I can't believe I almost drank it.*

A gentle knock comes from his front door.

Cephas shakes his senses awake and grabs his plasma gun. He peers out his peephole and sees no threat. He opens the door. Standing there is Linda, early fifties, athletic, with drooping but soft eyes that look like they have been crying. She holds a plate of cookies.

"I thought you could use these." Linda manages a smile.

"Linda," Cephas tries to hide his surprise. "Please, come on in."

Linda strolls inside and places the cookies on the coffee table.

"I am so sorry," she blurts out, almost stumbles, and hugs him.

Cephas is taken aback for a moment, until he gingerly wraps his thick arms around her, trying to hug her back, but not too tight. The last time he held a woman this close was his wife. Linda's auburn hair even smells like hers. Sensing he is uncomfortable, she steps back and places her hands to her sides.

"They are all gone?" she asks.

"Yes. All but me for some reason. I'm just glad you weren't there tonight."

Linda has been coming to Cephas's rehab meetings for nine months now. She was hooked on the Dust, and because of it, she lost her husband and two children. They now live in Zion East. She was instantly attracted to Cephas, and in his gruff naivete, he had no idea.

"And Red? Was Red there?" A single tear trickles down her hardened cheek.

Cephas simply nods and clears his throat, trying to keep his emotions at bay. Everyone liked Red. He was the group's youngest, and therefore everyone's unofficial son.

"The cookies are peanut butter," Linda tells him awkwardly, as if unsure whether she was too forward for showing up at his house. "Your favorite, if I remember correctly."

"Yes. Yes, they are. Thank you, Linda."

He peers around at his unkempt and dusty house and is suddenly embarrassed. "Excuse the mess. I, I wasn't expecting—"

"No need to apologize, Cephas. I am sorry for coming over unannounced. I probably should have called first." She then stares at the knives in the wall but turns away, pretending not to see them.

Cephas then realizes he hasn't showered since the bombing. He wipes soot and dirt from his clothes and face. "Sorry, I would have showered if I knew—"

"That's okay, Cephas. No need to apologize. I'm just glad you are okay."

They make eye contact and then look away like a couple of middle schoolers. Since his wife died, Cephas has never even entertained the idea of loving another woman. As far as he was concerned, he had hit the jackpot once already, and lightning doesn't strike twice.

Linda scans his bare walls and notices the crooked picture of his wife. "Perhaps I should leave. I hope you enjoy the cookies."

Maybe it's time to put myself out there again, Cephas thinks. *I have walked through enough storms and endured the thunder. Maybe I will see lightning again?*

Linda shuffles towards the door.

"Linda, wait." Cephas's voice flutters. "Perhaps you would like to stay for coffee? I can't eat all those cookies by myself. I mean, I probably could... but... but, I probably shouldn't." *You sound like a fool.*

"Sure, I would love to, as long as I'm not imposing."

"No, not at all."

Cephas heads to the kitchen and scans his empty cupboards. "Only thing is, I'm out of coffee."

"We will just have cookies then," Linda replies contently.

"Cookies it is, then." He sits beside her, grabbing one for him and one for her. "How are you managing otherwise?"

She shakes her head. "Good days and bad. When I heard the news of the bombing, I passed a narcdrop on the way here. I was tempted, Cephas. I really was. But I managed to pass it by."

Well, you did better than I did. "Lately, it has been more bad days than good."

"Sure is the truth."

Before Cephas can enjoy the company of a female for the first time in over twenty years, another knock on his door—more of a bang.

"Excuse me." Cephas trudges to the door and looks through the peep-hole. It's Jude. He swings the door open.

"It's Silas!" Jude exclaims, sweating and out of breath.

"What about him?" Cephas asks.

"They have taken him."

The thunder has returned.

Renatus

Zion East is growing on Renatus. If you walk the streets, it is starting to resemble Zion West of old, before The Defiance. Things are clean. Orderly. He misses his palace on the coast at Pt. Reyes. But the new digs he has occupied over the past ten years aren't bad: The White House. He loves the symbolism alone. It's where all the other leaders lived before The Wall. But at this very moment, Renatus is not perched in The Oval Office plotting the downfall of Asher and his only daughter.

He is ten stories underground.

Renatus marches the hallways of the new facility, which is still under construction. Scientists and doctors trail him. They try to keep up with his brisk pace; his walk is more like a jog. *Always be moving*, he likes to say. He feels another headache coming on and preempts it with four aspirins.

"And what of the LifePacks?" Renatus asks.

One of the scientists responds with a nervous stutter. "We have been able to accelerate the process successfully, sir."

"Hours?" Renatus lifts an eyebrow.

"No, my Sultan. Minutes."

"Excellent."

They pass by rows and rows of bodies in giant glass cylinders floating in the familiar pink translucent fluid. Two of the men are the addicts that Jude found earlier. Renatus has duplicated second-life technology. In fact, it's become something even more terrible.

"And we are ready for a demonstration?"

"Yes, my Sultan. Bring him in!"

A Lazurite elite, with no exoarmor, marches in front of him. Strapped to his back is a small canister filled with the same pink fluid. Floating inside is a white, spongy substance about the size of a golf ball. Renatus points to it.

"That's a LifeCell?"

"Yes. We can now extract it from our harvest, encapsulate it, and use it whenever, sir." His tone is clinical and scientific, with absolutely no regard for how the LifeCell was attained.

"This I have to see," Renatus declares, pulling out his plasma gun. He aims and shoots the elite in the chest. The soldier collapses to the ground, moans for a minute, then clenches his teeth and closes his eyes. One of the doctors checks his pulse.

"Expired, sir."

Then, the white substance travels from the LifePack on his back into a tube inserted into his chest. They wait. The scientist watches Renatus impatiently tap his foot and check his watch.

"Will be just a minute, my Sultan."

The elite begins to shake. His eyes flutter open with a loud gasp. He shrieks in agony, his body spastic. A moment later, dripping with sweat, he stands to attention. At first, the elite looks flabbergasted. He just died and was brought back to life. But then his look of shock turns to one of immortality. Renatus cannot hide his delight.

"Truly an invincible army, my Sultan," the scientist blurts with pride before checking himself. He dared to speak out of turn, and with Renatus's recent volatility, perhaps he should be wearing a LifePack himself.

"Can the LifePacks support more than one LifeCell?" Renatus wonders out loud.

"I don't see why not, with some tweaking."

Renatus's mood is now jubilant. Not only can he have a perennial army, but he can use this for himself during his non-stop adrenaline adventures.

No more waiting two weeks if his parachute doesn't open, or if he falls off the mountain while rock climbing. Instant regeneration and quickly back to doing what it is he loves doing.

"We must double our efforts on Operation Cell Sweep. We need to fill this place!" Renatus bellows at his men, referring to the tainted drugs and the HarvestDrones. The elite soldier, still awed at his miraculous recovery, turns to leave with a swagger of invincibility. A gait only a Lazurite can pull off.

"Uh, where are you going, soldier?" Renatus asks, his eyes narrowing.

"Home, sir."

"Home? You must have forgotten that you died, mate." And with that, Renatus shoots him again.

The scientists and doctors look on in horror. They have noticed Renatus's acts are ever increasingly heinous. Especially since his last protocol after a nasty motorcycle accident.

Renatus turns to the scientist and says, "See, if he had two LifeCells in his little backpack, he would still be bloody alive." Renatus still insists on his hybrid British-American vernacular, although it hasn't really caught on in the East.

"Of course, sir. We will get right on it."

"And see if you can make it not so painful." Renatus has been through protocol so many times that he is getting tired of the acute anguish the body goes through while being resurrected.

"Yes, my Sultan."

Another elite marches into the room. "Sultan, you have a visitor."

"Who?"

"Amos, sir. He tried The White House first, and they sent him here."

"Is he alone?"

"No, sir."

Renatus flashes his oversized, bone-white teeth. "Bring him in."

Ten minutes later, Amos waltzes in, brash and presumptuous. His gait is full of bluster. With him is Silas, a dark bag over his head.

Renatus rubs his hands together in anticipation. "Amos, who is your little friend?" He hopes his question is rhetorical.

With great showmanship and fanfare, Amos rips the hood off Silas's head. "I give you Silas, son of Asher."

Renatus watches Silas shake and stammer as he inspects him. The white blotches on his skin, the gaps in his teeth. *A wounded one of my own blood.* He has been waiting for this day for over twenty years. Finally, a match for his beloved Eleazar. His wounded prince. He will stop at nothing to bring back his son, even at the expense of his own grandson.

"Good work, *General* Amos." Renatus has just promoted him on the spot.

"Thank you, my Sultan. I will not disappoint you," Amos responds jubilantly.

"For your sake, I hope not again. Gather my newly formed first army and prepare for an offensive. It's time to end this war once and for all."

"Yes, my Sultan. And thank you, sir."

Renatus swats his hand at him. "I will send word of your promotion. Now off you go."

Still unable to wipe his smile off his face, Amos bows. "Yes, my Sultan."

As Amos leaves, Renatus sets his arm on Silas's shoulder. "I am Renatus, your grandfather."

Silas is more confused than scared at this point. "I know who you are. What am I doing here, sir?"

They stroll towards the back of the facility. "You are going to help your family, your uncle."

"I have an uncle?"

They turn the corner and reach Eleazar's cylinder. Renatus is surprised and impressed by Silas's calmness. His courage, actually. *Must be in the blood.*

"This is Eleazar, your uncle." Renatus points to his son, floating lifeless in the pink gel.

Silas studies him. "My uncle? He looks my age."

"Astute you are, my grandson. You do have my blood."

"What happened to him?"

"There was an accident in the ocean."

"What type of accident?"

Renatus always turns somber when he reminisces about that day. "He drowned. Your mother was supposed to be watching him."

The word "mother" sparks something in Silas's brain. "And where are my parents? My mother? Where is my father? Why am I here? I want to see my father."

Renatus motions to one of his elites. "You will see him soon enough, grandson. Now run along. You must be starving. We have an entire freezer full of ice cream."

The elite escorts a befuddled Silas through one of the doors. What a day this has been. First, the news of instant resurrection. Now, he has his grandson, who holds the keys to life for his son. Soon, he will have his wounded prince back. Soon, The Defiance will be wiped out. And Asher—the man who he once loved as his very own son, the man who defied him, The Traitor of Zion—will soon be dead.

Renatus places both of his palms against Eleazar's capsule. His head is bowed, his eyes clamped shut.

"Soon, my wounded prince. Soon."

CHAPTER FOUR

Asher

"How could this have happened!?" my wife cries, kneeling in the sand. She picks up handfuls of the smooth sand and watches the grains slip through her fingers. That is how we feel right now; everything we hold dear has escaped our grasp.

It's my fault. I should have seen this as a potential outcome. I mean, I used Amos's identity against Renatus. He simply did the same to me. How did I not anticipate something like this? It is so obvious. I became too complacent. Too war-weary to do the necessary. We became confident about our safety in the bubble that is this mansion.

I lift my wife and hold her tight.

"I'm so sorry, Sarai. It's my fault."

"Don't do that. Don't blame yourself. Don't you dare."

"I should have seen it coming, I—"

"No! We both should have seen it coming." Sarai wipes her tears, her tone becoming resolute. She turns and stares at the deceptively calm Pacific. It's the water in her eyes that is raging.

She wades into the sea, knee-deep, smashing the salt water with her fists over and over. "These waters have taken my brother from me, and now my son! Why!?"

I follow her in, the waves crashing over my legs, as they try to beat me back. She goes further in. "Sarai. Come back. Where are you going?" I catch up to her. The water is now up to our chests.

"Why!?" she shrieks.

"I don't understand. That's his grandson, his blood! You really don't think he plans on harvesting him, do you? I mean, maybe it's for a ransom; maybe he wants me in exchange," I say hopefully, knowing fully what Renatus is capable of.

"This is my father we are talking about. He killed me, in case you don't remember. Twice! He has been waiting twenty years for this. The only other person he cares about other than himself is Eleazar. His *wounded prince.*"

"But Silas is his own flesh and blood."

"So was I," she reminds me again. "Don't think for a moment he won't harvest our son to bring back his beloved."

Even though I know what Renatus is capable of, a little part of me has to believe he won't do it. Maybe when he sees Silas is also wounded, he will have a change of heart. Maybe Silas will remind him of Eleazar. Maybe it will cause him to change.

Too many maybes.

I grab her hands and pull her close. The salty waves crash into our faces, still trying to push us back. "I will find him, Sarai. I will get him back." My tone is not as convincing as I would like. My heart is fractured. I am doing my best to remain calm, but anger and fear are swirling inside me, taking over my thoughts. I have failed as a father, as a husband, and as a protector.

Sarai shakes her head, tears emerging once more. "Maybe we deserve this. Perhaps God is punishing us."

"What do you mean?" I say, surprised by her words.

"For protocol. I shouldn't be here, Asher. Neither of us should. We died! We shouldn't even have a son! Maybe God is just taking back what's His? Restoring the natural order of things."

"I don't think God works that way. Besides, neither of us asked to be brought back. It was gifted to us. We didn't have a choice," I rationalize.

"Yet here we are, living our lives as if nothing ever happened. We have naively thought we could have a life of our own, a family when fate has conspired against us from the beginning. I somehow knew this day was coming." She bangs my chest with her fists as another wave splashes over her head. Her long raven hair swirls around her like gathering seaweed. "He shouldn't even exist, Asher. And you are wrong. *You* did have a choice. *You* chose to bring me back."

"I didn't have a choice!" I raise my voice, trying to be louder than the ocean. "It was instinct. Either you lived or I did. That isn't a choice. That is instinct. You would have done it for me. And you would have done it for our son."

Her head shakes as she repeats herself. "Our son shouldn't exist, Asher."

"Yet he does. And I'm going to get him back."

Sarai peers at me. "Do you feel different? Since protocol?"

"I have headaches."

"Not just that. Ever since, I don't feel quite right. Not myself. Sometimes I feel like someone else."

I too feel strange at times. Weird thoughts and memories. Like my brain is now ruled by chaos. But I don't have time to ponder it. I must get my son back.

"I don't think any of us have been ourselves for a long time," I say. "Look at me. I'm going to get him back."

Sarai watches her reflection appear and then disappear with each wave that crashes against her chest. "Then I'm coming with you."

"You can't. Sarai. You have the election and an upcoming debate. I promise you I will bring him back."

"I don't care about the election anymore!" she wails. "All I care about is getting my son back."

"That's what he wants!" I raise my voice, feeling another headache coming on. "He wants you to give up. Look, Cephas has reason to believe that Neriah might be funded by your father. If she wins and Zion East is pulling the strings, we will just be handing the country back to him. You have to stay, Sarai. Your fight is here."

"No. How can you even say my fight is here when our son has just been kidnapped? How can I even focus on such a thing as a debate or politics?"

The frigid water is making us numb, at least more than we were when we first saw our son swallowed by that steel whale.

"You have to stay, Sarai," I say desperately. "And you have to win. Or all of this is for nothing. Everything we have accomplished in the past ten years will be for naught. Even if we get Silas back, if you lose, he will grow up like I did, in a divided country ruled by your father. We will be slaves, Sarai. Living in poverty on a reservation somewhere—that is, if we don't get harvested first." I cup her chilled cheeks with both hands. "Please trust me. I will find him."

She grabs my shirt until I can see the white of her knuckles. She spits out briny ocean water. Her eyes are fierce. "You don't come back here without him."

Asher

I make my way down to the weapons room to finish packing for my journey. I find Sarai cracking her scourge against a mannequin with unbridled fury. Both of us are still distraught with anger. Both of us are suffering from headaches even worse than before. Before I can say something, Cephas limps into the room, Jude with him. His legs, arms, and head are bandaged.

"What happened to you?" I ask, not yet knowing about the latest attack.

Cephas ignores the question. "I'm so sorry, Asher. I am at a loss for words. I mean, how could he? That's his grandson."

"This is Renatus we are talking about. What happened to you, Cephas?"

"More of the same." Cephas watches me as I look for supplies in frustration. "You going after him?"

"Yes."

"Let's not be rash, nephew. Let's think this through and devise a plan," Cephas advises.

"Think what through? It's only a matter of time before he kills my son to bring back his own. I am leaving. Now."

"Then I'm going with you," Cephas demands.

"You can't. Renatus's armies are mobilizing. I need you to stay here and prepare for war."

"Then take a platoon, at least. I will have Kenan gather the best men we have."

I shake my head. "My scouts tell me Renatus is building a new facility for harvesting. Surely, he is bringing Silas there. I need to stay under the radar. If I'm spotted with a platoon of troops, he will move him—or—worse, accelerate protocol. I am going small and nimble."

Cephas peers at Jude. "Which leads us to our next bit of good news. Jude, would you like to share?"

Jude clears his throat. "Sure thing, boss. It seems you're right about Renatus replicating second-life tech. I, uh, saw something... something a bit frightening—"

"Out with it!" Cephas taps Jude's forehead with his stubby fingers.

"Seems Renatus has put something in the demondust, causing users to become incapacitated to some extent, but not dead."

"For what purpose?" I ask.

"I found two addicts catatonic on the street. Shortly after, a massive drone—a HarvestDrone—flew over and sucked them up like a giant vacuum."

Cephas cuts in, "Seems he's harvesting again. On a scale we haven't seen before."

Sarai finally stops snapping her scourge against her obliterated target. "At this rate of harvesting, it has to be for something greater than just his personal use or for profit. Question is: what? I am betting it's something big."

Cephas's eyes widen. "It's for an army. An invincible army."

I say, "Maybe so, but protocol takes two weeks."

"Then, once the war begins, we have two weeks to finish it," says Jude.

Sarai wipes the sweat from her brow and catches her breath. Her eyes are narrowed and nettled, her hand on Cephas's meaty shoulder. "After Asher brings my son back, we end this. Once and for all. With or without Senate support."

"Yes, ma'am."

"That will mean a full-scale war," Jude adds.

Sarai spews sweat and spit as she snaps her scourge. "What's your point, Jude?"

"What if you lose the election? We won't have an army."

"She won't lose," I respond, my inflection huffy.

"I'm just trying to be realistic here. They are tied in the polls. We need a contingency plan in case we lose." Jude is now getting frustrated.

"She won't lose." My teeth grit as I grind out the words. But I fear that she might. Then what? I don't know. I can only think about my son right now. I can only take one step at a time without losing it.

Jude clears his throat. "Look, I understand this just got way personal for you guys. I just think we need to cover all of our bases."

I get right in his face. "She won't lose."

"Let's all just take this one day at a time. Silas is now our main concern." Cephas tries to keep the peace.

Jude paces the room. He is constantly moving, which is probably the reason he is so skinny. "If you don't want the old man to go with you, at least let me. I am stealthy."

I shake my head. "You're needed here."

Cephas approaches me. He eyes Sarai as she returns to her scourge with robust furor, then whispers, "You guys okay?"

"Other than our son just being kidnapped?" I reply, my tone biting.

"Before that, nephew. Lately you both seem a little... off."

"Is there something you wanna say, Cephas? Just come out with it. Beating around the bush isn't your style."

Cephas rubs his feathery eyebrows together until they grow wings, which he does when he wants to get something off his chest. "It's probably nothing, nephew; it's just that our scientists have been studying the effects that protocol has on the brain. It seems that every time someone is resurrected, the brain's structure is altered, especially the region that controls emotions and personality." He peers again at Sarai, who seems to still be in a frenzy, decimating her target. "Like anger, for example."

"We are fine," I lie.

"I am also told that in some cases, it can even affect memories."

"Look, our son just got kidnapped; what do you want from me? I'm doing as well as one might expect."

"Just looking after you, son."

"You want to help me? Stay here, watch over my wife, get our army ready."

"Of course, nephew. Just be mindful of your thoughts and your emotions. Don't let the demons get a foothold."

I watch my wife perspire and stew in her rage. "I am afraid they have slipped through the door."

"Then fight them, Asher."

I close my eyes. "I think I have forgotten how."

Cephas lifts his pant legs to reveal his chafed and scabby knees. "With prayer, nephew. It's the strongest weapon we have."

My faith has been shaken. "Will it bring my son back?"

Cephas exhales long and slow. "I don't know."

I change the subject and turn to Jude. "You got it? Is it finished?"

"Sure thing, Asher Liberator of Zion," Jude replies.

He likes to rib me with the different surnames he has heard. But as usual, his tact and timing are horrible. I don't have the emotional energy or bandwidth to respond. He hands me my ricochet and wrist strap.

"Programmable?" I ask.

"Yep." He points to the small screen on my wrist strap. "Access it here and set targets here."

Jude is very mechanical and good with electronics. I asked him to upgrade my ricochet, give it more range, and give me more control over where it goes. I am hoping he doesn't disappoint. I am hoping I don't have to use it. But that is unlikely.

"Thank you, Jude."

"Just hope he did a better job with that than his cooking," Cephas cackles.

"Maybe we should test it on him," I banter back.

Jude shakes his head. "Man, that's the last time I do you guys a favor."

Cephas places his paw on my shoulder. "Be careful."

"Not the first time I'm waltzing into the lion's den."

"Well, last time, they didn't know you were coming. At least let Jude go with you," Cephas pleads with me one last time.

"No. You need him."

"See that? You need me," Jude quips.

"I need you to shut it, buckethead." He turns to me. "You can't do this alone, nephew."

"I don't plan to. I'm off to find an old friend."

Asher

It has been two days since I loaded up my ElectroCycle and left Sarai once again. The massive cycle has three-foot-wide tires, suitable for off-roading and highways. My three battery packs should last me at least until I reach Reservation 15, or what used to be Kansas. I'm hoping I find him before that.

After a short break and a quick meal of bland OatBars, I arrive at my old stomping grounds, Reservation 9. I see where The Wall once was, and our tree. Our Weeping Willow. This is where Sarai and I married. This is where we first kissed. I feel at home here. At our palace out west, I have always felt like an outsider, like I don't belong—a Dreck living a Lazurite's life.

The wind picks up, and the long strands of the Willow wave at me in recognition. I return the greeting with a quick and cheesy half-salute. I would love to stay and enjoy the Willow's warm embrace, but I must move on.

My goodbye to Sarai was quick and cold. A short embrace and a peck on the cheek. Since they abducted our son, she has become all business. Her emotions scare her as they do me, so she holds them back. Then I think about what Cephas said about protocol. Maybe it has affected us even more than I realized. Perhaps she is struggling like I am. Maybe it's even worse for her, since she has been through it twice. It only makes sense; there has to be a consequence for immortality.

An hour later, I ride through town. Unfortunately, not a lot has changed in ten years. Demondusters trudge through the streets. I see multiple narcdrops falling like ash in the distance. A Dragger blows a stop sign and almost plows into me.

Déjá-Vu.

It's almost like I never left. Like The Wall never came down.

Sarai and I used to cruise this intersection. I savor the moment and think about how young we were. How innocent we were. Before the burden of becoming a leader and a warrior. Before the Canonization and the war. Before I was sculpted to look like Amos, before paying the tax of our destiny with mental and physical anguish.

Stop being so dramatic, Asher!

I gaze at the filth and debris of today's society and wonder what it was all for. Has anyone here embraced freedom? Are they still willing to fight for it? Do they know what we have forfeited for it? Or have they been controlled for too long? Are they now just empty souls filled with demondust? It has been ten years, and what did we accomplish? A loud honk wakes me from my philosophical musings.

"Ya gonna move or what?"

A rusted pickup barrels around me, and the driver gives me the finger as he kicks up dust and smoke. I want to remove my helmet and show him who I am, reminding him of all the sacrifices my family and I have made for him. For his freedom. But what's the point? He is probably racing towards the nearest narcdrop. My speeches and Sarai's campaign slogans can't compete with that. I can't force people to want to change, to want to be free. You shouldn't have to talk someone into fighting for their independence. I am figuring out that some people like to be imprisoned. That freedom is sometimes just too much work for them. And then there are those who don't even realize they are enslaved. They can no longer feel the extra weight of their chains.

And yes, if you must know, I am becoming more jaded by the day.

An hour later, I stroll through the outdoor market. I buy a slab of dried venison from an old hunter who has been here for as long as I can remember. As a kid, I used to loiter in these parts, and often, he threw me jerky scraps. I show him a picture.

"You seen this man around anywhere?"

His bristling eyebrows rise. His long, wiry arms reach for the picture, so he can get a better look. He shakes his head. "Ain't no one seen him around in a long time."

"Thanks."

As I walk away, he speaks with a raspy lisp, "The years have been rough on you, boy."

He recognizes me. I turn and smile. "And I have been rough on them."

His head rolls back, and he releases a loud, toothless cackle. "In my experience, the years always win."

Truth.

Unless you're Renatus and his ilk.

I dig into the dried venison and show the picture to a dozen more vendors before giving up. It's time to go to the next town.

Then I hear a commotion behind me. A rogue Lazurite patrol of about five men. They rough up the old man, selling the dried venison—stealing and eating his livelihood. Everyone just stands by and watches. They have been oppressed for so long that they don't know how to fight it anymore. Since the Senate withdrew funding for protection in The Middle, this is becoming more commonplace, I'm told. Renatus and his men have become emboldened. We have failed the people.

And they have failed themselves.

I need to remind them what freedom looks like. I march back to where the old man is being slapped around and his inventory devoured. I tap a Lazurite who is gnawing on a piece of the dried meat.

"Excuse me? Did you pay for that?"

He spits ground-up meat on my boots. "What did you say to me, you feckless Dreck?"

I smile. "I suggest you pay the man."

The five of them laugh in amusement. Then one of them turns serious. He recognizes me and the weapon on my belt.

"Wait a minute, that's—that's Asher! The Traitor of Zion!"

"That is one of my many names."

Before they can sober themselves to the reality of the situation, I slap the closest Lazurite to me with my ricochet. The shockwaves fizzle him to the ground. I hit another one in the back of the neck, and he, too, folds. We are so close that throwing it doesn't make sense. This brawl is up close and personal. One swings at me; I duck and kick at his knee. It inverts before snapping. He rolls on the ground in agony as I sweep my forearm and clothesline the fourth.

The fifth and last Lazurite sees his friends splayed across the ground, wriggling in pain. He turns and runs in terror. As I thought, they are cowards. I want the people to see that they are cowards and can be beaten, even when outnumbered. I let the final Lazurite feel that terror for a moment before I lob my ricochet in his direction. He plummets to the ground as my weapon returns to my wrist. I spin it like a cowboy twirls his gun in those old western movies and reattach it to my hip as those around me applaud.

"Stop clapping!" I yell.

My headache is returning. *Hold your thoughts captive.* But I can't.

They immediately stop. You can hear a pin drop. I guess I have the floor now. I wasn't planning on doing a speech, but I can't help myself. I can already picture Sarai shaking her head while concealing a half-smile.

"How many of them were there?" I ask rhetorically.

No answer; they know what I'm getting at. Some hold their heads down in shame.

"Five of them and one of me! There are a hundred of you! And you were all happy to just sit and watch them take this poor man's livelihood. His dignity! You don't think you're next? What will it take for you to stand up and fight against this tyranny? Do you enjoy being oppressed?" I hold up my ricochet and continue my lecture. "Are you content with how things are? Is this what you want for your children?"

"We don't have weapons!" someone in the crowd yells.

"Then make them!" I growl in response. "Giving in to oppression and fascism is the easy way out. Doing nothing is simple. Fighting back requires effort. Risk. I know I have risked everything! Including my family!"

A boy, about eleven, is paying attention. He is hanging on to my every word. I can tell he has never heard anyone speak like this before. If he is the only one I reach today, I consider it a success. I peer deep into his eyes and squint. "I can't make you do it. I can't make you want to be free. I can only hope it's something you want. Something you long for. I can only hope that the next time those pallets drop, you rush over to burn them before they burn you."

"But it was *your* Senate that withdrew our funding, our protection!" another squawks.

"Then it's your fault for relying on government for your protection."

"But we don't have an army!"

"Then form one! I see enough able-bodied souls here for a militia." I reduce my tenor a bit. "Look, if I have learned anything over my lifetime, it is that the over-reliance on government always leads to tyranny."

The eleven-year-old kid smiles at me like he understands and takes off. I see him in the distance throwing a wooden ricochet toy into the air. It gives me hope.

Then, behind me, I hear the whine of four ElectroCycles coming towards me.

The whir of a HeliDrone above me.

Asher

I dart to my own ElectroCycle, jump on, and gun it. The hum and loud whine of the electric engine isn't as satisfying as the rumble of the gas ones of old. But I love the instant torque. I hang a quick left. I want to lead them away from the outdoor market, away from the populace.

After a few minutes, I hang a right into old town. My old stomping grounds are now mostly abandoned. I know these streets and buildings like the back of my hand. I spent a lot of my youth here, hiding from my uncle's drunken escapades—as well as his never-ending chore list.

The HeliDrone drops plasma bombs that explode to my left and right as I zig-zag through the different alleyways. The shock waves reverberate off the decaying concrete buildings, causing dust and small particles to chip off. In my mirror, I see two ElectroCycles rapidly coming up behind me. Where are the other two? I turn the corner and have my answer for one of them. It is heading straight towards me, the rider firing his plasma gun.

I duck and gun it, heading straight towards him. He must wonder if I'm playing chicken; he doesn't back down. I didn't expect him to. They may be cowards, but they are also stupid. At the last second, I swing to the right and lean over, causing my bike's back tire to slide into his front, which sends him flying into the air and smashing into a brick building. That gave me a little bit of road rash, but it was worth it. I throttle to the next alley, where another Lazurite on his cycle awaits me. His friend shows up behind me. I am trapped.

So they think.

To my left is a locked door leading into an abandoned office building. I smash through it and quickly throttle my cycle up a flight of stairs, almost flipping backward on my way up. They take chase.

"You have nowhere to go, Dreck!"

I reach the top floor and watch them ride their cycles up the stairs. I peer around and spot a massive mahogany desk from better days gone by. I imagine the work that used to be done here. Suits and ties. Coffee and water coolers. An honest day for honest pay, then return to one's family, one's home. Safe and secure. I wonder if we can ever get back to that. Or is society too far gone?

Here I go again, philosophizing while in the middle of a dogfight.

I jump off my bike and roll behind a desk. As my adrenaline wears off, the sting of my road rash intensifies. With all that I have, I push the desk to the edge of the steps. With one last heave, I launch it down the stairs. Once used for business or to make some company a profit, the desk is now a battering ram. It slams into the first Lazurite, who was just turning the corner, and pins him and his bike against the wall.

I can't help but smile as I realize I am actually enjoying this. Either that, or it is taking my mind off my kidnapped son.

The last biker isn't deterred. He hops off his bike, throws it over the desk, which is now blocking his path, and then leaps back on his bike. Nimble and dedicated, this one is.

I race to the last door on the left, which leads me to the rooftop. I floor it to the edge and see that the building below me is about fifty feet away.

I can make it. I think.

The last Lazurite busts through the rooftop door and guns it towards me, firing away. He sure is an enthusiastic one, this Lazurite. Maybe he is training to be an elite? What the heck? I have done more foolish things in my time. *Let's see if he is afraid of flying.* I turn and punch it, sail through the air, and land safely on the next building. My leg feels better, as my adrenaline has returned in spades after pretending to have wings.

Now it's his turn.

His stubborn Lazurite zealotry doesn't disappoint. He does the same. Just as he hits the air, I pitch my ricochet at him. It hits him square in the chest, delivers a quick buzz, and sends him flying off his bike. He falls to the ground as his ElectroCycle crashes near my feet.

I hear something. To my left, on top of the building, is the same boy from the market. He is watching me, flinging his wooden ricochet into the air. I wave at him, but he points one of his dirty fingers to the sky directly above me.

I forgot—the HeliDrone.

It unloads its plasma bombs around me as I punch it towards the next building. In front of me, the explosions cause the rooftop to collapse as I sail through the air. At the same time, I chuck my ricochet at the drone. It smashes into the control center near its belly, and fries the electronics. It drops to the ground like a dead fly as I land on the next rooftop.

Without looking, I lift my hand, and the ricochet returns to me. The kid gives me a toothy smile, amused but aware that I am showing off a bit.

I peer around until I can assess that it is finally safe. Then I jump my ElectroCycle to the building on which the boy has been perched. He is obviously entertained.

"What's your name?" I ask him.

"Simon," he answers, scratching his dirty, matted red hair. His E.T. t-shirt is frayed and faded. He is in definite need of a bath, but so am I.

"Where are your parents, Simon?"

He wrings his hands. The sweat and dirt form a black paste underneath his long fingernails. "Dead."

"I am sorry, son. How?" I ask him. Then I think better of it. "You don't have to tell me if you don't want to."

"The Dust."

I nod. "The Dust. Of course."

"I live with my uncle now."

"Ya know, when I was your age, I too lived with my uncle."

"How did that go?"

He has me there. So I shrug. He reminds me of my Silas.

He tosses his toy ricochet again. "Tell me, what is it like being 'The Liberator of Zion'? 'The Slayer of Giants'?"

I shake my head, "'The Slayer of Giants?' I haven't heard that one before. The truth? Exhausting."

"Exhausting, but worth it, right?"

I nod. "Yeah, I think you may be the only one around here that gets it. But you know what, kid? I'm neither of those things. I am just simply a man trying to do the right thing."

"What do you mean?"

"Well, for one, I had a lot of help in liberating Zion. It wasn't just me."

"So why don't you say that?"

"I do. But, as far as the nicknames go, I think it gives people hope, inspiration." I hold up my ricochet. "This is more than just a weapon now. It's a symbol. One of freedom."

"Sometimes I paint it on buildings," he admits.

"Like I said, a symbol."

He nervously looks up at me. "My uncle says you have been dragging your feet, not living up to your promises."

I like this kid; he is straight to the point. "Your uncle is a little bit right."

"He is?" The kid sounds surprised.

"It's complicated."

"There are good people and bad people. Not so complicated."

I smile. "You're right, Simon. It shouldn't be so complicated."

"Well, I don't care what my uncle says. I wanna be like you when I get older."

I look at him, suddenly convicted. "Don't be like me. Be better than me."

He points to the dried blood on my ricochet.

"Is that blood?"

I smile. "That's the salty taste of freedom."

"How come no one else will fight them? At least not where I live."

I sit beside him. "Maybe they are waiting to be inspired?"

"By who? You?"

"Maybe, or maybe it's you?"

"Me? But I'm just a kid."

"So was David when he beat Goliath."

Sarai

I am supposed to be preparing for the debate. But I am still too furious about Silas to go over my notes. Instead, I crack my scourge at the air as I pace the training room in the underground bunker. I don't remember how long I have been down here, but I'm beginning to sweat, my face flushing. I grip my scourge so tight I can see the whites of my cracked knuckles. I suck in the brisk, musty air until I finally catch my breath. Ten years ago, this would have been light work. I dab my face and forehead with a fresh towel, when I hear her voice.

I turn to my left. On the HoloTube is Neriah, in the middle of an interview. Her calm voice may seem serene to others, but I think it's irritating. Almost too placid, with condescending, parental overtones. Neriah peers into the camera as if she's speaking to me directly. "Sarai is unfit to lead. She has been compromised. That fact that she is Renatus's daughter should automatically disqualify her, don't you think?"

"We shall let the debate decide that," the reporter tells her and his audience simultaneously. Neriah smiles at the camera; her hair is pulled back, exposing the pox marks on her forehead and the left side of her cheek. The Plague of 2070, or the DeathPox, as they called it. Neriah must have had it as a child. It affected primarily children under the age of twelve. It had over a fifty percent kill rate for those infected. Millions had died in the United States alone. In a way, this is how we got to where we are today. This is how my father came to power.

Just as the pandemic was at its height, protocol technology had arrived. The use of protocol and its merits were fiercely debated in the Senate as well as in the court of public opinion. My father ran for president on a pro-protocol platform. He had promised the American public to bring back the children that the pandemic had stolen. He played to their emotions and manipulated their bereavement. Grieving parents voted overwhelmingly in favor of protocol. Their emotional turmoil had swept Renatus into office. Once in, he promised protocol would be for all but only to be used once. He didn't let the public in on the dirty little secret: for each life given, one must be taken.

Coincidentally enough, the pandemic began to fade once he was elected. Then, as expected, first-lifers begin to squander away their lives and their livelihoods. An entire lifetime of recklessness was played out in a matter of months. Because of this, there was a growing resentment towards protocol. Families split apart, fortunes wasted.

Soon, a political opposition group known as The Defiance began to rise, led by Asher's parents. My father saw this as a threat, not only to him, but to his Utopian society—hence, The Wall.

How did we not see it? So many had asked. The towers were constructed first under the guise of a new transportation system. It was being dubbed an electric monorail of sorts. Until the very last minute, all we could see were the towers. We had no idea they would be connected by an electrical current that created The Wall. Soon after, first-lifers were bussed into The Middle, under the assumption they would only remain there until they had reached their second life. Then, they could emigrate to Zion as they pleased. But that, too, was a lie.

Shortly after, Renatus banned second-life rights under the pretense that it wasn't sustainable, financially or ecologically. But, of course, he secretly kept it for himself and his cronies. With The Wall up, he was able to consolidate power and begin the harvesting of Drecks. But how to keep the populace content without protocol? How to keep them preoccupied from what was really happening to their brothers and sisters, on the other side of The Wall?

The Canonization.

The ultimate distraction.

From Rome until now, whenever the people begin to question their government, just throw a little blood their way. Some fun and games, a little excitement. Get them involved; let them wager on it. Have them send their sons and daughters to be revered and honored.

But I digress. History is always different, depending on who is telling it. My mother and father's version of events completely diverges from the truth. The Lazurite schools will tell you Renatus is a hero, a savior. That he brought back our children and delivered us from the DeathPox. I didn't see the truth until I escaped to The Middle and stayed with my aunt Esther for a season. Not until I met Asher. Ironically, those deemed Drecks are the ones to hold, carry and perpetuate the truth. The ones who have to work the earth so they don't starve aren't so easily distracted.

I shut off the HoloTube and return to my notes. I am not ready for this debate, nor do I want to participate. But none of that matters anymore. I can sense another war coming. My wants and feelings have no place in this world anymore.

Asher

A few hours later, I reach Reservation 10, or what was called Breckenridge, Colorado. It was a dazzling yet charming ski resort before The Wall. I am still thinking about my conversation with Simon. At what age do we lose that simplistic view of life? At what age do we make things so unnecessarily complicated? When did we stop becoming humble and lose that sense of childlike awe and wonder?

I hop off my motorcycle and don't realize how cold it is until I turn off my suit heater. Even though the ski lifts aren't running, I spot people skiing in the mountains. Old school—they have to hike up. It seems The Wall and protocol have set us back a hundred years. It is ironic to see it was a technological advancement done under the guise of the betterment of the people. From my experience, whenever the government tells you that something will make your life better, it is usually the opposite.

The village is quaint, and I'm glad to see that the shops and restaurants are still open. I am also pleased that I don't spot any Lazurite patrols. I waltz into an old British-style pub with low ceilings and take a seat at the bar made of oak. A surly bartender with massive sideburns approaches.

"What can I get ya?"

"Just a lager, whatever you got."

He squints at me briefly, then recognizes me. "Asher?"

I nod.

He peers at my ricochet. "Damn, it is you! Beers on the house."

Not wanting to draw too much attention, I'm glad there are only a few others in the joint. He slams my beer down. The top layer of foam slides down the side and pools into one of the cracks of the hardened oak.

"If ya don't mind me asking, what's it like? To be, ya know—to come back to life?" He leans in and whispers, as if it's a bad word. "Protocol."

"Painful," is all I manage to say, as I don't want to have this conversation.

"I'd imagine so, seeing there is a death involved as well," he says wisely.

"That's what's so painful."

"Your wife gonna win this election? I don't trust that Neriah lady one bit." The words slither through his yellow teeth.

"Sure, hope so," I say plainly, not in the mood for politics either.

He glances down at my ricochet again. "Don't want to sound like a fanboy or an overly excited eleven-year-old, but can I touch it?"

I get asked this all the time, but I guess it is a good thing as it is a symbol of hope, a symbol of freedom. I release it from my belt, check to be sure it's deactivated, and hand it over to him. "Sure, just don't throw at it anybody," I joke. "I'm not insured."

He grins like a kid in a candy shop while pretending to throw it. "How many Lazurites have seen the blade of this thing?"

I tell him the truth. "I lost count. Too many."

He reluctantly hands it back to me. "Ya know you guys gotta crack down on those narcdrops. Damn, things nearly put me out of business, if ya know what I mean."

"Doing our best."

"Your best?!" a lanky, gaunt man in his sixties barks at me.

I turn to him. "Yes."

He wobbles towards me using a cane. "Do you recognize me?"

I don't.

He points his cane towards my face. "I fought with you. Did you know that? I was with Son's of Levi! I was there at Donner Lake, what was supposed to be the last battle! Lost part of my leg and two sons there. Two!"

"Sorry for your loss, sir, and I thank you for your service." I'm not sure what else to tell him. I'm not mentally equipped for this conversation right now. All I can think about is getting Silas back.

He spits at my feet. "What did my sons die for? You had ten years to finish the job, but your wife and your anemic Senate have done nothing. Now it's too late. Sometimes I wonder why that wife of yours would let that happen. Maybe because Renatus is her father." He spits again. "Neriah has got my vote."

"I respect that, sir, and again, I thank you for your service. And I'm sorry about your boys. I truly am."

He eyes me with bitterness and resentment. "Look around. Are we free now? No. It was all for nothing. You and your ilk are too damn daunted to go finish the job. Or too corrupt, maybe."

"Take it easy there, Frank. Here, have another beer." The bartender serves him another as he hobbles back to his table. "Speaking of Zion East. I heard their armies were marching north of here."

"Heard that too," is all I offer.

"Is that why you're here?"

"No." I lean in towards him. "And I would appreciate it if you didn't tell anyone I was here. Especially Lazurites or any of their sympathizers."

He senses by my vague answers that I don't want to talk about it further, and goes to help another customer. I take two aspirins with my beer to ward off another incoming headache. Then I think about what Cephas said, and how protocol changes the composition of the brain. That must be why some of my thoughts are more malignant than they used to be. And memories. I have thoughts and memories of things that don't seem real, of things I don't believe I have done. Of places I'm not quite sure I have been. Especially stuff about my father. Are they true memories? Or was it just my brain recalling stories he told? I wonder how badly it has affected Sarai. I have no doubt she has changed as well; I can sense it, though I haven't told her so directly.

I can only wonder what it has done to Renatus's brain, with the numerous times he has gone through protocol. It's a consequence of doing the unnatural, going against what God intended and what it means to be human. I must be intentional not to let these thoughts beguile me. Cephas says humanity striving for immortality is like the Tower of Babel. I think I now see what he means. These brain defects are synonymous with the builders who, out of nowhere, suddenly spoke different languages. We went where we shouldn't have, where we didn't belong.

"You wanna another?" the bartender asks me.

"No, I'm good." I am so lost in thought that I almost forget what I came in for. I pull out a photo and set it on the bar. "Hey, you know this man?"

The bartender studies it for a quick second. "You mean the big guy?"

"Yeah."

"The man of few words."

"That's him. You know where I can find him?"

"The mountains just east of here. I think he's got a cabin or shack up there somewhere, high up. Like I said, he doesn't say much. Eats a heck of a lot, though."

"Much obliged." I get up to leave.

"You two planning on having a rematch?" he asks, his eyebrows ascending into his wrinkled forehead.

I smile and drop some cash onto a table on my way out. "Not on your life."

Sarai

Neriah comes out swinging. Gone is the usual even-keeled tone. "If elected as Prime Servant, I will put an end to Renatus and his armies. This administration and its impotent Senate will be no longer. We will do something about Zion East! We will stop the bombings and the narcdrops. We will reopen the schools, the rehabilitation centers. Sarai and her cronies have floundered long enough. Her administration has become stagnant. Complacent with the status quo. And why wouldn't they? It's not them who are suffering. It's time for action!"

The crowd cheers. I am losing this debate.

"And your response?" The moderator looks to me.

"That is not entirely true. We have been doing all we can," I say plainly.

"Maybe she would do more if Renatus wasn't her father?" Neriah bangs it home.

The moderator raises an eyebrow. "What says the current Prime Servant?"

I take a deep breath. "Anyone who knows me knows that isn't true. Yes, he is my father, and yes, I don't want to destroy him, but I will do what is in the best interest of our new country."

Neriah shakes her head. Her short, wiry silver hair doesn't shift, as though every strand of hair is concreted to her head. "Why would you want to destroy your father, when you and your husband benefit from his technology?"

"Can you expand on that, please?" The moderator seems to be in the tank for her.

Neriah turns to me. "Prime Servant, how many times have you been through protocol? How many lives were sacrificed so you could grace us with your presence?"

When Asher died for me, that was common knowledge, but how would she know about the first time, unless my father told her? "I… I, neither time was by my choosing."

"So more than one?" the Moderator spits from the side of his mouth.

"Twice. Once by my father when I was young, and the second time when my husband gave me his LifeCell."

Neriah snorts. "Did he now? Did he? I mean, that isn't hard when you can just be brought back again at the expense of another."

This is why I hate politics; she is twisting everything in a knot of lies and half-truths. I try to defend Asher. "It wasn't his choice either!"

"So let me see if I got this straight: twice for you, and how many times for your husband?"

I take a deep breath and ignore the question. "How about we move on to a more relevant topic? Let's discuss how to make this country better."

Neriah pans the crowd. "Who here has been given a second life?" Silence. "That's what I thought. You have to be rich and well-connected, like our Prime Servant here. Besides, I thought protocol was outlawed. Doesn't seem that way for you and your husband."

I raise my voice. "My husband liberated this nation! Let's not forget, the only reason you are standing here participating in a free and fair election is because of that." Finally some applause in my direction. Although, I'm not sure how fair this election will actually be.

"And to the Liberator go the spoils. Isn't that right?" Neriah clasps her hands and softly walks towards the audience. She is as engaging as she is witty. "Ya know, I ran into a couple of young boys playing with wooden ricochets on the way here. They were arguing over who got to be 'Asher the Brave.'" She turns to me, "I will admit, your husband was a brave and valiant warrior. But that was many years ago. I mean, with the prospect of being resurrected, doesn't that taint his so-called bravery? Bravery is courage in the face of fear. What does he have to fear if death is no longer an adversary?"

"Why don't we stick to the issues," I suggest, rattled. Another headache arriving.

"You are the issue," she scoffs, scanning the crowd. "Can you really trust her to stop Renatus? I mean, that is her own father, flesh and blood. How do we know she isn't already doing his bidding? She just admitted that she didn't want to destroy him. Kind of explains why she has let him stick around for the past ten years and grow in strength."

"Not true. I have gone to the Senate on numerous occasions asking for war authorization," I retort, then go on the attack. "Or would you have illegally usurped the Senate?"

"A true leader leads. They don't blame others for their failures. If you were doing your job, you would have convinced the Senate."

"That's true," the moderator adds as they gang up on me. He shuffles through his papers and asks me, "Is it true that you contracted with a known terrorist entity at The Battle of Donner Lake?"

"No, that is not true," I reply resolutely.

The moderator raises an eyebrow. "So, The Sons of Levi aren't a terrorist group?"

I stumble over my words. My mind isn't here, it's on Asher and Silas. "They are, or they were. They came to our aid at The Battle of Donner Lake. That is true. But that was on their own accord. I didn't contract with them. And let's not forget, if it weren't for them, we wouldn't be standing here having this debate right now, as a free state."

Neriah waves her hands in the air. "Which way are the winds blowing today? One day, they're a terrorist group, and one day, they're your friends. I think it's time for a Prime Servant with unyielding moral character."

"Mine and my family's character is of the highest standing." My teeth slowly grind that sentence out.

I eye my campaign manager, who shakes her head and raises her hands, silently telling me to calm down.

Neriah turns to me. "And your husband's uncle, Cephas?"

"What about him?"

"He is an addict, is he not?"

I can't believe she dragged him into this, trying to defame his now solid character. "A recovered addict. Not sure what that has to do with the price of tea in China."

She speaks to the crowd in a manner reminiscent of a therapist or old friend talking to you on the couch in your living room. "Well, he is one of your main advisers, so I think it prudent we should be concerned with his mental health."

"Agreed," says the so-called moderator.

I intently stare at the crowd and then glare at the moderator. "We are talking about the same Cephas, right? The leader of The Defiance for all these years? The one who orchestrated the entire plan for my husband to win the Canonization and eventually bring down the Lazurites? The same man who has given everything to our cause?"

"The cause that would have lost if it weren't for the help of a known terrorist group. Not to mention Legion having a change of heart. He could lead, yes. But he is reckless."

The moderator adds, "Not to mention lucky."

She is demolishing me. I need to change the subject. "We are laying out a seven-point plan for the reopening of schools and businesses. We will stop the narcdrops, we will stop the terrorism, and we will stop Renatus."

Neriah rolls her dark, thin eyes. "Seven-point plan? Blah, blah, what a politician. Sounds like more bureaucratic nonsense. Actually, it sounds like your father. No more plans, no more double talk; the people want action."

More cheers from the crowd. This can't end soon enough. I am still on the defensive. "Neither Asher nor I have done anything illegal. All of our actions have been completely ethical and for the people."

"Ethical? If I can point everyone's attention to the HoloTube, we will see just how ethical Sarai's husband is."

Behind us, on the giant HoloTube, is security camera footage of Asher strolling through town, returning from battle. It shows my husband giving money to the mother of two children he took pictures with—the mother whose husband is an addict. Then, with the volume turned up, we hear her say, *"I am voting for your wife!"*

"See that!" Neriah points to the screen. "He is buying his wife votes!"

My anger is boiling inside me, and my headache is getting worse. I need to control myself and stay calm. I can't concentrate; my mind is still on my son, on Asher. My hands are trembling.

"Can you explain that, Prime Servant?" The moderator smiles.

"I... I, I uh, that was completely taken out of context. He was helping a woman whose children were starving and whose husband was on the Dust."

"Yeah, because your administration is unable to stop the drops."

She is a master at manipulation and deceit. Even though she is lying and twisting the truth, the damage is done. The optics are terrible. Edited versions of this debate will be played repeatedly on the news. Rearranged and assembled in a way that makes me look like the villain. Whoever can sway the perceptions of the people will win. This is not just a battle against Neriah. I am fighting the moderator and the media. The worst is yet to come. But what makes it so bad is that this last part is true.

Neriah takes a deep breath and grasps her podium with both hands. She lifts her head and peers into the heavens for a moment. She is putting on quite the show. "Look, some of you have heard, but many don't know my back story. I am just a simple woman, a simple mother. *Was* a mother. My son, who was eight at the time, used to play soccer at the bazaar while I would buy fruit and whatever else I could afford at the outdoor markets." A tear begins rolling down her cheek. "You might have remembered the bombing that happened there. Sure, it killed a ten-man Lazurite patrol, but it also took the lives of seven children. One of them was mine. It was ten years ago, but it feels like yesterday. And yes, even though The Sons of Levi took credit, guess who provided them with the explosives? It was Asher, her husband."

Murmurs and sounds of shock ripple through the crowd.

"Is this true?" someone yells out.

I should have gotten in front of this and preempted it. That way, we could have controlled the narrative—a rookie political mistake. But deep down, I'm not a politician. "Yes, it is true. But that was the Asher of old. That was before he took down The Wall and became The Liberator of Zion."

Boos from the crowd. I peer over at Neriah; she shoots me a quick sideways smile, then returns to feigning grief. Her performance is Oscar-worthy.

The moderator grins. "And one last question for Neriah: what makes you qualified to lead?"

She touches the pox mark on her cheek. "As a child, I survived the DeathPox, only to have my own child murdered. Like you, I know what it is to suffer. I believe pain and adversity are prerequisites for leadership. And unlike my opponent, I will not send your children to die for nothing, as mine did. And unlike my opponent, I will have only one life, and because of that, because I don't have any second chances, you get my all, everything I have."

The crowd chants her name. The moderator stacks his papers against the table with a smirk, as if to say, "We are done here." He is right.

I am finished.

CHAPTER FIVE

Asher

I HIDE MY ELECTROCYCLE under some brush at the base of the mountain. After three hours of hiking uphill, I stop for water and a break. The crisp, cold air renews my lungs. The pearly white snow looks like a bed of clouds. I just want to lay down in it and sleep. I am weary. Weary of fighting Renatus. Weary of trying to rebuild a new America for a populace who either doesn't want it or isn't trying as hard as we are. First soul slaves to Renatus, now bondservants to drugs. Captive to complacency. Perhaps empty hearts and lost souls covet such enslavement? Perhaps it's easier for some than fighting for their own freedom. It is something I don't understand, and I hope I never will.

I chew on an OatBar and wonder how the debate went. I know Sarai hates the political aspect of her work. I wonder if the bombing at the Bazaar came up. How could it not? I wonder if the voters will ever know what Sarai and The Defiance have sacrificed for the brittle freedom we are still fighting to hold. I hope the people see the Sarai that I see. I wish I were there for her.

Then, my son, Silas. Does he know what is happening to him? Yes, he is wounded, but I could not love him any more than I do, nor would I want him any other way. His heart is pure. He has no ill will toward anyone. No bitterness about his condition. He doesn't know that he is wounded, which makes him strong. My father used to say, "You can always do something until you can't." It took me a long time to figure out what that meant. Now I know: You're more apt to try something if you don't know you can fail. I don't see any of his physical abnormalities. I only see the inside. I see him as God sees us.

SNAP.

I spin around and hear the sound of a branch or a twig breaking. Then I hear the faint crunching of hardened snow. Before I know what's happening, it's on top of me.

A cougar.

Its claws dig into my shoulders as it snaps its jaws near my neck. I place both hands around its neck, trying to hold its head back. Its claws swipe at my face, digging in deep enough that I bleed immediately. I think about reaching for my ricochet, but dare not remove one of my hands from its neck. I try to roll it off of me as its front teeth scrape my nose. Then I remember the modifications Jude made to my ricochet. I tap the small screen on my wrist strap and yell.

"Throw!"

It is now supposed to go after the nearest warm-blooded thing other than myself. The ricochet unlatches from my hip, and instead of going after the cougar, it inanely flings itself into a pine tree! *Jude!* My arms are about to give out as the beast's jaws peck at my neck. I put my knee into its belly and somersault backward, sending the cougar flying over me, end over end.

I have a microsecond to ponder my options. I didn't come all this way to get killed by a wild animal. I have no choice but to scamper up a tree. Four branches up, one of them breaks. I swing my body around the tree trunk, grab a branch on the other side, and pull myself up further. To my dismay, the cougar scales the tree with relative ease. It swats at my feet as I lift my knees into my chest, trying to avoid its claws. Holding a branch with one hand, I grab my knife with my other and try to stab at its paws, as they swing up towards me. Leaving my plasma gun with my bike was a bad idea.

The massive cat inches up closer to me. I take another stab at him, but the branch I am clinging to doesn't hold. It severs in the middle, sending me tumbling to the ground, and taking out a few more branches on the way down. Before I can get up, the animal is on top of me again, jaws going for my neck.

My only chance is to try to hold it off with one hand, and reach for my knife—which is on the ground next to me.

Just before I attempt it, the cougar is suddenly ripped from my body. I peer up and see the animal being flung around by its tail like a rag doll. Then, finally, it is hurled back into the forest, with a chilling howl.

Legion.

He looks even bigger than I remember. He dons cargo pants and a ripped short-sleeve shirt. I can see my own breath in the cold air, but not his—even the cold fears him.

I take a deep breath and stand, my legs wobbly. "Thank you."

He grunts, rips my ricochet from the tree trunk, and hands it to me. "Asher, Son of Silas. What are you doing here?"

"Looking for you."

He studies the blood dripping from my face and arms and says. "Looks like you are trying to get yourself killed."

"It's a habit of mine. I had him, though," I joke.

"Her."

"What?"

"The cougar was a she."

"Oh, sorry. I was too busy preventing my throat from being ripped out to check what sex it was."

"Still a smart aleck."

"I'm trying to quit."

"I save you again," he snorts. He peers at the claw marks on my face. "You are starting to look like your uncle."

He refers to the scars striping Cephas's face, courtesy of a grizzly bear, so the legend goes. I knew that somewhere underneath all that muscle and testosterone, Legion has a sense of humor, albeit a dry one.

"I had it under control."

"Yes, it looked that way," he spits sardonically.

"You're forgetting at The Canonization, I killed a shark with my bare hands. Surely you don't think I can't handle a cat."

"You were lucky."

"Was I also lucky when I defeated you?"

But he doesn't answer. He is already making his way back up the mountain.

Asher

Legion's cabin is small. But it is well constructed. Various fur and pelts litter the floors and walls. We sit by the wood-burning stove, and he hands me a cup of hot liquid.

"What's this?" I ask him.

"Tea. Green."

"You don't seem like the tea-drinking sort," I jest.

"Because I'm the great warrior Legion? That I only drink the blood of my enemies?"

"Something like that."

A small lap dog waddles in and jumps onto his lap. Perched next to him, it looks like he is petting a small rat. "Ahh, good Buttons. Good boy."

"What is that? A Shih Tzu?"

He gently strokes his head. "A Pomeranian."

I can't help but see how absurd this looks. "If the cheering crowds could see you now. The great Legion, on his wooden rocker, drinking tea and stroking his Pomeranian named Buttons."

"I see not a lot has changed in ten years."

"You're a hard man to find, Legion."

"That was the plan. Did the guys down in the saloon tell you I was up here?"

I nod.

"I guess I have little chance of keeping a low profile. Why are you here, Asher, son of Silas?"

My tone turns serious. "I need your help. Renatus, he... he has my son. My son Silas."

"Son of Silas. Father of Silas," he quips, amusing himself. "Life is a circle now, isn't it? Let me ask, how did Renatus end up with your son? Surely you're not that careless, Asher the Great."

Is he still bitter about his defeat at The Canonization? Or has he been in the mountains too long? "Amos. He walked right into our house, disguised as me. Tricked my guards. Even fooled Sarai."

"Folly you didn't see that coming. Seeing as that was *your* ruse."

"I know, I should have. That's all I can think about. But I need your help getting him back."

"Hmm... 'Asher, Vanquisher of Giants. Defeater of the Almighty Legion' needs my help? I am almost tickled by the irony."

"Please."

"Why me? You are in charge of Zion's army. You could have brought an entire platoon."

I squeeze the bridge of my nose. "I wanted to be small and nimble. If Renatus caught wind I was coming..." I can't finish that horrible thought. "Besides, you eat platoons for breakfast."

"Why didn't you destroy him when you had the chance? Finish the job?" he asks plainly.

"No one had the constitution for it. The Senate was hoping the problem would just go away."

"Fools," he grunts.

"Politicians."

"Two in the same."

"Except for my wife, I can't argue with you."

"How is Sarai?"

"Her son has been kidnapped by her own father; how do you think she is?" I say bitingly.

"You know where your son is?"

"My spies inside Zion East tell me they are holding him in an underground facility in what was Virginia."

"Facility?"

"Protocol."

Legion squeezes his massive square chin. "Hmm... he is at it again."

I plead with him. "Renatus is going to harvest his LifeCell and give it to his own son."

"His own grandson's LifeCell?"

"Yes."

Legion shakes his head. "I'm done fighting. I'm finished with war."

"Listen, I know you have already done so much and that I can never repay you, but I beg you, for my son. I don't have much time."

He just stares into the crackling fire. "I was born with a warrior's body. That's what I was trained to do. That's what I was expected to do. That is all anyone ever saw when they looked at me. But that's not where my heart was. Not what I enjoy. Not what I want. It never was."

He is opening up to me, probably for the first time. "What do you enjoy, Legion?"

He takes a long pull of his tea. "Writing poetry."

"Maybe you're a warrior poet?" I ask him, then cringe after realizing how cliché that sounds.

He throws his cup against the brick fireplace. It shatters into a thousand pieces. Buttons jumps from his lap. "You are doing the same! Painting me with that brush. Putting me in a box. Judging me on how I look."

"I'm sorry, Legion, I truly am, but God has blessed you with a gift, a physical one. And a mental one. And I need that gift to help me save my son. I can't do it without you. I'm judging you on your ability alone."

"You sound like Renatus when he pulled me off the streets as a teenager. You speak many words, Asher. The more words spoken, the less that are truthful."

"I'm not trying to manipulate you. I humbly beg for your help."

Legion smacks his lips, and Buttons leaps back into his lap. "Don't hear from you for ten years. Now you need something, and here you are."

"It was you who left, Legion. I wanted you to come with us. I wanted you to be part of our new government."

"What? As your enforcer? Your bodyguard?"

"No. But if you were, I'm pretty sure I would still have my son." I stand so my face is close to even with his, even though he is sitting. "We would have had you in any capacity you wanted to serve. That is the truth."

"Doesn't matter. I can't help you even if I wanted to."

"Why?"

"My brother. My brother is with Renatus now."

"Brother?"

"Yes, my big brother."

"By *big*, I hope you mean *older*," I say, half joking.

"No. He is younger. But I am the runt," Legion says plainly.

I can't believe he has a brother and that he is even bigger than Legion. "What's his name?"

"Apex."

"Apex?"

"Yes."

I shake my head and can't help but smile. "Apex and Legion. I can't imagine what your parents were named."

"Never knew my parents."

"So he works for Renatus?"

"Yes, he is his new destroyer. He has fallen under Renatus's spell. And I will not fight my own brother."

"I can understand that, I do. But there is a good chance we are in and out without even seeing him."

"Good night, Asher. Stay if you want. For tomorrow, we hunt."

Sarai

It's 2:45 AM, and the moon shines a wide white swath across the Pacific. I can't sleep as I wade into the ocean. My torn, ragged Def Leppard shirt hangs below my knees. My feet are numb, and I feel a frost encapsulating my soul. I think of what this ocean has callously taken from me. In a different life, I would have probably recognized the beauty of this moment. I wonder where my husband is right now. I wonder what my son is doing and what he is thinking. How confused he must be. I need to shake this from my head, but once I do, my brain goes to the debate.

I can't stop thinking about my horrible performance. What I should have said. What I shouldn't have said. I have watched the replay at least five times, and the more I see it, the more vexed I am. Even my facial expressions could have been different. Then there is Neriah: a master performer for the camera. A simple yet elegant orator. She has the rare ability to convey a point without sounding like a politician. I envy that. Watching the replay on the HoloTube, I can see it now. She can stare through the camera and talk as if she is right in your living room. It's almost like having coffee with a friend.

But not everything was a performance for her. She *did* lose her son. Her emotions and tears were real. She has felt for over ten years the loss that I am feeling right now. In that regard, I can sympathize with her. Perhaps under different circumstances we would be friends? With shared grief, there is always a bond. But her son is gone. She watched him die and held his limp body in her arms. I still have a chance, and she hates me for that. Hates my husband for being an accessory to the bombing at the bazaar.

Asher would return to the bazaar every year on the anniversary of the bombing. He still carries that burden of guilt. I think going back there helps him with his penance. Maybe that is why I am in the ocean right now, exposing myself to its cold bite, trying to atone for the loss of Eleazar, still believing his drowning was my fault.

I close my eyes and think about last year. It was a happier time for us. We were shopping at that same bazaar. Silas was nine, and Asher was buying him everything in sight. I think he felt part of his contrition was to support the vendors and small family businesses here. Asher had already tracked down two of the families who lost children in the bombing to beg for forgiveness. That is the only time I have seen him on his knees in tears. I kept telling him that it wasn't his fault. But he would have none of it. *I greased the rails*, he would say.

Silas didn't understand it then, and maybe never will. But the one thing he did learn that day was how brave his father is. Asher is many things, but that day, he learned that he is a hero—someone who would sacrifice himself for others. Some would say Asher is trying to atone for that fateful day, but I know it is ingrained in his character. That is who he is. He is the only reason I am standing here today.

That day, it was about an hour before sunset, and we were getting ready to leave the bazaar.

"C'mon, one more shop? Please?" Silas begged.

I told him we needed to leave, but that was when Asher saw it. "Hey, look at those board games!"

He grabbed Silas's hand, and they rushed over to a vendor in the middle of the crowded bazaar. The man was selling all kinds of vintage games. Asher grabbed a Jenga box.

"What's that, Daddy?" Silas inquired.

Asher held up the game. "This. This here is a bunch of fun." He turned to the wrinkled man with bony fingers running the shop, "I'll take it."

I didn't notice him in the crowd, but Asher did. Asher could always spot a Lazurite. The man was tall, bronze. He had just shaved his head to try to blend in. His eyes fidgeted back and forth. But it was his gait that gave him away. Asher told me that the man walked like a soldier, an elite. There was no slog in his step. He trotted with purpose. Yes, we Drecks also have soldiers who march with purpose and vigor, but elites are pompous—they have aristocratic arrogance.

"Wait here a minute," Asher told us.

He weaved his way through a crowd of people until he arrived where the elite was standing—near a chair.

Tucked halfway under the chair was a bomb.

"Everyone clear out!" Asher yelled.

And instead of running himself, without a second thought, Asher jumped on top of the explosive device. He cradled it tightly in his arms, as though holding a child.

"Run!" he screamed, the bomb still nestled tightly against his chest.

The elite pressed his remote detonator multiple times. But nothing. Asher was protecting the people, while God was protecting him.

Silas looked at his father differently after that. As did I. I only hope God is protecting him now. One of the mothers who had lost a child at the bombing so many years ago was there to witness this act of pure, selfless bravery. Before that day at the bazaar, Asher had contacted this woman to ask for forgiveness, but she had refused. But that day, after the scene's chaos had dissipated, she approached him and offered her forgiveness for what had happened. I could literally see the weight lifting from his shoulders after that. His gait was a little lighter. No longer did he walk with a slouch of shame. It was a turning point in his growth and in our relationship.

Ironically, I open my eyes and think, *If only that scene were on film.* Suppose that footage was played at the debate. They would see the true Asher. A hero. A sacrificial lamb like his father before him. Maybe if Neriah had been there that day, she would have felt differently. Perhaps she wouldn't be running against us. Perhaps she wouldn't be under my father's spell.

Perhaps then I would have a chance.

Asher

I would have gotten more sleep in a den full of snoring bears. Legion's snoring is even louder than I could have imagined. Then, there's the sound of sizzling and dancing oil on a hot frying pan. I manage to open my heavy eyelids.

"Flapjacks?" Legion asks, looking silly, in a flower-patterned apron that barely reaches his knees.

"Where did you get the apron?" I rub my eyes, hoping he drinks coffee and not just tea. After the week I have had, I'm back on the coffee.

"My cousin made it for me. Coffee?"

"Yes, please."

I grimace when I see Legion let Buttons lick the pancake batter from the spatula, before proceeding to flip another pancake.

"Your dog likes pancakes?" I ask, my appetite waning.

"Only when I'm out of waffles." Legion wipes his hands down the front of his apron. He flops three Frisbee-sized pancakes on my plate and pours me a hot cup of coffee.

Lap dog. Flowered apron. He doesn't look like the killer that I fought in the Canonization. But then again, you don't just lose that instinct, either.

After a quick, relatively silent breakfast, we are following deer trails and elk scat.

"What are we hunting for?" I ask.

"Depends on what we find."

I notice he is not carrying a weapon of any kind. "What are you planning on killing it with?"

"Depends on what I find."

"Hope we don't run into that cougar again." I peer around with my hand on my ricochet.

"You afraid of that kitty-cat, shark slayer?" Legion snickers.

"I'm more of a dog person."

We stop at the top of a ridge and peer down. Legion bends over and points to some fresh deer scat. "This way."

We make our way down the trail. Fifty yards to our right, I spot a beautiful five-by-five whitetail buck. "There."

Legion licks his stubby finger and holds it up. "Winds are good." He then points to my ricochet. "You take him."

I have never hunted with my ricochet before, and seeing as I need to repair Jude's modifications, this will be a manual throw. I unhook it from my belt and reach back. The buck lifts its head, as if sensing us or perhaps smelling us. It peers at us for a moment, then starts to run. I fling my weapon; it slices through the air, and just before it makes contact, the deer jumps in the air, and I just miss. Its white, bushy tail waves goodbye to us. Legion grunts at me, picks up a rock the size of a softball, and hurls it at the animal, hitting it square in the head. Its front legs give out, and it flips over them, lying on the ground, lifeless.

"You rely too much on technology." Legion half smiles at me.

After a quick field dressing, Legion carries the deer back to his cabin, where we now enjoy freshly barbecued backstraps over his fire pit. It's been a while since I have had fresh venison.

"The key is not to overcook it; lean meat like this should be rare," Legion explains.

"I prefer Elk," I say. Elk tastes more like cow meat.

Legions laughs. "Then maybe you should kill one!"

While we enjoy some friendly banter near the campfire, I tinker with my ricochet's control strap on my wrist. I think I figured out a setting that Jude reversed. I need to test it. I remove three chunks of hot coals from the fire with metal tongs and place them in three different locations, each about fifty feet away.

"Now what are you doing?" Legion frowns.

"I'm testing my *technology*." I press a button on my wrist strap, and it scans the three heat signatures and their locations, as if they are humans or animals. I tap on the three of them, effectively marking them. I then hit a button that Jude has aptly labeled "Throw." The ricochet automatically unlatches from my belt; it spins through the air, hits all three chunks of burning wood, and then returns to my belt. I smile. Jude is more brilliant than I thought.

"Not bad," Legion admits. "But will it work when it counts? Against flesh and blood?"

"We'll soon find out."

Legion tears off another piece of meat. Apparently, he doesn't believe in silverware. "I would keep it on manual if I were you. No computer can compare to human instinct."

I shrug. "Sometimes."

"So tell me, what have you been doing the past ten years?"

"Trying to rebuild this country. Sarai on the political front, me militarily. Cephas on the social front, trying to get people off the poison."

With his bare hands, Legion again grabs another strip of venison and rips a piece off with his large teeth. "And how is that working out?"

"Terribly," I reply honestly. "We are still at war. There are still narcdrops. EMP's. OD's. Bombings."

"Narcdrops only work if people use them," he states astutely.

"That's part of the problem; people are rushing for the Dust and Tonic faster than they are for their own freedom. It's not just civilians either."

"Can't force people to be free, Asher."

"Who wouldn't want to be free?" I ask, astonished.

Legion shakes his head. "Too many people are trapped by their own demons. Before you can long for external freedom, you must liberate yourself first." He feeds a piece of venison to Buttons. "That used to be me, Asher. I was at war with myself. That is why I was a slave to Renatus. A slave to the Canonization. A slave to violence. To killing. A slave to acceptance. I don't want it anymore, Asher."

Buttons waddles in my direction. I give him a small pat and look to Legion. "Sometimes, to rid yourself of your internal demons, you must slay the external ones."

"Renatus," he says simply, knowing who I'm referring to.

"Yes. He haunts you and me both, doesn't he?"

"I'm over it, Asher. I'm over him. For the first time in my life, I am at peace. The only thing I kill now is what I eat."

I can't waste any more time here. I must get to my son. "I appreciate the hospitality and the meat, but I must be off. Just me, myself, and my technology."

"How old is your son?"

"Silas. He is ten."

"I was fighting for my life at ten."

"So is he," I say a little louder. "Ya know my son. He is... he is special. He is different. Some might even say 'defective.' But I say he is perfectly flawed. It's those 'defects' that make him who he is. That makes him strong. I have found there is not a lot of character to be found in someone who has lived an easy life."

"Nor is there any integrity in the ones who think they are immortal," Legion refers to Renatus. "You know, I, too, was different, an outcast. Made fun of, then feared, which I think was worst of all."

"To be feared?" I ask, a bit confused.

"Having all your friends respect you only because they fear you is worse than having none at all. Friendship, respect, and love should be earned."

"I don't argue with that. And yes, your enemies may fear you, but your friends love and respect you for who you are, what you have done, and for your heart—a heart that is just like my son's."

"I know what you're doing, Asher. Trying to guilt me into coming with you, trying to connect me with your son."

"I am not!" I half-lie.

"Shut up. It worked," he spits.

I stare at the licking flames of the fire and humbly accept his help. "Thank you, Legion."

"We leave at first light. I need to drop Buttons off at the bar down below. Then we must stop on the way and pick up my cousin."

"Cousin?"

Neriah

Neriah grew up impoverished. And even though she had little schooling, she was very astute and shrewd. She was the one who taught her parents how to read and write. Mostly her mother, though, as when her father was actually sober enough to learn, his pride wouldn't allow his daughter to be above him. Growing up as the child of an alcoholic and abusive parent, Neriah tended to see things in black and white. She was also good at negotiating the peace, making her a proficient debater. Also, because of her father, she learned just the right things to say that would make him happy, to stave off another alcohol-fueled beating. This also made her a great politician: knowing what to say, and when.

But now she was swimming in a gray area. Her son was dead, but she had the opportunity to do something about it. She didn't particularly like the idea of hitching her wagon to the likes of Renatus, but right now, she had no choice.

Neriah has her security detail drive her to where The Wall once stood, while Renatus took a helicopter. She is nervous about meeting him face-to-face for the first time, but she is also resolved to get what she wants—no, what she needs.

"The debate went bloody splendid!" Renatus belts out in a fiery tone. The rain is torrential, but Renatus doesn't care. In fact, he loves it, as he only wears a short-sleeve shirt and jeans. It isn't uncommon for him to be shirtless and walk barefoot in the snow. "It's the elements that let you know you are alive," he likes to say. "Don't hide from Mother Nature; embrace her!"

"I couldn't have done it without your help, my Sultan." Neriah clears her throat and hopes she is not being too forward. She has heard wild stories about Renatus's mood swings and his never ending appetite for blood. *Perhaps they are exaggerations?* she wonders. The wind picks up. "Did you get the body?"

"My men dug it up yesterday. It is being transferred to our facility as we speak." Renatus circles her cadaverously thin body like a vulture, sizing her up. Based on her performance at the debate, he looks as if he is quite proud of himself for choosing her.

"Him." Neriah almost chokes on the word, her timbre teetering on the edge of boldness. But to Renatus, it nearly sounds insolent.

"What?"

"You said *it.* It's a him. My son was a *him.*" Neriah winces, either from pushing it too far with Renatus, or from the thought of them digging up her son's dead body. *I hope they were careful. I hope they showed respect. I hope I'm doing the right thing.*

Renatus almost appreciates her audacity. Not many people speak to him in this manner. "Not yet. Not until I am done with *it* will he once again be a *him.* You see, *it* is dead now. But *I*, the bringer of life, shall bring *him* back."

She gulps down her pride. "Of course, my Sultan."

"Assuming that you win, of course."

His pacing circles around her begins to make her nervous. She shakes out her hands, her mouth feeling suddenly dry. "Why am I here? This is dangerous. If we are seen together, then the ruse is up."

"I'm amending our deal," Renatus announces through a waterfall of rain that slides down his shaved head and over his mouth. He gives her a look, as if she is weak for using an umbrella.

He has her son's body. He has promised his resurrection in return for her cooperation, if she wins the election. Her help in taking down Sarai, Asher, Cephas, and the rest of what once was The Defiance. There isn't much she can do or say now; he holds all the cards.

She presses her lips together in a slight grimace and tugs on her hair. "And what would that be?"

He stretches and swings his long arms, still circling her like a predator cornering his prey. "The moment you are elected, you will give me control of Zion West's nuclear arsenal."

Neriah is not expecting this. Sure, West and East have been at war, but there was an unspoken rule of not going nuclear. Mutually assured destruction, for one. Too many innocent civilian casualties on both sides. Besides, why would Renatus want to wipe out his source of LifeCells? You can't harvest dead bodies.

"Why?" Neriah asks, her voice trembling.

"Aren't you suddenly the curious one? I give you what you want, and you give me what I want, very simple. You say yes or no, never *why*. I can always find someone else to beat Sarai. And your son will remain an *it*."

"Yes," she says quickly, scrunching up her round mushroom-like nose.

Renatus claps his hands together. "Well said! You are a quick learner."

A gust picks up, and Neriah shivers in the cold. "And what assurances do I have that you hold up your end of the bargain?"

Renatus's face tightens. "None. There are no assurances in life. Only trust. I trust you to win; you trust me to give you back your son."

She closes her eyes and thinks back to the day he died. The explosion. His limp body in her arms. How they almost didn't go to the bazaar that day. It is all a blur, yet vivid at the same time. *How has it been ten years already?* She turns and faces him. "And what if I don't win?"

"There you go, getting inquisitive again." Renatus is beginning to become unsettled. The wind now blows rain into his eyes, causing him to blink incessantly. But he refuses to move his head or cover his eyes. He won't break his stare.

His maniacal glare is making her nervous. She wants this conversation to be over. "I'm just wondering what happens to our bargain if I lose."

"You will win."

CHAPTER SIX

Asher

"**W**HAT'S YOUR NAME?"

"Aspis," Legion's cousin responds, her voice dry.

Aspis was the name of an ancient shield used by Greek soldiers. It's also another name for the venomous snake, an asp viper. I inquire if she was named after either.

"Don't know," she spits out indifferently. Her thick forearms bounce up and down as she sits in the back of the Jeep, for which we traded my ElectroCycle. Her short, dense, red curls dance in the wind. Like Legion, she has a pronounced chin and chiseled cheekbones. She was also living in a cabin in what used to be Nebraska. She readily agreed to go with us when Legion explained the situation. She said she could use some adventure.

But, unlike Legion, she is easily bored. I remind myself not to shake her hand anymore; her grip is like a vice. Her biceps are larger than my calves.

"She is both," Legion chimes in from the passenger seat. Well, technically, the back seat. He ripped the front seat out so he could fit his legs in. "Both shield and snake. I like to stay on her good side."

She is not as big as Legion, but she is bigger than I am, "Don't forget, cousin," she says.

I wonder who her parents are and how big they are. I'm about to ask but then think better of it. Legion already told her he thinks I talk too much. But everybody talks too much for Legion's liking.

I do want to know about the weapons she brought, though.

"Why the crossbow and not a plasma rifle?" I ask her.

"Why a ricochet?" she retorts.

"I'm just used to it, I guess."

"Me too. Besides, I hate technology."

"You two *are* related," I joke.

She pulls out one of the arrows with a metal tip. "These here can pierce exoarmor." Her smile resembles a set of piano keys: long ivory teeth with significant black gaps.

I notice a slingshot hooked to her hip. "And that?"

"This is for shooting dazzlers."

"Dazzlers?" I inquire.

"I told you he talks too much," Legion breaks in.

"For someone who hates talking, you're sure doing a lot of it," I counter. "Besides, what's wrong with a little curiosity? And don't say it killed the cat."

"It was the cat that almost killed you," Legion amuses himself, referring to the cougar incident.

"Funny, I think it's about time we let that one go."

"I'm gonna use it for at least another six months." Legion grins.

Aspis places a small round steel ball inside the slingshot and fires off a shot from inside the Jeep. It flies about two hundred yards in front of us, then explodes in a *dazzling*, blinding, bright light. I have to squint my eyes and slow down the Jeep.

"If you're close enough, it blinds you temporarily."

"Not always temporary." Legion points to his blinded left eye.

"You did that to him?" I ask her.

"It was an accident. Besides, you should be thanking me; if he weren't blind in one eye, you would have never beat him in The Canonization."

"Fair enough." I smile. I like her.

She sizes me up like I'm a steer at an auction. "I still can't believe you beat him; you're nothing but a shaver. Thought you'd be bigger."

"I got lucky."

Legion chimes in, "Yes. Lucky."

"And you did all of this for that wifey of yours?"

"Yes."

"She must be something special."

"She is," I say with gravitas.

"She gonna win this election or what?" Aspis asks, juggling two dazzlers in one hand, as if they are acorns and not deadly weapons.

"I don't know. I hope so."

"You lack confidence in her?" she asks, surprised.

"Not her. The system. She is a wonderful leader, but not much of a politician, I'm afraid."

"Great leaders usually aren't," Legion bellows.

Aspis smacks him over the head. "Hey, just because you don't say much doesn't mean that it's something deep and profound every time you do. And why are you yelling?"

"That's how I speak."

"I think he's quite insightful," I say, adding to their playful banter.

"Yeah, well, maybe his brains are catching up to his brawn," she blurts, tongue in cheek. She turns back to me. "I, for one, can see right through that Neriah. A politician through and through."

I sigh. "I wish the polls said the same."

"I trust polls about as much as I do politicians."

I point to Legion. "You two grow up together?"

"Both our parents died a month apart—the Dust. I was put in an orphanage. Legion was out on the street. We were twelve."

"Then what?"

She looks up at the cobalt sky, her tongue squeezing between the gap in her front teeth. I can't tell if she is trying to remember, or gauging what she should or should not tell me. She clears her throat. "Let's just say that they didn't particularly like children."

"I'm sorry," is all I manage, disgusted at the evil that exists in this world.

She twirls her ruby curls with her left index finger and shakes off the memory. "Yeah, well. Last I heard, that place burned to the ground."

"Then what?"

"Hooked up with Legion. Did our own thing on the streets for a while. That was until"—she peers over to Legion, who betrays the slightest of grimaces—"until Renatus plucked him off the streets."

"You didn't go with them?"

"Are you kidding?" she scoffs. "The man promising riches and fame? My uncle used to say, 'Beware the prophet, promising profit.'"

I smile. "My uncle used to say the same thing."

She taps the back of Legion's head with her knobby knuckles. "But this lug-head, he fell for it. I tried to tell him he would become a slave. Used for the riches and entertainment of others. In Zion, it was always about who you could kill, never who you could help." She cracks her neck. It is so loud it sounds like bones breaking. "Heck. I'm glad you beat him. He needed a good humbling."

I am amazed at how patient and humble Legion has become since I last saw him. He grits his teeth. "I let him win."

In a way, that is true. If he'd believed in what he was doing for Renatus and the Canonization, he would have won. If he fought the way he did at Donner Lake, he would have demolished me. No question. "And what about Apex?"

"Apex was adopted. Haven't seen him since we were young. Soon after Legion left, Renatus sought him out and convinced him to go east with him."

"Where are we headed anyway?" Aspis asks nonchalantly. I wondered when she would ask about the details. When we picked her up, she didn't seem to care; she just wanted some excitement.

"Virginia," I tell her. "My son is being held in an underground facility used for protocol."

"How are we getting in? You got someone on the inside?"

"No."

"You have a plan?"

"No." I shake my head.

"You know about its defenses?"

"No."

She shrugs, then juggles the dazzlers even higher this time. "Smash and grab job. All righty then."

Asher

Two days later, we arrive on the outskirts of Renatus's new harvesting facility. For two straight days, there was no end to the bickering and banter between the two giants. For the most part, it is entertaining, and it keeps my thoughts away from Silas.

I pray that he is actually here. That my spies are correct, and they haven't moved him yet. Or worse, that his LifeCell has already been harvested. *Harvested?* Such a clean and sterile word for murder. Sounds like something a politician would come up with. Or a dictator.

There is a massive translucent electric fence, much like The Wall, that surrounds the area. Sentries are posted at four guard towers at the four corners. Construction is still happening on the east side. Flecks of snow begin to float lazily to the ground. Like reaching for my son, I hold out my hand, trying to grasp the fragile flakes before they melt between my calluses. Just like Sarai and Silas, I can never hold them for long.

"Not going through the front door," Aspis asserts, looking at me like she would be absolutely okay with this. "Are we?"

Legion motions to the construction crew. "We can disguise ourselves as workers, then go in through the front door."

Aspis frowns at him. "You plan on shrinking and growing long golden hair in the next few minutes?" Her timbre is full of zest. She is referring to the Lazurite workers' similar appearance.

Legion points his bulky index finger at me. "He can go, and then let us in."

"Too risky, I might be recognized." I peer around. "If they are underground, they must get oxygen and perhaps water from somewhere."

"The reservoir," Legion suggests.

About two miles back, we passed a small reservoir.

"Let's check it out, boys," Aspis proposes.

We hike back, and I peer around. "Look for any manhole openings."

Maybe it is because all three of us have our eyes on the ground, but at first we don't notice the three Lazurite guards patrolling the reservoir. I spot them from the corner of my eye and whisper, "Get down."

We crouch down behind a thicket of thorny bushes. One of the thorns scratches Legion's arm.

"Ow."

Aspis frowns. "Ow? Really, big man?"

"They're sharp."

"You not so much."

I turn to both of them. "Can we concentrate for just a minute here? Or do I need to separate you two?" I then begin to formulate a plan. "You two flank them, and I'll—"

Aspis stands. "I got this, boys. Stay put. Oh yeah, you might want to put on some sunglasses."

As she casually wanders towards the guards, twirling her fiery locks, I look to Legion. "She always like this?" He simply nods and hands me a pair of sunglasses before putting on his own.

The guards don't notice her until she is about ten yards away. "Freeze!" one of them shouts, holding up his plasma gun.

She continues to saunter towards them, sliding on her own dark glasses. "You're a bit small for a Lazurite, aren't ya?"

"Don't move." His finger is on the trigger.

She sizes him up. "Definitely not an elite."

The other two guards don't take her seriously and, in fact, laugh at the one she is talking to.

"I said, don't move."

"Here, catch." She tosses a dazzler at him. It hits him square in the chest, and the blazing light burns through their eyes. They fall to their knees muttering and sobbing, groping the ground for their guns. She quickly finishes them off with her crossbow.

"Why couldn't she just use her crossbow to begin with?" I ask Legion.

"This is fun for her. She likes to be up close and personal." He then gives me a look. "The orphanage she grew up in was run by a Lazurite."

I am seeing that her animosity towards them runs deeper than most.

After a two-hour search, Aspis finds the manhole closest to the facility. We dig around the large metal top, fully exposing the opening. The excavation reveals a massive lock, which prevents us from opening it.

"It's locked—"

Before finishing my sentence, Legion grabs the manhole cover and rips it free from the lock. I peer my head inside the large, enormous pipe, where water is rushing towards the facility.

"Water slide, eh?" Aspis snickers. "That's not risky at all."

"Who's good at holding their breath?" Legion looks to me.

But the giant metal fan pushing the water is what worries me. "If we can stop that, just for a moment, perhaps I can squeeze through."

Aspis puts her palm in the air. "What about us?"

"Once inside, I'll see if I can open a portion of the wall. Get you guys inside."

"You always do things on the fly?"

"Usually."

I turn and see Legion pilfering a large metal pipe from some of the construction debris nearby. He lowers himself into the water pipe and jabs the small pipe into the spinning fan. It slows for just a second, then breaks the pipe in two, and the fan immediately spins again at full speed.

"I'll hold it, and you swim through," Legion tells me confidently.

"You sure you can hold it?"

He simply grunts and shrugs.

"If not, you'll be fish bait pretty darn quick," Aspis murmurs.

I lower myself down the manhole into the crisp, frigid water. Legion follows me in with another metal pipe.

"If I'm not able to open the wall or you don't see me within an hour, go back home."

"Or I save you again, little man," Legion crows.

"Angel on my shoulder," I say, feigning confidence. I throw up a false thumbs up, take a deep breath, and put my head under.

Legion does the same. The pipe isn't large enough for us to fit side by side, so Legion stands directly behind me, holding me with one of his massive arms, preventing me from being sucked into the fan. With his other hand, he drives the pipe into the fan. The spinning blades slow down just enough for Legion to grab hold of one of the blades. With all his might, he is able to stop the fan entirely. I dart through just as the massive blades slip from his hands, barely missing my feet.

The sudden rotation of the fan hurls the water toward me and gives me a much-needed nudge down the tube. Along with the current, I swim with all my might, looking for an exit. There must be some access point to the water pipe inside, perhaps where the filtration system is. I have yet to see anything and wonder if this was a good idea, as I'm not sure I can hold my breath for much longer. It doesn't help that the water is so cold that it feels like tiny lances are piercing my body. I wonder if this is how my son felt when he was tossed into the cold Pacific. Or Sarai's brother, who died in that same vengeful ocean.

I'm quickly pulled out of those thoughts as I turn a corner, and waiting for me about twenty yards ahead is another fan, illuminated by the lights on the ceiling of the tube. I really am going to be fish bait. Then I see it—metal rungs. As the water whisks me past, I reach out and barely grasp one of them. The water pushes my feet towards the fan, which is about six inches from cutting off my toes. With all my strength, I am able to pull myself vertically up the rungs of the ladder and into the tube. I gasp for air as my head finally emerges from the water. I reach the top of the tube, where another manhole cover blocks the exit. I try to open it, but it's locked. I reach into a pocket in my utility belt and stick a small explosive to the metal cover. It's risky, as it will definitely make some noise. I set the timer for ten seconds and quickly climb back down the ladder, submerging myself just as the manhole cover is blown off.

I only hope this leads inside the facility, and that I was pushed through the tube far enough. I also hope no one is waiting for me at the top.

I hope Silas is still here.

Sarai

Jude and Cephas sit with me as we anxiously watch the HoloTube. I am not optimistic after that last debate, but today is the day they announce the election results, whether I like it or not. Cephas can clearly read my apprehension and tries to assuage my worries.

"The people are smarter than you think; they know better. They know Neriah is a politician, plain and simple. They can see right through her. You, my dear, are sincere."

"You got this, no worries," Jude adds.

I wish I felt the same. She did seem sincere to me. What mother who lost a child wouldn't be? You can't fake that kind of anguish. Besides, she has had the media on her side from the beginning.

"And we now have the results," the newscaster announces on the Holo-Tube.

"Turn it up," I ask Jude, realizing my tone was snappish.

The newscaster opens a sealed envelope, just like they used to do for the Oscars, I'm told. "Zion's next Prime Servant is Neriah!"

"What!?" Cephas whoops.

"Can't be," Jude joins in.

A silent shock engulfs us. The quiet lasts only a minute, but it feels like an hour. The pundits on the HoloTube can't be happier. Smiling and excited, as if they themselves won. So much for an impartial media. They don't realize everyone has lost today, not just me.

Cephas finally places his hand on my shoulder. "I'm sorry, Sarai, I—"

"It's okay," I tell him calmly. I actually feel as if a weight has been lifted off my shoulders. The loss suddenly slips my mind, and all I can think of is Asher and Silas. As long as they both come back to me alive, I don't need this job. I don't need to be Prime Servant. I just want their love and to love them. Neriah can take this palace for all I care. I smile inwardly at the thought of a simple home with just my family. Somewhere in the woods, far away from this vile ocean. Asher, chopping wood outside. Silas, on a swing attached to his tree fort. Me, on the porch, watching them, sipping tea as the hued and vivid first leaves of fall sprinkle to the ground. A stillness and quiet peace that we Drecks haven't seen for a generation. Asher's ricochet and my scourge permanently packed in the basement, collecting dust.

But if I'm being honest with myself, I know as long as my father still lives, that can't be. Until he is gone, protocol destroyed, and The Wall is a distant memory, it is just a dream.

"They cheated!" Jude spits.

"No, it's okay, Jude, really."

Jude peers at the HoloTube. "No, I think they did. A friend who works at one of the ballot counting stations said that at the last minute, six of his workers were replaced with six men he had never seen before. They looked and spoke like Lazurite elites. He also said they counted their ballots in secret."

"What can we do about it now?" I ask, not wanting to play politics anymore.

"We can contest it," Cephas answers.

"Look, she is on the Tube already," Jude points.

"That was quick," Cephas says in a tone indicating that he, too, believes it was rigged.

Neriah stands behind a podium. "I am here to humbly thank you for making me your next Prime Servant. Things are about to change. Help has finally arrived. Be certain that I will serve the people and that the people will always come first. I will follow the will of the people. You will lead. You will be my boss, so to speak. I wish I could say the same for my predecessor. In fact, I just spoke to Sarai in what I thought would be a congratulatory call."

"What!?" I say, jolted.

Neriah clears her throat. There is evil in her eyes. "She told me under no circumstances will she relinquish power. She is refusing to concede her throne, if you will. She has skirted mortality and believes she can forever hang on to unelected power."

Cephas bangs his fists onto the oak table. "I don't believe this!"

Neriah stares directly into the camera. "You, the people, must not let this happen. Power has corrupted her and her administration. Rise up and let her know! Let your thoughts be heard loud and clear. She wants to be her father. We will not stand for another dictator. Another tyrant. Another Renatus of his own blood. The apple doesn't fall far, my friends. Rise up! Rise up before it is too late! Freedom and democracy will prevail. Don't let your children suffer as you have. As mine did. Rise up!"

"We can't contest it after that," I say solemnly, shaking my head.

"We must now more than ever. You still have another three months left in office," Cephas pleads with me.

"All we would be doing is reaffirming her lies. The optics of it would be scandalous." Neriah is smart. Very clever, actually. I recognize this political ingeniousness. This is a Renatus maneuver; I am now certain he is the one pulling her strings. Make the populace believe that your opponent is what *you* really are—projection at its finest.

Just when I think it can't get any worse, my security team bursts in.

"My Prime, we have a situation out front."

I switch the HoloTube to show us the surveillance footage of the compound. Hundreds of protesters are gathered there, holding signs and screaming, "Dictator! Dictator!"

One of my guards informs me, "There are too many protesters for our security team to manage."

"Those aren't protesters; they are paid agitators," Cephas growls.

"Gee, almost as if this was planned," Jude says sarcastically. "They sure got here quick."

These people may be paid, but soon, others will believe these false-hoods and follow suit. All they need is a spark. Everything is twisted and backward. What are truths are lies, and what are lies are truths. With enough money and the media on your side, you can convince people of anything. People want a hero, and they want a villain. Someone to root for and against. At this moment, Neriah is their hero, and has convinced the populace that I am the villain.

Then we watch in horror as they storm the gates, climbing over and busting through, throwing Molotov Cocktails at my security detail and shrieking, "Dictator!" I turn and see that the events are live on the Holo-Tube. The media had a heads-up on this planned and false protest. My downfall has been carefully coordinated and predestined.

"We have to go now," my head of security demands.

"I'm staying," I counter.

Cephas squeezes my hand. "I think we should go. Fight another day."

"'Live to fight another day'—a Dreck's maxim," I say to myself more than to Cephas.

Asher once said, "Life is a series of moments. Not months, years, or even decades. But moments."

I have come to realize it only takes a moment for everything to change.

In a moment, everything we have done in the last ten years to rebuild this country vanishes.

In a moment, our sacrifice means nothing.

In a moment, we are Defiance once again.

Asher

I emerge from the tube and find myself in a compact water filtration room. The blown-off manhole cover still spins in the corner. I am relieved that the room is empty. I take off my clothes, wring them out as well as I can, then put them back on. I open the door and sneak into a hallway. I tread lightly as my wet shoes squeak on the sterile tile flooring. I hear footsteps, and dash back into the filtration room. I watch a lone guard march past me through the small window in the heavy, thick door. Once he turns the corner, I exit the room and follow him.

Squeak.

Wet shoes. I slip them off and follow him to the corner. I sidle up behind him and tap the back of his neck with my ricochet. The electric current is ingested through his shaking body, and he drops to the ground, unconscious. I quickly drag him into the room I just emerged from, and swap clothes with him. His pants are a little tight, and his boots a bit loose, but I will pass for a Lazurite guard. More importantly, I have his laminated badge, which I'm hoping will get me where I need to go. I slide my ricochet under my shirt behind my back, where it hooks onto a belt strapped to my chest that I use to conceal it.

Minutes later, I'm marching into one of the main common areas. About a hundred prisoners wait in line for food. This must be the staging area before they are transferred to their Cryo cells and prepped for harvest. They all wear large, heavy metal boots, like the prisoners did at SeaPen.

I search frantically for Silas but do not see him. And if I do find him—no, not if, *when*—I'll certainly need help. Legion and Aspis must be getting impatient by now. I have to find a way to let them in. I shiver at how cold it is. I hope Silas is warm. I hope they have at least given him a blanket.

After about ten minutes of ambling through half the facility, I find the control room. This must be where I can open a portion of the wall. If not, it's something important, as there are five armed guards and two operators. The guards are elites. I can tell by their size, red sashes, long flowing hair, and an aura of smugness that permeates through the door.

Okay, time to try this thing out. *Don't disappoint me, Jude.* I stroll by the control room and hold my wrist up to the window in the door. It quickly scans the room and the people inside. I hear a slight BEEP from my ricochet, telling me it's armed and ready. Now, I hope my badge has access to this room. I take a deep breath and scan it.

It buzzes and turns red—usually not a good sign. I try again. Same thing. One of the guards notices me and comes to the window.

"This is a restricted area. Step away," he says in a tone that conveys disdain for my idiocy. Typical pompous elite thinking they are better than everyone else. His highbrow attitude will be his downfall. When you think you are above everyone else, you don't perceive them as a threat.

"There has been a situation. I must speak to one of the operators," I lie.

He unlocks the door and cracks it slightly. Frowning, he asks me, "What's your name and number?"

Apparently, all guards are assigned a number. But at this point, it doesn't matter; the door is open just enough for what I need to do. I reach behind my back, unhook my ricochet from underneath my shirt, and toss it into the crack of the open door. I watch as it takes out all seven men in the room before slipping back through the crack in the door, and into my hand. *Way to go, Jude!*

I slip into the room and shut the door. I step over the unconscious men and make my way to the computer terminal. I can see security footage of the entire place, inside and out. I access a grid of the outside wall. I could use Kenan right now, but after some wrangling with the computer keys, I figure out how to open a portion of the wall where Legion and his cousin await. I also figure out how to unlock all exterior doors. I watch as they enter the facility through one of the side doors.

In a moment, all hell is going to break loose. I need to find Silas. I search the footage of all the prison cells until I find him. He is alone, sitting on a cot, his knees to his chest, his thin arms hugging his legs. A meager blanket wrapped around his small frame. I am overcome with relief. But it doesn't take long for anger to well inside of me, watching my son shiver in his frigid cell, confused and scared.

Then I hear a footstep. The barrel of a plasma rifle is pushed against the back of my head. "Hands up, filthy Dreck." I put my hands up. He spins me around in my swivel chair to get a better look at my face. "It is you! Asher, The Traitor of Zion."

I see the scorch marks on his neck. Apparently, my ricochet didn't incapacitate him for as long as I thought. Perhaps it is size. He is larger than most elites. He holds out his hand while digging his rifle into my forehead. "Your ricochet. Hand it over. Easy now, Dreck."

I slowly unclasp it from my belt and hold it up. He snatches it out of my hand with delight. His vast smile reveals chalky, wide teeth. I can see the dollar signs in his eyes. "You know what the bounty is on your head, traitor?"

"Probably more than you can count."

He doesn't like being made fun of; after all, he is superior to everyone else. He slaps me in the face with the side of his barrel. "Watch your mouth, Dreck."

He has been told he has been an elite his entire life, and probably never had to earn the title. It probably doesn't even register in his puny brain that I defeated Legion and that I have commanded armies. He sees me as a simple Dreck and, therefore, not a threat.

"I only have one more thing to say," I tell him.

"Oh yeah? And what the bloody hell would that be?"

I stare at him straight-faced. "Activate."

The ricochet he holds in his left hand vibrates to life; a second later, it sends a shock wave of electricity through his entire body. He folds to the ground.

I scoop up my weapon and turn back to the computer. I see that Silas is now pacing in his cell, beginning to cry. It almost numbs me. His head rocks back and forth, something he does when he is overwhelmed and disoriented.

I steel myself. It is time to cause a ruckus.

And just like at SeaPen, I open all the cell doors.

Asher

Alarms blare. Inmates exit their open cells, but due to their heavy boots, they slog every which way. Below me, on the main floor, I watch two guards fly across the room. It looks like they were launched out of a catapult.

Legion.

I sprint to the stairs to join them. When I reach the main floor, it is pure pandemonium. Plasma blasts everywhere. Legion swings his massive club, knocking guards to and fro. Aspis adds to the carnage as she flings dazzlers into the air with her slingshot. I close my eyes as the blinding flashes emanate everywhere. I hurl my ricochet, taking out guards at every turn. In the chaos of the moment, it's almost easier to throw it manually than try to have it scan for targets and operate it on an autonomous level. Besides, I'm still working out its quirks.

"Glad you could make it!" I yell to my friends.

"What took you so long?" Aspis barks back, firing her crossbow at the same time.

"I thought I did pretty darn well," I bellow back through the havoc, while grabbing an elite and tossing him down to the floor below.

She turns and screams back, "Duck!"

I do, and she takes out a guard behind me with her crossbow.

"I can't remember the last time I have had this much fun." Aspis smiles. She is serious. Dancing around, she looks more like she is at a disco while I am trying to trudge through the discord. I am starting to feel my age. My arms are sore, and my back is tight. I'm not as swift or mobile as I was ten years ago. I hope that what I have lost physically has been compensated for in mental acuity. Cephas always used to say, "Fight smarter, not harder."

I charge ahead of them. "Silas is this way, in the detention area."

Moments later, we reach a bridge leading to the prison cells. Some prisoners are crossing it, coming towards us. Underneath us is about a two-hundred-foot drop into what looks like a storage area. We start to cross when I hear Legion yell.

"Grenade!"

A guard perched above us has thrown a grenade onto the bridge directly in front of us. We dive down and take cover as it explodes. Aspis turns and takes him out with her crossbow.

"Everyone okay?" I ask, dusting myself off.

Aspis peers across the newly created chasm. "No way we can jump that."

"You won't have to!" Legion declares as he picks me up. Before I can protest, he hurls me across the gap like a stuffed bear.

I just reach the other side, and land on my knees, tuck, and roll to my feet. I would be lying if I said that didn't hurt. Legion smiles. Like his cousin, he is beginning to enjoy himself. He then grabs Aspis.

"Don't even think about it, cuz." She gives him a death stare.

Despite her unwillingness, Legion grabs her by the arm and spins her around like he's throwing an Olympic discus.

"Legion!" she howls angrily as she flies across the gorge.

She is not going to make it. I nudge myself to the edge and hold out my hands. Almost like we are trapeze artists, she reaches out her hands, and I grab them. With all my might, I'm able to pull her hands up onto the ledge. She pulls herself up, spits, and stomps her foot. "Legion!"

He smiles, takes a step back, and sprints towards us. His giant quadriceps flex and pulsate like a thoroughbred's, as they propel him into the air. We move out of the way as he lands right in front of us, causing dust to puff up around our feet. I am quickly reminded of the giant killing machine he can be. Gone are the images of him in an apron, flipping pancakes and petting his dog Buttons.

"Darn, you, Legion!" Aspis smacks him, "You could have killed me!"

"You could have just waited for us and missed all the fun," he japes, almost merrily.

"I'll show you fun," she snarls, pulling out a dazzler. Is she actually going to use it?

I try to calm the situation. "Okay, let's settle down; we are almost there."

"This is me being settled. If I weren't settled, both of you would be under this bridge right now," she bristles.

I would hate to see their family fights. I forgot all about his brother Apex. I am relieved that Apex has not been seen so far. If they fear him, I can't imagine what kind of savage he must be.

"See? This is fun, right? Aren't you glad you came with me?" I try to join in, but my sarcasm dwindles the closer we get to where my son should be. Fear and hope battle inside my chest.

We turn the corner and run into three more guards. I grab my ricochet, but before I can throw it, Legion simply points and demands, "Leave."

They take one look at him—his bulging muscles, angry grinding teeth, and massive flaring nostrils—and do precisely that. More prisoners trudge their way left and right, looking lost, looking to escape, and looking confused to see me and Legion there.

"Silas!" I yell, peering all around for him. "Silas! Where are you, son?"

"Are you sure we are in the right location?" Aspis asks.

"Yes, he was just here right before I opened the cells."

"Maybe they took him already, seeing how valuable he is," suggests Legion.

I refuse to believe that. He must be here. He has to be here. If Sarai is the reason my heart beats, he is the reason I breathe air. My heart is racing; beads of sweat form on my brow.

Then I see him. He can barely shuffle across the floor with the heavy metal boots locked to his ankles. He is confused by the bedlam engulfing him. He is covering his ears to protect his sensitive hearing from the oppressive, piercing howl of the alarms. Then he sees me.

"Dad!" he cries.

"Silas!" I rush to him.

"Dad! You're here."

I grab and pull him into my arms. "I'm here, son. It's okay now. I'm here. You're safe now." I can't let him go, as tears stream down my face. I never understood how much God loved us until I had a child of my own—a father's love.

He turns and looks behind me.

"Is that Legion?!" Silas says excitedly, already forgetting the horrible situation he has been put through. I'm amazed at how resilient kids are, especially mine.

Legion gets on one knee and leans into him. "Silas, son of Asher, grandson of Silas, it is a pleasure to meet you."

"Pleasure is all mine, Mr. Legion." Silas smiles, shaking his hand. Then he notices Aspis. "Who are you?"

"I'm Aspis. Legion is my cousin."

"Wow, you're big!"

She laughs. "You will be the first to ever say that to me and live to tell about it."

I cup my son's beautiful face. "What do you say we get outta here, buddy?"

"I wanna see Mom," he states plainly.

"Me too, buddy, me too."

"Where is she?"

"Home. Where we are going," I reassure him.

I try to remove his metal boots, but they are locked on. I pick him up and we continue down another hallway until we find a rear exit. Moments later, we are outside and heading towards the opening in the wall.

I can't believe it. We did it. I have him in my arms. Soon, Sarai will also. We will be whole again.

"Look!" Aspis points to three HeliDrones swooping in on us. "Run."

We exit the facility's perimeter through the opening in the wall and sprint towards the forest, the trees somewhat hiding us.

"Split up," I tell them.

Legion goes to my right, Aspis to my left. A HeliDrone follows each of us. I head towards a thick cover of trees and find a small trench that I jump in, covering Silas's head and eyes. A HeliDrone hovers above us like a hummingbird. Then, I don't see it until it's too late. A massive magnet dangling at the end of a cable. I try to run with Silas, but his feet are being sucked towards it, because of his metal boots.

"Dad!" he wails.

"Hang on to me, son!" I grip him with all my might as I try to sprint away from the drone. But it's just too powerful; his feet are now above his head, and I have to resort to grasping his arms.

"Daddy! Help!"

"I got you, son." But I don't.

He is being pulled closer. Closer to Renatus, further from my chest, my heart. Further from Sarai.

"Help me!" he screams. "What is happening?"

I pull him back towards me, worrying I may rip his arms out of his sockets. He is above my head now. I am trudging backward, trying to pull him away from the giant magnet. My foot hits a rock, and I fall backward. That's all it takes. He is finally ripped from my arms, and his boots latch onto the magnet. The cable then retracts, feeding him into the HeliDrone.

And just like that, it is gone. I had him. I had him in my arms. Once again, Renatus has taken everything dear to me. My heart might as well be made of steel, so that magnet could have taken that, too. How can I forgive myself?

How will Sarai?

Surely, Renatus won't risk losing Silas again. Surely, he will accelerate protocol to bring back his son. I drop to my knees and shriek in anger as my son disappears into the sky. I don't even flinch when the dozen or so elites creep from the trees and form a circle around me.

With them is Amos.

Asher

I bounce up and down in the back of the army Jeep. It is a makeshift prison, with two benches and bars over the windows. From what I can tell, we are part of a convoy, with two Jeeps behind and two more in front of us. Across from me sit Amos and two elites. My hands are cuffed behind my back. Amos studies my ricochet, then pretends to throw it at me.

"First your son, now you. You're lucky Renatus wants you alive."

The loss of Silas has me crestfallen. My eyes are despondent. My heart is at my feet. "Is that where you're taking me? To see Renatus?"

He nods.

I don't care what they do to me anymore; I just want my son. I just want him alive and returned to Sarai. "Good. You saved me an extra trip." I spit on his shiny boots and say defiantly, "That way, when I retrieve my son, I can kill you and Renatus both."

He slaps me across the face, then charges me from his seat, slamming my head into the metal bars that cover the windows.

"Do you know the humiliation and ridicule I received after you pretended to be me? You have any idea, stupid Dreck?" He slaps me in the face again. "Do you know I spent a year in SeaPen? A year of drinking filtered seawater and wearing cast iron boots for shoes? Try sleeping with those on. A year eating OatBars while being a daily target from the other inmates. A year of beatings for giving the keys to the kingdom to the Traitor of Zion. To see my face on you makes me sick. I have half a mind to sculpt you before you are killed. You have disgraced my family. My father wouldn't even speak to me!"

I blow the blood from my lips. "Sounds to me like your people aren't very nice to you. Maybe you should come play for our team."

He slaps me again. "I'm a General and a Lazurite elite!"

"Elite at what exactly?" I say sarcastically. "Except for being my Trojan Horse."

"How about stealing your son from right under your nose?"

I lunge at him in rage. His two guards push me back and force me down onto the hard metal bench. I change tactics. "What's my bounty up to?"

"Why does that matter?"

"If you let me go, I'll double it."

He leans in. "You think this is about money, Asher?"

I seem to have piqued his guard's interest, though.

Amos doesn't notice. "I knew you would come here looking for your son. Now that I have you and Silas, I will be given what money can't buy. Prestige. Power. Eternal life."

"Be careful what you wish for," I warn him.

He holds up three fingers. "We are one short of the whole family."

"What?"

"Next will be your wife." He smiles.

"You stay away from Sarai," I croak in fury.

"No can do; it seems Renatus wants a little family reunion. Soon, he will have his daughter and son back. And me? I will finally be hailed as the hero that I am. My family name will be restored. I will get back what you have taken from me."

I close my eyes and take a deep breath. I feel like the oxygen is being sucked from our steel enclosure as our ride gets bumpier. My headache has returned. I do my best to slow down my heart rate. A rise out of me is what he wants. Getting angry won't help me escape. It won't help me get Silas back. I do my best to calm myself.

"On the other hand, we don't want you. If you're too stupid to see that Renatus is using you, you would never make it as a Dreck."

"Now, Asher, everyone is being used in one capacity or another. You don't think your uncle used you when he sculpted you to look like me?"

I smile through bloody teeth. "Like I said, you're stupid."

He sits back down and laughs. "You and your Sarai are hypocrites. You know that, right? You disparage our use of protocol, yet you have both benefited from it, haven't you? You sit on your high perch and chastise us? We tried to make a better life for all, but you Drecks were reckless with what was given to you; that is why we had to take it away. I know all about the bombing at the bazaar. It was you who created your wife's opponent. And you probably wonder why someone like Neriah is running against her. You are probably naive to the fact that she will win. And what about those children? Don't they deserve a second chance more than you or your wife? More than your son, who shouldn't even exist?"

I try not to dignify anything he says with a reply. Besides, he is not totally wrong. That is the problem with the bad guys; they only need a pinch of truth to amplify their lies and lead them to believe in an unjust or evil cause. I glance out the window. "In a moment, none of us may exist."

"What are you talking about?"

I smirk. "You remember Legion, right?"

Then Amos sees what I see. A big-rig semi-truck barreling towards us. Legion behind the wheel, Aspis next to him, a large grin plastered on her face.

CHAPTER SEVEN

Sarai

USUALLY, I'M NOT NERVOUS when I address the Senate. Am I so rattled because I lost the election, or is it because I can't stop thinking about Asher and my son? I take a deep breath like it's my last and peer at the fifty Senators before me. Most of them I know personally; some are even my friends, and share my ideals and goals.

But today is different. They stare back at me with flustered disdain. Is it because they don't want to be associated with the loser of the election, or is it that they believe Neriah's lies? Or are they typical politicians wanting to hitch their wagon to the winner? These types tend to follow the contrails of power, not caring who or what is causing the foul vapors.

"We will continue our destruction of the narcdrops and—"

"Resign!" a young senator with a perfectly manicured goatee yells from the back.

"Sarai the Corrupt!" another bellows.

Cephas, seated to my right, stands, his red cheeks pulsating with anger. "She may have lost the election, but she still has three months left in office. Show your Prime Servant some respect!"

"We respect freedom," declares an aging Senator with long white hair and a gaunt frame.

"Sarai has brought more freedom to these lands than—"

I cut Cephas off and whisper to him, "It's okay, Cephas, I'm fine. I can handle this." I turn back to the Senators. "As I was saying, we will continue the—"

I stop when I see what is happening. Before I can finish my speech, about half the Senate rises at precisely the same time, as if it's been choreographed. They turn simultaneously, like robotic, brainwashed ants, and slowly but deliberately march out of the Senate building.

Neriah has gotten to them. Or maybe my father has. Either way, this is unfortunate and unexpected.

"This meeting is not adjourned!" Cephas barks.

"What? Is the *dictator* going to force us to stay?" another Senator spits. The word "dictator" echoes through the chamber. In my mind, I hear Neriah's voice. Nothing is more maddening than being accused of something I am not, especially coming from someone who is. How did everything get so backward so quickly? It seems like yesterday that we won this war. But maybe there is no winning?

I exchange nervous glances with Cephas. Kenan is to my left, shaking his head. Something is going on, and it's not good. Cephas spoke to me earlier about the possibility of a coup. I have extra guards inside and an entire platoon waiting outside to help stave off that possibility.

As the Senators file out, Neriah and a platoon of soldiers march in. With her are three of my six top generals.

"How did you get in here?" Cephas asks.

"Your platoon outside has pledged loyalty to me," Neriah states plainly. Surely, she has bribed or threatened them in some manner.

"This meeting is for elected officials only; you are three months early," I tell her, betraying no emotion. Then I turn to the generals. "This is a civilian matter."

"Abdicate now, and I will not charge you and your husband with corruption," Neriah says quietly.

My contingent of guards leaves my side and falls into formation behind Neriah.

"This is ridiculous," Cephas snarls.

Neriah feigns like she is reading from a list. "Buying votes, illegal use of second-life protocol, illegal arms sales, funding terrorist organizations. Shall I go on?"

Kenan steps up. "None of which is true. And you know it."

Neriah's soldiers form a circle around us. "Step down or face charges. I hope to do this peacefully."

"This is an illegal coup!" Cephas is steaming now, his nose turning blood red.

"What will it be, Sarai? Either way, I take power today." She feigns the look of a loving sister. "You have served long enough, Sarai. It's time to move on. Spend time with family."

Kenan draws his gun and marches towards Neriah. "This is treason, and you are illegitimate. We do not recognize you as Prime Servant."

Cephas follows suit. Neriah's soldiers raise their weapons.

"Wait," I tell them. "I vacate my position as Prime Servant. I formally step down from my post and recognize Neriah as the rightful winner to serve the will of our people."

Kenan turns to me. "But, Prime? This isn't right. We must fight this."

"Not today," I tell him. Cephas and Kenan look at me, shocked and disappointed at my capitulation. But I don't see another choice. Not doing so will only lead to more deaths. We must live another day. I have lost this battle so we can regroup and win the war.

"Very well." Neriah peers at the remaining Senators still in the chamber. "Any Senators still loyal to Sarai, please stay in the room, and we can *talk*."

They all sheepishly file out one by one. None of them dare look at me as they pass by. In a way, I'm relieved; none of them has shown any backbone to begin with. If they had, I likely wouldn't be in this situation to begin with.

I slowly approach Neriah. I eye my treasonous generals like a disappointed mother. I can't tell if they believe Neriah or if they are being coerced. They step back to give Neriah and me some privacy.

"I am sorry about your son. I truly am." I feel empathy for her loss, but there is something else lurking in my brain that also wants to strangle her.

She smiles. "I hear I'm not the only one who has lost a son."

She is referring to Silas. She knows! Was she involved? I have to clasp my hands behind my back until my knuckles are white to avoid clamping them around her neck.

"Look, Neriah. Listen to me when I tell you: you don't know my father like I do. He is using you like he is my son. Believe me when I say this—it won't end well for you, one way or another. Renatus is in it for himself and only himself. Once he has what he wants, he will toss you aside, or even get rid of you."

She leans into me and whispers, "You. Like me. Would do anything for their child."

I shake my head. "Not this."

"Easy words spoken from someone whose child is still alive."

Does she know where Silas is? I get on my knees. "I beg you to reconsider. We can work together. We can stand up to Renatus and end this once and for all."

Neriah clears her throat. "Please escort the ex-Prime and her colleagues out of *my* Senate chamber. And be sure they never return." She turns to one of the generals. "Secure the command center. I need immediate access to the weapon's cache and nuclear arsenal."

The general bows. "Yes, my Prime."

Her soldiers, who were my soldiers mere minutes ago, push their plasma rifles at our backs. How quickly the political winds shift, propelled by fear and power. I realize now it's all an illusion. Politics and power. Control. We control nothing. And everything you have and hold dear can be taken from you in an instant. There is nowhere to store the earthly things we covet, aside from in a house of sand. Sooner or later, the foundations will crumble.

I need to regroup. I can't think straight right now. So much has happened so fast. I need to see my son.

I need Asher.

Asher

Before any of us can react, the semi-truck slams into the side of our Jeep. Legion tapped the breaks at the last second to help lessen the impact. But he hit us hard enough to send the Jeep end over end at least three times, until we finally landed upright again. Blood drizzles from my forehead and into my left eye. With my hands cuffed behind me, I can do nothing but blink out the salty sting. I understand he had to hit us hard, but not this hard. Legion.

I peek out of the window and watch Legion approach the back doors. He tries to open them, but they are locked.

"Rip the doors off!" I scream at him.

From the other window, I can see Aspis fighting off the Lazurites from the four other Jeeps in our convoy. She is using her crossbow and dazzlers, but it will only take so long before she is overwhelmed.

"Get me outta here!" I yell to Legion.

He grabs the handle as if he is going to rip the door off, but before he does, Amos puts his gun to my head. "Back away, or Asher dies!"

"Ignore him! He won't do it!"

Amos smacks me in the side of my head with the butt of his gun. "Shut your mouth! I will kill him! Back away from the door!"

"He won't kill me. Renatus wants me alive; get me outta here, Legion!"

"I'll do it!" Amos threatens. I can tell his guards are getting nervous. They certainly don't want any part of Legion.

Legion bristles, unsure what to do, as he sees he and Aspis can hold off the elites for only so long. Legion grabs the door handle like he is going to rip it off. Amos digs his gun further into my temple. Legion backs off.

"Rip it off, Legion! He won't kill me! Do it! Now!"

Legion contemplates. It's unlike him to hesitate.

Then I remember the upgrades to my ricochet, which Amos holds in his left hand. With my hands cuffed behind me, I tap the screen on my wrist strap controller and yell, "Throw!"

The ricochet rips itself from Amos's hand; it takes out the first of the two guards before hitting the second guard in the neck. They both fold to the ground. But instead of hitting Amos, it malfunctions again and sticks to the side of the Jeep, next to his head. *Jude!*

It does distract Amos long enough for me to jump into the air and kick the gun from his hand.

A second later, Legion tears the back door off and squeezes his massive frame inside the back of the Jeep. Amos fires his plasma gun at him. Legion falls to the ground, the shot just missing him. Amos takes the opportunity to jump over Legion and out of the truck, and sprints into the bushes.

"Don't let him go!" I yell at Legion.

"There's no time. Drones will be here any minute. We need to go. Now."

"Wait, my ricochet."

Legion pries it free from the side of the metal Jeep. "You need to aim better."

"And the cuff keys," I tell him.

He peruses through the pockets of the dead guards with no luck.

"No time," he grunts. Then he grabs both of my wrists and pulls them apart, breaking the chain between the two metal cuffs. I won't lie, that hurt again.

I grimace, and he grins. "Did that hurt, Mister Canonization winner?"

"I'm starting to wish I lost."

We jump out of the Jeep and join Aspis near the semi-truck.

"What took you guys so long?" she says in a saucy tone.

I fling my ricochet at an approaching elite, but we are outnumbered, with more on the way, I'm sure.

"Get in the truck," Legion orders us.

Legion jumps in the driver's seat as we cover him. Aspis is next, and I jump in next to her. He fires up the engine, and I notice on the long flatbed trailer attached to the truck is a massive backhoe tractor excavator.

"Where did you find this thing?" I ask them.

"I'm sorry. Would you rather we stole a Porsche?" Aspis spits, elbowing me and jockeying for more room in the cab of our big rig.

Legion punches it and smashes into two Jeeps blocking the road in front of us. Plasma blasts fly by us as the elites jump into the remaining two Jeeps and take chase. Amos is driving one of them. We should have gone after him, but everything happened so fast. It only takes a minute for them to gain on us.

"A Porsche would have been faster," I quip.

"Next time, we'll just pass you on by."

Aspis looks at me, then at the backhoe tractor in the bed behind us. "Why don't you get out and do something about it?"

I see what she is getting at. I climb out of the passenger side window, ducking plasma blasts, and jump onto the trailer. The truck swerves, and I lose my balance, falling to one knee. I get up and duck and weave until I make my way into the driver's seat of the backhoe, as plasma explodes from the backhoe's cage surrounding me. I turn the key and quickly take inventory of the controls. A Jeep flanks our left side. An elite holds a plasma rocket and is about to shoot into the cab and essentially obliterate us.

I pull a lever that swings the giant hydraulic arm of the backhoe across the freeway. The clawed bucket smashes into the side of the Jeep, sending it tumbling into the concrete median.

I turn towards the cab, "Did you see that?!"

Aspis is smiling; she is enjoying this. Legion, on the other hand, is inert. "Still one more of them."

Amos's Jeep creeps up right behind us. An elite sitting next to him shoots at the hydraulic cables of my backhoe. Red hydraulic fluid spews from one of the hoses. I try to swing the bucket towards him, but I can't. It will only move up and down. As Amos gets closer, his passenger tosses pulse grenades at us. Legion swerves out of the way, just avoiding the concussive blasts.

"Get rid of them!" he barks back at me.

"I'm sorry, this is my first time controlling a backhoe attached to a trailer while going seventy on the freeway!"

"Well, a minute ago, you were so proud of yourself."

Amos is right behind us now, his cohort about to toss another pulse grenade, when I slam the clawed Backhoe bucket into the Jeep's hood. The large metal teeth sink deep into the engine—smoke, and oil belches from the hood. The wind blows some of the hot oil into Amos's face. He squeals in pain, then wipes the oil from his face, along with some of his skin.

"Now we're talking!" Aspis cheers me on.

I pull the lever back but cannot lift the clawed bucket back out of the Jeep. It's stuck! The Jeep is essentially being dragged, and is now an extension of the Backhoe. This isn't good.

Amos grits his teeth in pain, slams on the brakes, and pulls up on the emergency brake. With his wheels no longer spinning, the friction pulls on the backhoe chained to the trailer.

The Jeep's tires have melted away to the metal as sparks emanate from the rims, causing even more friction. I desperately try to free the backhoe claw from the Jeep. Hydraulic fluid still gushes from the hoses, and again, the wind blows it into Amos's burned face, plastering him with what looks like streaks of blood. I work the controls again with no luck.

"C'mon!"

"What's the problem back there?" Aspis asks. This is the first time I actually see a concerned look on her face. She tosses a dazzler towards Amos's Jeep, just missing.

Just before Amos can toss another pulse grenade, the chain holding the backhoe tractor to the trailer snaps. The tractor begins to lift into the air, and is about to slide off the trailer and onto the freeway, due to the extra weight of the Jeep attached to the clawed bucket.

"Slow down!" I yell to Legion.

He doesn't hear me. Before it falls off the trailer, I jump out of the cage and onto the trailer, grabbing the back of the semi-truck's cab. Just in time. The backhoe slides and bounces off the end of the trailer, Amos's Jeep still connected to it. It hits the freeway, going seventy, and flips—taking the Jeep with it.

The Jeep, still connected to the bucket of the backhoe, protects it from being slammed into the freeway. The tractor does a one-eighty onto its side, leaving Amos and the Jeep dangling unharmed, eight feet in the air. I climb back into the truck's cab, and squeeze in next to Aspis.

"Stop, and we'll finish him off," Aspis suggests.

I shake my head. "No, keep going. I'm sure drones will be here any minute."

"It will only take a minute. I mean, c'mon, that man took your son."

I can't think about revenge right now. I am too deflated. "Another time. Just keep going. There is no time to stop."

Aspis peers at the carnage slowly disappearing behind us, then at me, a wide grin on her face. "Did that just happen?"

Legion makes his foray into the banter. "This was nothing. You should hang out with us more often." I can't tell if he is joking or serious.

I turn to Legion. "Thanks for coming back for me."

"Now we are even," Legion replies.

Aspis pats my head. "Yeah, but you owe me."

My joy is short-lived, because now I have to return to my bride empty-handed.

Asher

An EMP has fried my SatPhone. This is probably good because my coming home without our son is not phone-worthy news for my wife. This has to be in person. I am overcome with dread as I think about losing my son and how terrified he must be. If I'm to get him back, I must bury my anger and refocus.

I first try to go home, and discover it is no longer my home. My resident guards pretend they don't even know me. I'm exasperated at how fast they switch their loyalty. Does fealty even matter anymore? Does righteousness? I cannot get into the Senate building either.

On my trip home, I heard about Sarai's loss. But it wasn't until an hour ago I heard about the coup—the false corruption charges. People eye me in the street as if these charges are true. Legion, Aspis, and I stroll through the market, and this time, there aren't any kids asking to take pictures with me. No one wants to hold my ricochet. Massive HoloScreens display an image of Neriah with the words, "Your new Prime Servant. Honesty and integrity." I guess if it's advertised enough, they somehow get the masses to believe it is true. Some people will believe anything that they see or hear on the HoloTube.

A man limps by me and barks, "Asher the Corrupt!"

Aspis lifts her hand like she is going to backhand him. I stop her. "It's okay. I'm used to it."

I can't let what's not true bother me. The time to restore our reputation and reveal the truth will come later. I only hope my army is still with me. Loyalty cannot wane this quickly, can it? Or maybe it can, as these same folks were hailing me as a hero mere weeks ago.

"Where to?" Legion asks me.

"The place I thought we would never have to return to."

Two days later, we are descending into the musty underground facility. Even the smells bring back bad memories. These are the tunnels I was forced to dig as a child. This is where Cephas led The Defiance. This is where I was sculpted and bloodletted. You can sense the feeling of defeat and fear slowly wafting by. The air is stuffy, depressing. I have always equated this place to hiding.

To losing.

The closer I get to Sarai, the more I want to hide. The more I feel like we are losing. I am dreading the look on her face when she sees me without Silas. I promised to bring him back, and I haven't. I don't break promises often.

I do have another idea about how to get our son back, but it's one she won't like.

We turn down another hallway, where Cephas is waiting for us. He is surprised to see Legion and Aspis. "I see you found help."

I nod.

"Silas?" he asks.

I shake my head.

"Oh dear." Cephas sighs, and his forehead descends into his hand.

"Where is she?" I ask him.

"She is waiting by the fire. Jude is with her." He places his chapped palm on my chest. "Maybe you should wait a bit. She has had to digest a lot of bad news lately."

"You know as well as I do, I cannot hold this information from her. She needs to know now."

He nods in agreement. "Asher. I am sorry, nephew."

"Not as much as I am."

I have had many bad moments in my life. A lot of terrible things have happened. I think telling Sarai this news will be the worst. I turn to Legion and Aspis, both whom have to duck because of the low ceilings.

"Could you give me a moment?"

"Of course," they answer in unison.

I trudge down the hallway with Cephas. We turn the corner, and there are Sarai and Jude. The fire licks at their ashen faces. For a moment, she seems peaceful. Maybe it's the burden that has been lifted from her shoulders, of no longer being Prime Servant? Perhaps she believes Silas is with me? Or maybe I have mistaken her tranquility for resignation.

Suddenly I feel as if all the oxygen has been sucked out of the room. I find it hard to breathe. That happens a lot when I'm around her.

She spots me. She stands, smiling. That smile transforms to tears the moment she realizes I'm alone. I gently shake my head and close my eyes. I cannot stand to see her this way. I approach her slowly. I'm hesitant, unsure how fragile or angry she might be at this moment. I feel guilty for losing him. Even more guilty for not bringing him home. Words escape me. My lips won't separate. How do you break such news? How do you tell the mother of your child you lost him? Twice.

But she knows. How could she not? She could always read me like a book. Her legs wobble for a moment. The air is suddenly thin. The room is smaller. She looks behind me for a moment, as if Silas might be hiding somewhere. Time slows to a crawl. I peer down at my empty hands and hold them to her, half-way expecting her to turn and run.

But instead, she rushes into my arms. We both start bawling.

"I'm so sorry. I had him. I had him, Sarai."

"It's not your fault. Don't do this to yourself. It's not your fault," she manages through tears.

"I had him in my arms. I had him; then I lost him. I couldn't hold him, Sarai. I couldn't hold him anymore. I lost him."

"Just stop. You have to stop, Asher."

I show her my hands, as if in some weird way it can prove what I'm saying. "I couldn't hold him. I tried, but I couldn't. I even had Legion with me. And I still failed."

She grabs both of my hands and places them on her heart, then slowly looks up at me with bloodshot eyes. "Is he... is he still alive?"

"Yes," I lie, unsure if Renatus has harvested his LifeCell yet.

She pulls away from me, her voice full of grief and tinged with anger. A switch flips. "Then why? Why are you back here? You told me you weren't coming back here without him."

"I haven't given up. I'm going back for him," I try to reassure her.

"Then why are you here? What are you doing here, Asher?"

I am hesitant for a moment, but then I finally say it. "I need something."

"What could you need more than our son?" she asks, her eyes full of anguish.

"Eleazar, your bother. I need to know where he is."

Sarai

I am confused. What does my husband want with the body of my dead brother?

"Eleazar? I don't understand."

Asher grabs my shoulders, his eyes still bloodshot. "His body. Do you know where your father keeps him?"

I bite my lip and blink rapidly, still befuddled by the question. "Why? What does this have to do with Silas?"

"Do you know where?" he asks again.

"He used to keep him in a bunker underneath The Mountain, but of course, he is no longer there. Why are you—"

"Where do you think he would be now?" Asher asks me. I wish he would just get to the point.

"I don't know, his new facility maybe? Maybe somewhere in The White House, so he can see him more often? Why? Why are you asking me this?"

He stares at the ground for a second, then pinches his nose the way he does when he has to say something hard, something he would rather not tell me. "I'm going to kidnap him."

My eyes narrow in befuddlement. "What? Why? What are you talking about, Asher?" Yet, I do know what he is thinking. I just don't want it to be true.

"I'm going to hold him ransom in exchange for Silas."

"That's... that is my brother." Out of the corner of my eye, I see Cephas raise an eyebrow; he is intrigued by the idea. I look at him. "Can we have some privacy, please?"

"Of course." Cephas slowly wades through the tension before exiting the room.

"Look, he can't perform protocol on our son if he doesn't have Eleazar. And he'll definitely want him back."

And even though I am standing near the fire, I suddenly feel a crisp chill move up and down my spine. "No, no, you can't. How could you even think it? That is my brother!"

"Sarai, he's dead already." Asher is a matter of fact; his tone is icy.

"So were we!" I declare.

"What are you saying, Sarai?"

"I'm saying nothing. I'm saying he is my brother."

He shakes his head. I can see he is working up to a lecture. "We can't do it, Sarai. You know we can't."

He is implying that I still hold hope, like my father, that we can bring Eleazar back. And maybe I do. He paces the floor, and I can tell his stress levels are rising, as well as his anger, or is it disappointment? I am so cold.

"We can't ever bring him back, Sarai. Ever. If we go down that slippery slope of protocol, we are no better than your father. Humanity has excelled at taking life. But only God can give it."

"You're a hypocrite!" I snap.

"Hypocrite? I didn't ask to be brought back!" he retorts.

"That's not what I'm talking about. You used protocol to bring me back."

"Yes, by sacrificing myself to do so."

"It was still selfish."

"Selfish?" Asher gasps.

"Yes. Selfish. Bringing me back so I had to live without you, instead of you having to live without me! That was selfish."

Asher snorts. "I don't believe this."

I hold back tears. "And what if it was Silas? Would you say the same thing if it was our son?"

"I would do anything for our son. I would move heaven and earth. But I... we, we can't do that. You have to trust me. I was sculpted and fought in the Canonization just to have the chance to be with you once again. Imagine what I would do for Silas." He buries his face in his hands, then slides his fingers down to the bottom of his scruffy neck. "I will bring our son back to us. I promise you, Sarai. But I need Eleazar to do it."

I know deep down that he is right. We can't play God and bring back protocol, not for anyone. But I can't bear the thought of my brother's body being used for ransom. As a prop. Maybe it's because I still harbor guilt for what happened to him. That his death was my fault, and that my father was right; it should have been me instead.

"Please find another way," I urge him. "There has to be another way."

He turns his back on me. "I'll do what I must."

We are in uncharted territory. We have not been on the same page since Silas was taken. Is my subconscious blaming him? Am I doing to him what my father did to me when Eleazar drowned? I feel again, quite strongly that protocol has done something to my brain. To both of ours. We aren't who we used to be. It's a daily battle to keep our integrity and virtue intact. I can't think clearly. My spirit is restless. My soul anxious. I close my eyes and turn towards the cold concrete walls. So much has changed so quickly. Before I can turn around, he slips behind me, his arms under mine. He pulls me in tight.

"Please, Sarai. It's the only way. I have gone over every possible scenario. It's the best way. It gives Silas the greatest chance. Your brother may be dead, but he can still do some good."

I grasp his hands and pry his arms off of me. I guess now is a good time to tell him I'm leaving.

"I need to pack."

He steps back, confounded. "Pack? Where are you going?"

"France."

His words can barely creep from his bewildered frown. "France? Why would you go... how could you leave at a time like this? And France?"

I have been contemplating this for a while now. "I'm going to ask their government for help. I no longer have the resources that I did yesterday. As you saw, a lot has happened since you left."

"What kind of help? And last time I checked, they aren't exactly our friends these days."

"I know their Czar. I have met him on numerous occasions."

"Yes, when you were Sultana, he was friends with your father, wasn't he? But why would he help us now? We are Defiance, not Lazurites." Asher retorts.

I try to summon my leader's tone. "Look, although I technically have three months left in office, we just lost half of our army to Neriah, who is no doubt working for my father. We no longer have access to the treasury or our weapons cache. Renatus's armies are at full strength. We can't win this alone. And you know it."

Asher shakes his head. "You think they're just going to give us weapons? Money? Soldiers?"

"They helped us win our first war; perhaps they will do it again. I have to try."

"You're not thinking straight, Sarai. I can't let you go. It's too dangerous. We don't need their help. Besides, Amos mentioned something about your father wanting to get the family back together. He has this absurd notion that we can all be a family again. What if this is a trap?"

"That's a chance I'm willing to take. Besides, you don't even know if you have an army left to command! You think because Legion came back with you, that we can accomplish what we did ten years ago? We don't have the people anymore. Drecks are a dying breed."

"I can get the people. I can rally them like I did before."

"They don't care like they did before!" I yell. "They would rather be imprisoned than sacrifice. You just bring Silas back and let me handle this."

Asher tries to gently touch my back, but I step away. He says softly, "When this is all over, I can bring Eleazar's body back if you want. You can finally have a proper burial for him. Finally, some closure."

"My plane is being fueled." Without looking at him, I walk out.

Asher

For the first time since we met, I don't understand her. She is not being reasonable. Would she really not risk something happening to her brother's dead body to save our son? The fact that my brain just formed that sentence tells you what a crazy world we now live in. And now France? She's not thinking rationally. Then again, nothing is rational anymore.

"You can't trust Czar Percival," Cephas confirms from the other side of the fire. "I fear for her safety."

"I can't stop her," I admit. "You know that."

"Y'all just now figuring this out about her?" Jude jokes, his tongue in his cheek more often than it is not.

Cephas plucks a hot coal from the fire and tosses it at Jude. "Buckethead!"

Usually, I enjoy their back and forth. But today, I'm not so easily cheered up as I think about my son. That doesn't stop Jude, of course. He—as is the case for most Drecks, has never been accused of being good at reading the room. Legion and Aspis eat in the corner. I wince whenever Aspis lackadaisically throws one of her dazzlers in the air and catches it like a baseball.

"Could you stop that?" I say, annoyed. She doesn't. I turn to Cephas and Jude. "One of you should go with Sarai. I don't trust Percival either."

"Already suggested it. She won't have any of it. She said we are needed here." Cephas places his hand on his creaky knee. "Sound familiar?"

I ignore the dig and peer back at him, "One thing I don't understand. Why didn't Neriah just arrest you guys at the Senate chamber? Why did she let you go? Why would she risk us forming another Defiance?"

"I'm guessing because half of our army is still loyal to us. Besides, the optics would have been bad; it could have made it look like Neriah was actually attempting a coup. This way, it looks like Sarai and her 'corrupt government' have been exposed, and are just giving up early. Quite brilliant, actually."

"So she is going to wait us out. In three months, Neriah will control all of our army," Jude adds.

"And by Neriah, you mean Renatus," I say disgusted. "He has the capacity, and the will, to play the long game."

"When you have eternal life, you can afford to do so," Jude spits. "At least he thinks he can."

"Soon we will be Defiance once again," Cephas pronounces.

I raise my head towards the ceiling and exhale. "I'm so tired of labels. I just want to live in peace. I just want to be Asher, husband to Sarai and father to Silas. No more Asher the Traitor or Asher the Liberator." I turn to Legion and say dryly, "Or Asher, Slayer of Giants."

Legion flicks a hot coal at me. "I think you mean Asher the Lucky."

Yes, I'm worried, and yes, I'm in pain. But we Drecks have always dealt with adversity and heartache with sarcasm and humor. In fact, the worse it gets for us, the more biting the banter—a coping mechanism, for sure. I learned it from Cephas and Jude. A bit from my mother. From my father, not so much.

Jude picks at the fire with a stick. "Defiance again? Well, that didn't take long. Oh well, I think Dreck life suits me better."

Legion nudges closer to the fire. "Maybe it's time to head back to the mountains."

Jude frowns at him. "And run scared? Didn't think of you as the type."

Legion's eyelids pinch; you can hear his teeth grinding as a nonverbal warning. Jude puts his hands up. "Whoa, whoa, big guy, just stating facts is all."

"There is a difference between running scared and consciously choosing to live without war."

Jude shrugs. "I, for one, don't like to argue with the biggest guy in the room."

Before Legion can respond, Aspis yells, "SHUT YOUR EYES!"

The blinding light of a dazzler consumes the room. The shock wave snuffs out our fire. "Sorry, it slipped," Aspis says with a smile, her lips smacking while she chews some kind of gum or candy. All we can do is grimace at her.

After a while, Cephas retreats to a corner with his Bible.

I approach him. "My parents, Zion, the election, Silas, Sarai. Why does it seem that everything I love turns to dust?"

"Eventually, *everything* turns to dust." Cephas holds up his Bible. "Good thing this isn't our forever home."

"Why does everything have to always be so difficult? I feel like Job," I say in a tired voice.

Cephas clears his throat. "This... this is all temporary. Your tears, my tears, our suffering—temporary. Listen to me, nephew. I'm not going to pretend that I don't get bothered, angered, or live without sin."

"That's an understatement," I say with a healthy dose of cynicism.

"Nor am I perfect. I never will be. Neither will you. Neither will Sarai. Neither will anything that happens on this earth. I don't think God is so much interested in our health, daily situations, or financial well-being as he is in our souls, our character. I believe every trial produces more character."

"Then I'm becoming quite the character."

Cephas smiles and peers at the motley crew before him. "I think we all are."

Before we can ponder anything more spiritual, Kenan storms in, sweating like he has just run a marathon. He places his hands on his knees to catch his breath. "I have good news and bad news."

"Bad news first, please," Jude sighs.

"I just spoke to one of my commanders who has feigned loyalty to Neriah. He tells me our nukes have been hacked."

"What do you mean hacked?" Cephas stands.

"That we, or Neriah or whoever is in control now, no longer have control of them."

"Hacked? Or has it been made to look that way? I'm thinking Neriah has given Renatus direct control of them," I presume.

Cephas peers at me. "Makes sense. He gets Neriah elected with a fraudulent vote; in return, she gives him access to our military and its arsenal."

"We should have seen this coming. Renatus's ten years of small skirmishes and terror attacks lulled us into complacency." I turn to Kenan and ask, "And the good news?"

Kenan turns to one of his soldiers. "Bring her in."

A teenage girl with short, dirty hair is escorted in. She wears ripped jeans and a grimy "Breakfast Club" T-shirt from the 1980s.

"This is Helah," Kenan introduces her.

"How old are you, Helah?" I ask.

She is timid and quiet. She mumbles a number, but I can't quite hear her.

"I didn't quite catch that."

"Fifteen," she stammers.

"She's a contra mule; works for Boaz," Kenan informs me.

I lean into her. "Ya know, I used to be a contra mule. I, too, worked for Boaz."

"Really?" she says, surprised. "Asher, the Savior of Zion, a contra mule. Go figure."

It seems I will never get away from the monikers. "Hungry?"

She nods.

I hand her a chocolate bar, and she devours it.

"Where are your parents?" I ask her, handing her another chocolate bar.

She shrugs. "The Dust."

Another family torn apart by Renatus's demondust. It is so commonplace now that our orphanages are at capacity. Even though we tried to destroy every narcdrop we could, some out there say Sarai and I have failed our people. Maybe that is true, but then again, we can't be responsible for their choices. They were never forced to use the Dust.

Seeing what used to be contraband here is now legal since The Wall came down, I wonder what Boaz has her doing. Knowing him, it's something illegitimate.

I hand her another chocolate bar. "So, what brings you here?"

"Eden," she manages to say while inhaling the chocolate.

"I'm not sure I heard you correctly. Did you say Eden?"

She just nods.

Cephas, Jude, and I exchange glances. We are all internally asking ourselves if it is the same Eden we're thinking of.

Kenan hands her water. "She said she overheard Boaz talking about it, that he had a map to it, and that it also had clues on how to get inside."

In light of recent news, Eden could be our savior.

"Eden's a rumor," Cephas declares.

"So was the Fort Worth Armory, or so we thought," Jude counters.

"Well, this is different," Cephas grunts. "I mean, this is Eden we are talking about; you actually think it's there?"

I stand. "We won't find out just sitting around talking about it."

I think I need to pay Boaz another visit.

Asher

If you believe the rumors, Eden was established around 1980. It is said that the United States government created an underground bunker somewhere on an island in the Pacific that houses trillions in gold, as well as nuclear weapons. The idea was that if there ever was a nuclear holocaust or any other doomsday scenario, this is where we could start over. Along with gold and weapons, it is also reputed to have frozen seeds, similar to those in the Doomsday Vault near Norway.

We could really use the gold and the nukes about right now. Especially since Renatus now has control of all of Zion's nuclear weapons.

Funny that when humanity decided to construct a place to start over after a potential nuclear event, they decided nuclear weapons would be the first thing stored. I guess the scenario makes one become an immediate superpower, even if you are alone on an island!

We arrive at Boaz's lavish estate. I brought Legion with me. At the very least, I figured the mere sight of Legion would help *motivate* him. If, in fact, he has the map and Eden is even real. Jude and Cephas believe it is. Me, not so much. But I am running out of options.

I'm also running out of hope. Besides, the Fort Worth Armory existed; why not Eden? I guess we will soon find out.

As we walk up his steps, I spot him in the garden. He dons an orange satin jumpsuit, gold chains, and a Rolex watch on both wrists. Who needs one on both wrists? He looks ridiculous. Then again, he always has. But I guess he can afford to.

"I see business is still good."

Startled, Boaz rises to his feet and almost falls over. "Asher, you scared the life out of me." He peers up at Legion. "Is that... is that Legion?"

I ignore his question. "Seeing that there is no longer any contraband to speak of, what are you up to these days, Boaz?"

"I am completely legitimate, if that's what you are aiming at," he stammers.

"Then why the need for fifteen-year-old contra mules?"

He watches Legion pluck an apple from one of the trees and devour it in one bite. "I do antiquities now, Americana, that sort of thing. You wouldn't believe what sort of treasure is thrown out."

I eye him, tap my head with my ricochet. "I almost don't."

"You can come to my shop and have a look-see if you like."

"You mean your cover for your illegal arms trade?" I am making an educated guess here, but by his reaction, I can tell I'm on to something.

"I have no idea what you are talking about," he protests. "My business activities are legal. This is harassment! Come see."

"So you're not selling arms to contingents of Lazurites at the border? You're not brokering weapons deals between The Middle and Zion East?"

"I told you, no. I'm into antiques and—"

"Boaz, relax; you're not in trouble. Not yet."

He uses both hands to scratch his paunch. "What is it that you want, Asher? I'm a busy man."

"Just been kind of wondering where you have been these past ten years? A resourceful gentleman such as yourself could have been useful to our cause. Your services could have come in handy."

He waves me off. "I'm not one to delve into politics or war."

"Ah yes, a man always on the sidelines. Or too busy lining your pockets? Besides, why would you want to end this war when you profit from it?"

"Can I help you with something, Asher?"

I watch Legion pop a few more apples into his mouth like grapes. "I hear you're the man with all the maps."

"Maps?" He then points to Legion and his mouthful of apples. "I hope you will reimburse me for those. Apples are at a premium right now."

I approach him and tap the end of my ricochet against his barrel chest. "Eden."

"Ah, the myth of Eden." Boaz smiles, looking up at the bright sun. "Many have tried and have never found that fabled place."

"You saying you don't have a map?"

"I do, but that doesn't mean Eden actually exists. It's a mirage. A cold war fantasy. Something out of a movie."

"Give me the map, and I'll go find out."

"Can't just take it from me," Boaz pleads, his face turning maroon. He is a creature of greed and gluttony. He always has been. I will appeal to the former before moving on to other motivational tactics. "Eden may not exist, but the map is an expensive piece of Americana."

Legion marches up to him and drops a bag of gold at his feet. "This should cover it."

Boaz's greedy, beady eyes peer into the bag. He holds it up, guessing its weight. "Eden is worth much more than this."

"You just said it was a myth," I retort.

"And if it's not, we are talking trillions."

Legion approaches him. He squishes an apple between his thumb and index finger. "I said this will cover it."

Boaz swallows while shuffling backward.

I change tactics. "It's okay, Legion. He is right. Consider this a down payment; I will pay you a hundred times this upon our return." Boaz contemplates it. "Besides, are *you* going to find transportation there? Are *you* going to figure out how to get in?"

"Ah yes, the cipher. You one for riddles?" Boaz asks.

"No, but I know who is," I reply.

Boaz smiles and gives that look he loves to give when he knows something no one else does. "Because getting there is only half the battle."

"You're starting to sound like a believer."

Boaz holds up his index finger as if to say just a minute. He retreats into his palatial estate.

"You trust him?" Legion asks me.

"No. But he was right about the Fort Worth Amory."

Legion sniffs as if he can smell one's character. "I do not trust a man that lives for money and nothing else. They can easily be bought off."

"Isn't that what we are doing?"

Five minutes later, Boaz waddles his way through the garden holding the map. He must have gotten cold, as he is now wearing a fur coat and a ridiculous-looking Shapka—one of those furry Russian hats. He is about to hand over the map, then stops. "Under one condition."

"What?"

"That I can come."

"You want to come to Eden? Why?" I ask, a bit perplexed. Boaz was never the risk-taker. He always had someone else do his dirty work. Not once did I ever see him digging through the trash or actually handing off merchandise.

"I want to see it for myself. I want to see if it actually exists. Besides, I think some fresh sea air will do me some good. I don't get out much anymore."

Legion pulls me away and whispers, "Not a good idea, Asher. This man is disloyal at best, treacherous at worst."

"I don't trust him. But he knows the map better than anyone and might prove useful. Besides, this way, we can keep an eye on him."

Legion growls, "You're the boss, but Cephas won't like it."

"There isn't much Cephas does like."

I stroll back over and take the map from Boaz and study it. "Alaska in the winter? Better keep that hat on, and you'll need your sea legs as well."

CHAPTER EIGHT

Sarai

AFTER THREE STOPS AND twenty-seven hours, I finally land in Paris, France. We had to go around Zion East to avoid any potential EMPs taking down my jet. I nodded off for a couple of hours, but that was about it. I have never been able to sleep well outside of my bed.

I ponder the state of the world and how much of it is a wasteland, especially Europe. The financial meltdown and BitTender crash were almost worldwide. A digital currency provides too many opportunities for corruption and hacking. Mass famine, war, and The DeathPox became a breeding ground for dictators worldwide. Luckily, we are still the only ones to have protocol. At least for now.

I must focus on the meeting ahead, but I can't stop thinking about Silas. And Asher. How could he not see how using my brother's body for ransom would bother me? I know that Eleazar is dead already and that he thinks he is just being practical, but still. That is my brother. Or am I being ridiculous? Do I secretly want my father to resurrect him? Not at the expense of my son, of course, but how I miss my brother. Maybe it's the guilt I still carry for his drowning on my watch; perhaps that's why I am so strongly against Asher's plan. Possibly, one day, as my father initially intended, we will have the technology to bring him back without sacrificing another human being. I can have my son and my brother.

But.

It would still be wrong. Unnatural, I know. Once again, my feelings and morals are going head to head.

I squint and shake these thoughts from my mind. I slip into my black formal dress with red sashes tied to my waist and biceps. Czar Percival is a vain man who is a sucker for these types of events.

For the first time in months, I apply makeup to my face. It feels weird. Like I'm brushing on a different person. I figure it can't hurt while I make my requests. I peer closer into the mirror; my eyes are droopy, my face downtrodden. I have never felt so alone. Once again, Renatus and this never-ending war have managed to separate us. All of us. I am in France. Cephas and Jude are in search of Eden. And my husband, looking for my dead brother. All long-shots.

Thirty minutes later, my entourage of guards and I are escorted up the grand steps of Percival's mansion. Asher insisted I take a more significant security force, but I didn't want to look imposing or dominant. I must walk a fine line and not hurt Percival's fragile ego, if he is still who I remember him to be.

I shiver as a light breeze blows through before his Sentries open the massive double doors and wave us inside. The floors are marble, and the ceilings are at least fifty feet high. It seems every dictator's mansion has to have marble. I recognize paintings pilfered from the Louvre. Including the Mona Lisa.

Czar Percival strolls in. Skinny and extremely short, he reminds me of Napoleon. His black hair has blond streaks highlighted down the sides. I am guessing he is in his late fifties. His hazel eyes are wide set, and his nose is a tad crooked. His feet are large for his height, and his teeth, unlike the Lazurites', are a sandy brown. He grabs my hand and kisses it.

"Sultana, it has been so long. Welcome to Paris. Some call it the City of Light." He gently squeezes my hand. "I like to say the City of Love."

"Czar Percival, you look well." I feign a smile. I hide my nervousness by retaining direct eye contact with him. "And Sarai will do." I pull my hand away from his smooth, silky one. His long fingernails slightly scratch my palm. On purpose?

He rubs his smooth, round chin. "Yes, of course. You are no longer a Sultana. Shall I call you Prime Servant? Or is that no longer the case either?"

News travels fast, and my election loss will complicate things.

"Sarai is fine."

"You must be famished, my dear. Let's eat!"

The dining room table is even larger than the one my father had. Servants pour us the finest wine. Lobster, crab cakes, and filet mignon grace our plates. I feel like a Sultana once again. As skinny as Percival is, he eats like Jude. Unlike my father, his table manners are impeccable.

"I was so sorry to hear about the war with your father. How is he, by the way?"

I clear my throat and conceal my glare at his stupid question.

"Never mind, that was a foolish question," he concedes. "Family can be tough sometimes."

"That's quite all right, Percival," I lie.

"And I'm sorry to hear about the election," he adds, dabbing his chin with a silk napkin.

I gulp my wine. "Didn't like politics anyway."

He laughs and holds up his glass. "Those who do usually aren't fit to lead."

I cheers him with mine. "Well said." Then I think to myself, *A dictator doesn't have to worry about politics. Or votes.*

"So, Sarai, to what do we owe the pleasure?"

I have been dreading this moment, but I swallow my pride along with my wine. "I... I have humbly and respectfully come to ask for your help."

"Help? What is it that you need?"

"I'm afraid we are about to be in the midst of another civil war. One where we are out-gunned, out-manned, and out-spent."

"You want money from me?"

"And weapons and troops."

"I would be lying if I didn't say I am a bit bewildered by your petition. You want me to assist you in fighting your father?"

"I want your assistance in fighting for freedom. Our countries have a long history of being allies. Look, I know Renatus, and you are friends."

He nibbles on a crab cake. "No longer. I asked him for a favor long ago, and he refused. Anyway, I'm unsure why I would waste valuable blood and treasure helping you. You and your administration are on their way out—or chased out, is what I hear. A coup, was it?"

"I was cheated," I tell him.

"Isn't the loser always? Look, when I first heard you were coming, I honestly thought you were coming here to live in exile. With the corruption and all."

"There was no corruption in my administration; that was a complete lie."

"Does it matter now, Sarai? Give me one good reason to throw money at a lame horse."

He is right, true or not; the damage is already done. This is going to be more challenging than I thought. I bite my lip and fight back the urge to shiver. Between my thin dress and the fan above me, I suddenly feel cold.

"Look at me as a buffer between you and Renatus."

"Buffer?"

"If Renatus reclaims power, I assure you his ambitions reach further than the Americas."

Percival swirls the wine inside his glass. "The sea is my buffer."

"Even so, he certainly wouldn't be an ally. I would."

Marcus, one of Percival's advisors, whispers something into his ear. Percival runs his tongue on the inside of his lip; he is pondering.

"Perhaps we can make a deal, Sultana?"

"What kind of deal?" I ask, not liking the way he gawks at me.

He jumps up. "First, let us dance!"

"And what of dessert?" I try to bring up anything other than dancing with him.

He eyes me as if I'm dessert. "Later, my dear. Give the main course a chance to settle."

He grabs my hand, and not wanting to be rude, I reluctantly join him. His soft hands squeeze mine. As he queues the music with a snap of his finger, we tango. No man has held me this close since I met Asher, and I hide how uncomfortable it makes me.

"Where did you learn this dance?" he asks, surprised.

"I grew up a Sultana, remember?"

"Ah, yes. And Asher? He did not want to join you on your trip?"

"He is busy elsewhere. Besides, he hates to dance." I'm unsure why I let that information slip from my mouth. That has always been between me and Asher.

"That's a shame." He smiles, staring at me for a bit too long. "Trouble between you two?"

"No trouble."

He is a good dancer, probably years of practice and pampering. Plus, he is French, after all. I am a good four inches taller than him, so I bend my knees just a bit to try to remain at eye level, again not wanting his ego bruised.

I want to get back down to business. "So, what kind of deal are we talking about?"

"Protocol," he whispers into my ear. His breath smells of wine and shellfish.

"You have the wrong person; you should talk to my father."

"I did. That is what he would not help me with so many years ago. You give me protocol, and I will give you troops, tanks, fighter jets, gold, BitTender, you name it."

I make the mistake of telling him the truth, in an attempt to appeal to his good nature. "I'm sorry, but we no longer have it."

His tone is suddenly hostile. "That is not what I hear."

"We destroyed it."

He immediately stops dancing. The music comes to a halt. He clasps his hands together and paces in a circle twice, like a dog before it lies down.

"I think you're lying to me, Sultana."

"I swear, we no longer have it." Perhaps I should have lied about it, but I don't want to make a promise I cannot and will not deliver.

"Only a fool would destroy such a gift!" he snarls. "Yet, you fly halfway around the world and ask me to give you the world, and you are offering nothing in return. Perhaps you are that fool." He sniffs the air. "Perhaps you are a Sultana turned Dreck."

Asher and Cephas were right. I am a fool for coming here. I slowly step away from him and perform a ridiculous curtsy. "I'm sorry to end the evening early, Czar Percival, but I must be getting back."

Percival claps his hands. In barge a dozen soldiers.

"I think you'll be gracing us with your presence for a while longer, Sultana."

Jude

The Aleutian Islands are a chain of islands in southwestern Alaska. If Boaz's map is correct, Eden is on Sitka, a quaint little fishing town on Baranoff Island. Cephas vomits over the side of the hundred-and-twenty-foot vessel. It used to be a crabbing boat.

"Chumming the water, eh? Didn't know you got seasick." Jude laughs.

"I don't. It was your cooking," Cephas jokes, hurling again.

"Can I get you some ginger ale or something?" Jude can't help himself. "Maybe a pastrami sandwich with hot mustard, pickles, and sauerkraut?"

Cephas retches again.

They didn't have a plane big enough to fit the amount of gold and nuclear warheads they were hoping to recover if they did, in fact, find Eden. So, they had to take a ship instead.

Jude hands Cephas a towel to wipe his mouth. "You need to lay off the coffee and orange juice; the acid in your stomach doesn't help."

Cephas wipes the remnants from his mouth and beard and tosses the towel at Jude. "You and your mouth don't help."

Jude dodges it. "Sure you don't want that sandwich?"

They both disdainfully watch as Boaz waddles across the deck, stuffing his face with pastries. The sun reflects off the massive amount of gold jewelry he is donning. Even his shoes have diamond studs on the side.

Jude shakes his head. "Diamonds on your shoes? Someone tell me why?"

"Someone tell me *why* he's here," Cephas growls.

"Asher thought it might be a good idea," Jude replies.

"He's not to be trusted."

"True, but Asher thought this way we could keep an eye on him—that he can't run off to Renatus and tell him what we are up to."

"Just look at him, dressed like some fancy Lazurite. No more contraband, but business seems good. And look at that. A Rolex on each arm. Why?"

"What if he loses one?" Jude loves playing the devil's advocate any chance he gets.

"What? An arm?"

Jude laughs, then spits, "Heard he's dealing arms these days."

Cephas raises a bushy eyebrow. "To who? To us or to Renatus?"

"Both."

"Figures. I still think he should be in jail."

"I agree, but he knows more about the map than anyone. Not to mention the cipher," Jude informs him.

"Cipher?"

Jude unfolds the map. "Once there, assuming we find it."

"And assuming it exists." Cephas frowns at Boaz. "I still think this is a snipe hunt."

"Assuming it exists, and we find it, there is a cipher to get in. Or, more like a riddle."

"Riddle?"

Jude flips the map over and reads the riddle, "Father of the Sun. Was neither Fat nor Little. Could see and divide the invisible."

"What the heck does that mean?" Cephas asks.

"No idea."

"You don't know?" Cephas can barely get the words out as he hurls over the side again.

"I hope to figure it out before we get there," Jude replies.

"Wonderful, this will make the Fort Worth Armory seem like a trip to the market." Cephas scratches his chin, then clears his throat as Jude throws the towel back at him. "Neither fat nor little? Guess they're not talking about Boaz. I'll leave it to you, my friend. Good thing you're good at puzzles."

Another rolling wave hits them, and Cephas darts back to the railing.

Jude is good at puzzles. And he loves riddles. His parents died when he was eleven. He grew up in an orphanage that was short on toys but had stacks upon stacks of puzzles. When he wasn't puzzling, he was studying human behavior. Maybe it was how the nuns spoke about his situation at the orphanage, almost in code. Or perhaps it was how potential new parents acted when they visited—never choosing him. He was too old, they would say. He stopped listening to their words, and instead paid attention to their subtext and body language. He was more interested in what they weren't saying. Or, to be more exact, the words behind the words. There are very few people who always say precisely what they mean.

Many riddles are just figuring out the subtext of the words. By the time he was eighteen and went off on his own, Jude excelled at them. It wasn't long after that he met Cephas. He had Cephas pegged immediately.

Gruff on the outside, softy on the inside.

Tough but fair.

A born leader who pretends he is a bad one.

An imperfect man who strives to do what's right.

Firm yet yielding.

Does hard things because they are hard.

Few people know this about Jude, and that is how he likes it; reading people without their knowledge gives him an advantage.

The one person Jude could never figure out was himself. Perhaps that is why he hides under a blanket of sarcasm and wisecracks. Maybe the lack of a real childhood is why he sometimes still acts like one. In spirit, anyway. He craves human interaction and attention even though he pretends not to. As a child, he was ignored and marginalized. As an adult, he wants to be recognized. And above all, loved. Since he doesn't have a father, Cephas has filled the gap, and is that father figure to some extent. And Cephas is the only person he feels comfortable being himself around.

Jude reads the riddle to himself repeatedly, until he spots Boaz heading back to the mess hall.

"Hey Boaz, can you come here a sec?"

A wave hammers the side of the boat, and Boaz almost loses his balance as he trudges over. Cephas grabs his arm to hold him steady.

"Thank you. Still finding my sea legs, I'm afraid." Boaz is winded already. He takes a wide stance to help with his balance.

"Maybe if you didn't have all that gold weighing you down," scoffs Cephas.

Jude hands him the map. "The riddle? You know anything about this?"

"I don't believe I have figured it out yet."

"Any ideas?" Cephas orders more than asks.

Boaz shakes his head. "Someone tall and skinny, perhaps?"

Jude stands. "How long have you had the map?"

Boaz rests both hands on his plump belly. "About five years. I found it hidden behind a picture I purchased from the museum."

"You mean stole," Cephas barks.

"Purchased. Fair and square," Boaz corrects him.

Jude shuffles back and forth, "Doesn't matter now how you acquired it. You saying after five years, you still have no idea?"

Boaz nods. "I was afraid to show it to anyone else. I was afraid they might steal it."

"That would be ironic," Cephas's words slide from the corner of his mouth.

"Listen, I know you two don't like me, but I'm here to help. I am here at the behest of Asher."

"Bullpucky! You're here for the gold."

"That too. But at least I'm honest. Unless you have forgotten, The Defiance's success was predicated upon my ability to procure the contraband you needed. Weapons. Exoarmor suits. Intelligence."

"At a hefty profit."

"We all have to put food on the table," Boaz says, turning and heading toward the mess hall.

"I don't trust him. If this map isn't real, I'm feeding him to the sharks."

"I don't trust him either," Jude agrees. "But if his map was fake and he knew about it, he wouldn't be here."

"He's still a buckethead."

After a few more decent-sized waves, Cephas runs to the side and once again retches overboard.

Renatus

The Atlantic Ocean is calm today. Renatus's massive yacht is anchored just offshore. Blue skies and intermittent bloated clouds hover above them. The wind is almost nonexistent.

"Nice cast!" Renatus yells, barefoot and shirtless.

Silas reels in his line and prepares for another.

"Your father taught you that?"

"Yes, sir," Silas answers as if everything is normal. He is actually enjoying himself, as evident by his smile. He either doesn't know better or has quickly become entangled in Renatus's web of deceit. To him, it's just a day out fishing with Grandpa. Asher and Sarai knew firsthand that Renatus is a master at selling all that Zion has to offer.

Renatus studies the child's face and the alabaster stains on his body. The gaps in his teeth. The two boys have the same eyes and similar mannerisms. How it made him miss his *wounded* one.

"You look like him, my son. Eleazar."

"I want to meet him," Silas says naively.

"Maybe someday," Renatus lies.

"So he is my uncle?"

Renatus smiles. "Smart and a good fisherman."

"How old is he?" Silas asks while flinging his pole for another long cast.

"Why, he is your age."

"He is my uncle, and we are the same age?" Silas asks, perplexed.

Renatus rubs his head. "It's complicated, grandson."

"Does he like to fish?"

Renatus is in deep remembrance. "Yes. Yes, he did. He used to love these waters." Then, to himself, "They didn't love him back."

Renatus wants to get to know his grandson before he takes his life. For every pound of evil, he still has an ounce of humanity. But that is fading by the day. Every time he goes through protocol, virtue seeps from his soul. With immortality comes the loss of morality. The longer he lives, the more earthly he becomes.

Silas studies him. "My mom and dad say that you are an evil person."

"Oh yeah? What do you think, grandson?"

Silas's tone is matter-of-fact. "I don't know yet. You seem nice. I think you are afraid, maybe."

Renatus can't help but laugh. "I see that you are definitely not."

"Fear is from the devil," Silas pronounces, casting his line out once again.

"Tell your parents that I have many lives. I have nothing to fear. Especially death."

"Then why did you build The Wall, Grandfather? And why do you need more than one life? Isn't one enough? My father says life is hard enough to have more than one."

Renatus can't believe he is even entertaining these questions, but since no one else dares ask him, he is pleased in a strange way that he gets to explain himself and his perspective, especially to someone so non-threatening.

"You know, grandson, I created second-life protocol to give people a second chance. Life as designed is just too fragile. Take my mother and father, for example. I was your age when they both died in a horrible car accident, along with my little sister. She was only seven. Was her one life enough? To die at seven? Didn't she deserve a second chance?"

Silas has no answer. But his ten-year-old brain is processing the infor-mation, albeit at a slow rate. "My uncle Cephas says, 'If God called them home, who are we to snatch them out of his hands?'"

"Perhaps it was God who gave us second-life technology?"

Again, Silas is quiet yet contemplating. "Maybe."

"And then The Wall. Why did I put up a wall, you ask? You see, Silas, not everyone treated my gift with the respect they should have. Their reckless-ness was exuberant." Renatus doesn't see his hypocrisy in that statement as he casts his line back into the placid cobalt sea.

"Like how?" Silas's curiosity is never-ending.

"Protocol was supposed to be a backup, a contingency for honest mis-takes and accidents, like what happened to my parents and sister. It wasn't meant to give you a license for negligence. A free pass to do whatever you wanted. To waste your first life just because you knew you had a second. Unfortunately, that was the Dreck way. I had to separate those people from those of us who wanted to live rationally. That is why I built The Wall."

What Renatus doesn't see is that is precisely what he is doing. The devil will always accuse you of what he is doing himself.

"Sort of like the Prodigal Son?"

Renatus again studies him, then nods, impressed. "Sort of."

"My dad says you put up The Wall because you are afraid of freedom."

"If freedom is being free to hurt people, being free to get drunk and decide to drive right before plowing into an innocent mother and father, a precious and beloved sister, then yes, I am afraid of freedom. At least that kind of freedom."

"My mom says freedom is messy but always worth it."

For a moment, Renatus has forgotten that he is speaking to a child. Instead, he speaks as if Silas is his intellectual equal. "A lot of blood has been shed in the name of freedom. Not everyone deserves freedom, young Silas."

Silas ponders that momentarily, and then his pole is pulled down with a massive tug.

"I got one!" Silas yells.

"Good, good. Keep reeling. Keep the pressure on it."

Silas pulls and reels. Pulls and reels until his arms burn and his back tightens.

"I'm getting tired," he admits.

"Keep going, grandson. Don't give up. It's not a Lazurite virtue. You sound like a Dreck, complaining like that. Be strong, boy."

Silas continues to reel and pull for another ten minutes until the massive four-foot Striped Bass makes its way to the boat.

"Look how big it is!" Silas gives a toothy smile.

"Keep your tip up; it's not in the boat yet. You're celebrating too early."

"It's so heavy."

"Keep that tip up, or you'll lose it!"

Renatus reaches over the side with his net and pulls the trophy fish in.

"Got him! How about that?" Renatus pats him on his back. "Well done."

"My biggest one yet. Can't wait to tell my dad."

"Me too," Renatus replies, something sinister in his tone.

Renatus peers at him and remembers fishing with his beloved, his *wounded* prince. *It's a shame I can't have both my son and grandson. Or maybe there is another wounded one out there? Perhaps I should keep looking? I'm sure Eleazar would like to have the company of another wounded one.*

Then again, he is not sure if he can wait any longer.

"Can we take a picture? Please, Grandfather?"

"Absolutely." Renatus snaps a photo of Silas struggling to hold up the fish.

"Now what?" Silas asks.

Renatus turns to him, a vile look in his eyes. He exhales as if being gracious has suddenly worn him out.

"Now we gut him."

Kenan

It's time to step up and lead. It's time to step up and lead. Asher's words were ringing in Kenan's head like a broken record. Kenan has wondered if he is ready. Hours before Asher set off again to find his son, he made Kenan a general.

If Kenan's father could only see him now. Yet his father is in Zion East. He still serves Renatus. He would consider Kenan a traitor, fighting for Asher. He cringes at the irony of the situation. He has finally become what his father wanted, but it is for the other side. If they were to meet on the battlefield, they would be enemies.

It is 2:21 AM, and the downpour is torrential. His boots are worn and torn. His thick alpaca socks are damp and squishy. *We can't keep our feet warm; how will we win a war?* Kenan is on his way to meet his army. The army for which he was made a new general, in the cover of night. Neriah declared it illegal for any military to exist that hadn't pledged allegiance to her. He wonders how many will be there. How many are still loyal to Sarai and Asher?

The sound of rotors.

A HarvestDrone emerges from the downpour. *There must be demon-dusters around.* Kenan ducks behind a tree and watches through his night vision goggles, as the drone's long vacuum tube is lowered toward a young man passed out on Dust. The youth of Zion West was being hooked, then sucked away, literally. An entire generation has essentially disappeared.

Kenan aims his plasma rifle and fires at the HarvestDrone before it can take the addict. The drone changes course and fires back at him. The blast hits him in the shoulder, causing him to somersault backward. He slides underneath some bushes, grimacing in pain. The drone hovers right above him. The vacuum tube dangles mere feet from his head. The suction starts.

He hangs on to the roots of the bush while his feet are being pulled over his head. He manages to grab his plasma rifle, aiming it directly up the tube, and fires.

Whatever is at the end of the tube must be sensitive, because the drone immediately explodes. Kenan jumps to his feet and sprints to the left to avoid the raining debris. Then he thinks of the addict who was inside, the person he just blew up. *But he was dead already*, Kenan rationalizes. Not physically dead. The Dust goes after your brain, then your spirit. After that, it goes after your will to live.

I can't even get to my army; how will I lead them? He spends twenty minutes dressing and bandaging his wound. He also takes this opportunity to wring out his socks.

Two hours later, Kenan stands in front of five thousand men. His shoulder is stinging, his legs wobbly, and his feet cold. He *rarely* stutters anymore, but *rarely* does he speak in front of thousands.

Be a servant leader, Asher told him. Stand with them. Fight with them at the front. It is the only way to earn their respect. A man fighting for someone or something they believe in is ten times stronger than one who fights only because they have to. Cephas told him: *Lead from the back, get stabbed in the back. Be the first and last off of the battlefield. Never put your men at risk for your own vanity. Only lead them where you are willing to go yourself. Make decisions as if they were your own children, not someone else's.*

Kenan climbs onto a rock and takes a look at his drenched army. He clears his throat. "I... I... I thank... " He stops to recompose himself. *Don't stutter now! Deep breaths; get yourself together, Kenan.*

"I want to thank you for coming out in the rain and the dead of night. We are grateful—"

A soldier interrupts him, "Where's Asher?"

Another one says, "Who are you?"

"I am your new general, Kenan. I have come—"

"We want Asher! We didn't come to fight for you!" another yells.

Another shot to Kenan's confidence. He begins to stutter. "I... I... I understand. Asher sent me instead. He, he..."

Some of the soldiers start to pack up and leave. Another yells, "You don't look like a general!"

Another: "He looks like a frightened kid!"

It's time to step up and lead.

"Wait!" Kenan hollers with renewed tenacity. "I am not Asher. And I don't pretend to be. All I can do is lead you the best I know how. Neriah is a fraud who cheated her way into office. She is working for Renatus."

More soldiers leave. Another yells, "Next time, tell Asher not to send his lackey!"

"Look, I realize I am young for a general, and I may not look the part. But I was there at the battle of Donner Lake. I—"

"So was I!" another blurts out.

Kenan does his best to project his voice even louder. "I was there when The Wall came down. I was there when Asher gave his life to Sarai. And I am still here, ready to finally end this war!"

"We are done with war!" More begin to turn and leave.

Kenan can hear Asher's petition to him: *You must win their allegiance and loyalty; everything we do from here on out depends on it. I am counting on you, Kenan.*

"Please don't! Our freedom is at stake! You have a choice before you right now, and I know it isn't an easy one. If you fight for Neriah, you are fighting for enslavement. Renatus duped all of us the first time. Do not let him do it again. I am here at the behest of Asher. Following me is following him. I promise that I will fight with you, side by side. I don't ask you to fight for me. In fact, I don't expect you to fight for Asher, or any man for that matter. Instead, aren't we fighting for a cause? For an ideal? For our freedom? For yours and your children's? I don't know about you, but twenty years from now, I don't want to look into the eyes of my offspring and tell them I had a chance to prevent their enslavement but instead did nothing."

The exodus stops momentarily. Kenan's eyes narrow, and his cadence is now crisp and confident.

"If we give up now, everything we have been fighting for will be lost. We can stand up to tyranny and corruption and make a difference! I need you. Asher needs you. Sarai needs you. Our New America needs you! Freedom needs you! Leave now, and you may never have this chance again. Leave now, and I promise you, you will regret it for the rest of your lives."

Kenan doesn't quite get the hoots and hollers one of Asher's speeches might elicit, but most of the soldiers stay. A win.

For now.

Asher

Finally, a stroke of luck. My spies inside Zion East informed me that Eleazar's body was to be transferred to Renatus's new protocol facility in three days. That was two days ago. I had a delay in the communications, as we had to procure new SatPhones from the black market. Our old phones were once again rendered useless by a localized EMP.

We have made camp for the night. Legion stokes the fire. Aspis juggles her dazzlers. I have twelve other soldiers who volunteered to go with us. In fact, I had ten times that amount willing to go, but I wanted to keep this force small and nimble. The last thing I want to do is attract any attention. If Renatus catches wind of my coming, he may accelerate protocol on my son.

With an increased frequency in narcdrops and EMPs, Renatus has also stepped up his drone patrols.

I hold up a map. "We will snag him in transit. This place should give us the best vantage point for an ambush."

"Your wife's brother? How does she feel about that?" Aspis asks me, trying to stir the pot.

"How would you feel about it?" I ask her, curious to hear another female opinion.

"All I know is that there's a lot of fuss being made about a corpse." She shakes her head.

"Right you are," I agree. Then I feel a tinge of guilt talking to Aspis about my disagreements with Sarai, while she is not here to defend herself. I also feel guilty for promoting my opinion against my wife's. Sarai and I are on the same side; why must I remind myself of that?

How absurd it must all sound. I want Eleazar's body so Renatus won't kill my son. Renatus wants his body so he can resurrect his son by killing his grandson. Cephas says when you leave God out of society, this is where you end up. It used to be that money was the root of greed. Now it's time. Time was the one thing you could never get back, until now. When time isn't limited, what is there to cherish? Isn't love more meaningful when one's time is limited? The last thirty-five years have been hard enough; who would want to live forever?

"Man, I don't envy you. You have the father-in-law from hell," Aspis spits into the fire.

"Literally."

Aspis almost drops a dazzler.

"Please stop!" Legion points to Aspis and her dazzlers.

"What?"

"The dazzlers, you're making me anxious."

She laughs. "The almighty Legion, anxious over a few firecrackers."

Legion points to his blinded eye to remind her what happened.

"Okay, okay. You guys aren't any fun," she says, returning them to her satchel.

I am in no mood for their banter or blood rivalry. "How are my explosives coming?"

Aspis rubs her hands together, "Done." She is a bit of a pyromaniac.

"Will it be enough?" I wonder.

"Should be," she says casually.

"If it's not, we're hosed."

"It will be enough."

I turn to Legion. "And the shovels?"

"I found ten."

"Once we have Eleazar, then what?" Aspis asks me.

"We trade him for my son."

"How? You just going to march his body up to The White House and demand a trade?"

"I don't know yet." I won't admit it, but I'm surviving one step at a time.

"And if he doesn't deal?" Legion asks.

I never thought of that. I can't think of that. "He will."

"Well, when I die, don't anyone ever try to bring me back," Aspis asserts.

Legion's wide tongue pushes out his left cheek. "Don't worry, we won't."

This stirs some fireside laughter from the troops as Aspis feigns like she is going to throw a dazzler at Legion.

"Big day tomorrow. Let's get some sleep," I order.

"Yes, Dad," Aspis jokes back.

Three hours later, everyone around me is asleep despite Legion's snoring. The raven sky is littered with shimmering stars. One streaks across the sky, and I think how even stars die. Who are we as humans to believe we can surpass the wondrous beauty and lifespan of God's created universe? Sometimes, I think we have become too clever for our own good. With technology, we have taken a step forward and backward simultaneously. The brighter and more inventive the human race becomes, the more destructive we are.

I wonder how Sarai is managing in France. I wonder how long she will stay mad at me. I know what I am doing is the right thing—the only thing—I can do for Silas right now. I think of Cephas and Jude and wonder how smart it was to take a boat to Alaska in the winter. I wonder if Eden actually exists. Then I think of Silas and how terrified and confused he must be.

I have to focus on one thing right now: getting him back. I also desperately need sleep. An hour later, I'm finally out.

My dream has returned. Or my nightmare.

The bombing at the bazaar. The smoke. The smell of burned flesh. The wailing mothers. The anguish. The haze. Everything happened so fast, yet I can see it in slow motion.

But this time, it's a little bit different. I can actually see Neriah. I could never see her face before. She is carrying her dead son, her tears raining upon his lifeless body. I walk close to her. The weight of the guilt pushes my shoulders forward as I slog towards her. Then she approaches me.

"I'm sorry," I tell her, my tears matching hers.

She holds out her hands as if she is handing me her dead child. I take him. Then I look down, and it's not her offspring. It's Silas. He opens his eyes.

WHOOSH.

I am awoken in a lagoon of sweat, to the sound of rotors. HeliDrone.

"Get up. Get up," I whisper and yell at the same time.

"What is it?" Aspis murmurs, half asleep.

"HeliDrone."

Moments later, they are up and scampering under trees and bushes.

"If it spots us, it will report our location."

It hovers above us like a flying reaper. It knows something is amiss. Its AI system has advanced in recent years.

One of my men aims his plasma rifle towards the sky.

"No!" I tell him. "It will bounce right off."

"I got this," Legion says evenly.

He roves towards a massive tree fifty feet behind us. He begins to rip off one of its huge limbs. It makes a loud cracking sound, almost like a bone breaking. The drone hears it, and immediately comes to hover right above us.

"Quiet." I grit my teeth. I am wondering what he is doing, but I have learned that Legion is going to do what Legion does, and stopping him is like trying to stop a locomotive with an ElectroCycle.

He then proceeds to climb the gigantic tree with one hand, the other gripping the thick branch. To him, it's more like holding a baseball bat.

"See if you can get it to come lower," Legion asks.

I flash my flashlight three times—enough to get the drone interested, but not enough to give it evidence to report. It is working. It slowly hovers lower and lower until it is right above the tree Legion is scaling. Man, he is nimble for his size.

Then, as if the tree itself is swatting at it, Legion swings the massive log and smashes the front of the drone. That did the trick. For him, it was like swatting a fly. It comes crashing down next to us. I quickly jump into the smoking pile of debris and cut any remaining electrical that might still be functioning. I don't want it communicating.

"You think it had time to transmit the video?" Aspis looks at me, concerned.

"If it did, let's hope it looked like it hit a falling tree."

Legion scampers down the tree with the log resting on his shoulder, a proud look in his eye.

"Oh, look, the monkey has found himself a stick," Aspis teases.

"You're just jealous," he quips back. She likes smashing things more than he does.

I peer at the stars. "We have a few more hours until daylight. Let's see if we can't get some more shuteye. I have a feeling tomorrow we are going to need it."

CHAPTER NINE

Cephas

JUDE FLIES FROM THE top of his bunk bed and hits the hard floor with a thunk.

"What the?"

Next up is Cephas, who is rolled from the bottom bunk but lands directly on top of Jude.

"Get off of me, you lug!" Jude yells.

They both try to stand but are knocked to the ground. Cephas peers out of his porthole window.

"Those are some thirty-foot swells."

He is knocked backward and again lands on top of Jude, taking him down also.

"Oh, c'mon!" Jude spits. "Will you get off of me? I can't breathe, for Pete's sake."

Next, a chest of drawers crashes on top of them. Cephas's underwear spills out and lands on Jude's head.

"Are you serious? C'mon!"

Cephas again rolls off Jude. "Just be lucky they're clean. What time is it?"

"Three in the morning." Jude stands, steadying himself with the pole attached to the bunk bed.

"Now you know why I made you take the top," Cephas chaffs.

They are rocked back and forth as the ship continues to take a beating.

"How you feeling?" Jude asks him.

"Not too bad. Think I got my sea legs."

The ship creaks and moans as it knives its way through each hammering wave.

"Maybe we should check on Boaz?" Cephas is actually feeling cordial.

Jude squints. "You think I want that guy falling on me? You were bad enough." He pulls out the map. "How about we work on this?"

Cephas shrugs. "Can't sleep in this chop anyhow."

Jude reads it again. "Father of the Sun. Was neither Fat nor Little. Could see and divide the invisible."

Cephas also repeats it while he runs his fingers through the massive scars on his face. "Fat and Little. Why are they capitalized?"

"Maybe they are names and not descriptions?" Jude suggests.

"And who can see the invisible?"

"As well as divide it? Maybe it's the name of some mathematician?"

"Sun is a Chinese surname, is it not?"

"So, a tall, skinny mathematician named Sun?"

"You know any?" Cephas asks.

"Nope. I doubt that is it, though."

"What makes you say that?"

Jude steadies himself, grabbing the bed frame. "Because if it is, we're in trouble."

Another wave hits them from the side, almost knocking them both down.

"Maybe we should be praying about now," Jude ponders out loud.

"What do you think I've been doing since we walked onto this floating crate?"

Jude's eyebrows furrow.

"What is it?" Cephas asks him.

"You think the mess hall is open now? I could use a sandwich."

CRACK! Another wave sends them sliding across the room. "How can you think about food right now? Isn't your stomach spinning?"

"It helps me think," Jude proclaims.

Cephas seems like he has a realization. "Wait a minute. Father of the Sun. Maybe it's Son like the Son of Man. Maybe it's God. He can surely see the invisible and divide anything He wants."

Jude nods. "That's not bad. But the Fat and Little. What does that mean? Doesn't make sense."

"I still think Boaz knows more than he's telling us."

"Maybe he has information on who designed Eden and could give us some clues on figuring out the cipher."

"Let's go wake him," Cephas suggests.

Two minutes later, they stumble towards Boaz's room and storm in without knocking.

"Hey! What are you doing in here?" Boaz practically screeches like a child.

"Figured you were awake." Jude plops at the end of his bunk. Boaz sleeps in a purple silk robe with fleece at the neck, wrists, and ankles. "Nice jammies."

"What time is it?"

"Time for you to start talking."

"Please leave my room," Boaz begs.

"Not until you tell us everything you know about Eden and this cipher."

"I told you everything already."

Cephas has had enough. He yanks him out of bed and pushes him against the wall. "And don't tell me you got it from inside some picture at some museum!"

"I'm telling you that's the truth!" Boaz quivers in terror.

Jude is calmer, the good cop. "And the cipher? What do you think it means?"

"I have no idea. I am as stumped as you are."

Cephas releases him and stares at the raging storm through the porthole. "Always in the storm."

Jude shrugs. "Dreck life. Besides, what do you always say? 'Weathering the storm builds character.'"

"And wrinkles."

Boaz straightens his robe. "I have told you everything. Will you please leave now?"

Then, a loud siren blares. A deckhand pushes open their door. "We got a leak in the hull!" He tosses them three survival suits. "Put these on."

Jude looks over at Cephas. "Ready for some more wrinkles?"

All three struggle to slide into their red survival suits as the ship is knocked every which way.

Jude gets his on first, grabs the back of Cephas's suit, and pulls it up. "Let me help you."

Again, Cephas falls backward with his suit only halfway on. "What's the point?" he bickers. "I mean, if we fall in, instead of freezing to death in ten minutes, it will take twenty."

"Just stop squirming for a moment, will ya?"

Boaz stammers, "We are going to die in this tin can, aren't we?"

"You're not gonna die on the boat; you're gonna drown in the freezing water," Jude corrects him.

"I don't want to die. It's not my time." Boaz whimpers.

"Will you shut it?!" Cephas barks.

Jude sees Boaz is having more trouble getting his suit on than Cephas. "Don't worry, I got you next."

Thirty minutes later, they are able to patch the hole with marine epoxy. Cephas stands on the boat's back deck, soaked from the rain and the waves still crashing overboard. His knuckles are white as he grips the railing. He watches the seething sea, and he rages back at it. Can anything else go wrong?

Just as the hull is almost flooded, he himself is flooded with thoughts of his deceased wife. He remembers how her hands were rough but her heart soft. Her wiry, long red hair, and how her tongue was acid if you pushed her too far. How badly she wanted children, but they couldn't have them. Sometimes, he feels as if he is Job from the Old Testament. He wonders if he is still being tested. Is God still molding him through his many trials? He thinks about the Tonic and how he could use a drink right now. The daily struggle. He prays for the Holy Spirit to give him the power and fortitude to overcome. It's a daily prayer. It seems every year, his strength wanes. Sometimes, he wants to give up and let someone else take on this fight. But there are so few like him, so few willing to sacrifice anymore.

Finish strong.

"You crazy? Get inside, knucklehead!" Jude yells at him. "You're gonna fall overboard, and I ain't fetching ya!"

"Coming."

Just as he turns, he thinks he sees something out of the corner of his eye—something black emerging from the water, that disappears again.

"Did you see that?"

"What?" Jude squints in the night sky.

Cephas wipes the rain from his eyes. "I don't know. It looked like—like, a submarine."

"Submarine? It's dark and storming out here. I think you're seeing things."

"I don't know, maybe."

"Look, it's understandable for your brain to go there. Silas was taken by a submarine, after all. But c'mon, you think we're being followed?"

"Yeah, you're probably right. Probably just a wave."

Asher

A few angry gusts propel snow flurries our way. Perched on a ridge, Aspis buries the explosives underneath the snow.

"All set, twenty of them," Aspis informs me as she audits her handiwork.

"Will it be enough?" I ask her for the fifth time.

"Better be. It's all we have."

I peer down into the valley below us. There's a small battered road, where a Lazurite convoy is supposed to be transporting Eleazar's body to Renatus's new second-life protocol facility. I know Sarai disagrees with me, but I'm convinced this is the right thing to do. The only thing I can do. I am prioritizing right now. Save my son first, then work out my differences with Sarai later. I am certain that once she has her boy in her arms again, she will see this was the right choice. If not, I'm not sure what I could say.

Aspis pats me on the back. "Conditions are good. Snow is wet and heavy. Just give me the signal."

We are going to create an avalanche, hence the shovels. If we time it right, the convoy will be buried under the snow, and then we will simply dig out Eleazar's body. He is already in a cryogenic chamber. He can't freeze twice, right? I only hope that the cryogenic cylinder in which Eleazar's body is housed isn't damaged during the avalanche.

Legion approaches me from the very top of the ridge, where he has a view of the other side.

"They're coming."

"Get into position." I peer over at Aspis. "On my mark."

I scan the valley through my binoculars. A convoy of nine Jeeps emerges. In the middle of the Jeeps is a covered army truck.

I point to the truck. "I'm guessing the body is in that one."

Legion is counting, "Sixty Lazurites." He spots red sashes on some of them, "Twenty elites."

"Child's play," Aspis states confidently.

I point to Aspis, who holds the detonator. "On the count of three."

She nods.

"Two. One." She is about to press the button when I spot something. "Wait!"

She removes her thumb, which was hovering over the remote detonator.

"What?" She frowns.

Through my binoculars, I spot an old blue Ford Pickup heading towards the convoy on the same road. A mother is driving, her two small girls wedged in the front seat beside her, and a pile of their belongings tied down in the back.

"Down there. A mother and her kids."

"It's now or never. Our window is closing," Aspis warns me.

I can't sacrifice innocents, even if it is to save my son. "No, wait for them to pass."

"It will be too late by then. Maybe we can just dig them out."

"Too risky," I argue back, not believing our bad luck.

"When is the last time you have done anything that didn't involve risk?" she questions me. "It's the Dreck way, as far as I can tell."

Why is she so concerned about my son? Is it because I spared Legion? Is helping me a way of paying me back? The truck is about halfway past the convoy at this point, and my window of opportunity is closing. Then I have an idea. One of those ideas that is, as my wife would say, very Asher-like. Jude would call it Dreckish. And Cephas isn't here to talk me out of it.

I turn to my men behind me. "Anyone have a Tracker?"

One of the Drecks holds one up. "Got one."

A Tracker is just what it sounds like. They are about the size of a silver dollar and are sticky on one side. My spies use them by sticking them to enemy vehicles or clothing. Then, with a handheld monitoring device, you can track it within a three-foot radius. I am going to use mine much like an avalanche beacon. I grab the Tracker, switch it on, and stick it to the inside of my shirt.

Both Legion and Aspis gape at me like I'm crazy.

"Like you said, 'when is the last time I have done anything that didn't involve risk?'"

Aspis grins. "I knew you were my people."

A brave young Dreck marches up to me. "Sir, let me trade places with you."

"Appreciate your courage, soldier, but you know my policy concerning the battlefield. First one on and the last one to leave. Or, in this case, to be buried." I don't have time for a rambling speech about courage and sacrifice, even though my heart wants to. I point to Aspis. "Stay down, and wait until I raise my left hand before you detonate."

Before I turn to leave, I have second thoughts. "Isn't anyone going to talk me out of this?"

Legion places his mighty paw on my arm and says with a straight face, "We will dig you out first."

Thanks. "Just watch my head with those shovels."

I turn and trudge down the hill as fast as possible, raising my knees high through the deep snow. I flail my arms about.

"Hey! Hey! Stop!"

The Jeep in the front brakes to a halt, stopping the rest of the convoy. I am about a hundred yards above them. The heavy, wet snow and explosives are right above me. There is no turning back now.

"Stop!" I shout. "Please stop!"

A few Lazurite elites point to me and begin to slog up the mountain.

"Who goes there?" one of them asks.

"I'm an elite," I lie. "There are Drecks over that ridge. I just escaped."

As they get closer, they wearily scrutinize me. I eye the old Ford and wait until the mother and her children have cleared the danger zone.

Is this the craziest thing I have ever done?

Hard to say.

"An elite, you say? You look more like a feck-witted Dreck to me."

The other elite sniffs the air while raising his plasma rifle at me. "He smells like one too."

I grin. "I hope you two like to ski."

They both give me puzzled looks.

"Or perhaps making snow angels is more your thing?"

They frown at one another. "This Dreck is out of his gourd."

"You're not lying."

I give Aspis the signal and raise my left hand. Aspis closes her eyes and presses the button. Within seconds, a chain of twenty explosions goes off.

It worked.

A wall of snow comes tumbling towards me. It looks like pure white smoke. Like a cloud exhaling after puffing on a cigar. It's surreal to know that I'm about to be purposely entombed under an avalanche I created. Just before it crashes into me, I gobble up as much oxygen as possible. The Lazurites in front of me turn and unsuccessfully try to outrun it. Moments later, everything goes white. You would think that my life would flash before my eyes or that I would be flooded with thoughts of Sarai and Silas.

But instead, for some reason, all I can think about is Cephas calling me a buckethead.

Sarai

Eleazar is drowning. And I can't reach him. Every stroke my arms take in the cold Pacific brings me no closer to my dying brother. The more I kick my legs, the more irate the ocean becomes. I scream his name as the current takes me further and further away, until he becomes just a bobbing buoy somewhere in the distance. I yell his name, and he yells mine back. I don't know if we have been in the water for five minutes or fifty. Then a boat.

It's Asher!

I scream to him to save my brother. He doesn't. Instead, he watches him drown while casting in a fishing line. I shriek and howl for him to help, but the louder I try to scream, the more I am punched in the mouth by the indifferent waves of the bitter Pacific. The icy salt water is pushed down my throat. Asher ignores my flailing brother and continues to man his fishing pole, remaining aloof as Eleazar and I are dragged out to sea. I think I even catch him smiling as he reels in a Chinook salmon.

I wake up from the nightmare lathered in sweat and choking on my spit. My heart is racing. It doesn't take too long for the cold concrete floor of my prison cell to cool me off. My wet, sweaty hair is practically frozen to it. Percival has held me against my will going on three days now. Each day, he asks me about giving him protocol technology. My answer is always the same.

I have no idea what time it is. There are no clocks. I'm guessing it's the middle of the night. I am afraid if I go back to sleep, my nightmare will continue, so I force myself to stay awake.

Why? Why did Asher let him drown? And why am I asking why? *It's just a dream.* Maybe this is how my subconscious has manifested my feelings: that Asher is not interested in Eleazar, aside from using him as a bargaining chip.

A bargaining chip to save my son. Maybe it is the only way? I don't know. I can't think straight. What if Percival never lets me out? I think claustrophobia and panic are starting to set in.

Click.

My cell door unlocks. In walks Marcus, Percival's adviser from dinner the other night. He turns to the two guards that are with him.

"Leave us."

I am a bit worried, as I can't imagine what he wants with me in the middle of the night. But I size him up. I'm pretty sure I can take him. I know I can. Before he comes any closer, I jump up and take a defensive position.

"What do you want?"

He shows me both of his palms. "Easy, Sarai. Don't you remember me?"

I scrutinize him again; he looks vaguely familiar.

He paces in my cell, his hands now clasped behind his back. He looks about my father's age. His hair is charcoal black. He is lanky and emits nervous energy.

"How is your mother?" he asks, his green eyes droopy and kind.

"My mother?" I'm confused.

"We shared a dance, once or maybe twice. Is she still a stunner?"

Then, the memory comes back to me. It was one of the many fancy balls or dinner parties at my father's mansion. Czar Percival was also there. My father and Percival had retreated to the back room for a glass of scotch. I was probably about eight or so when I snuck onto the terrace. There, my mother and Marcus were dancing. Slow dancing. Her head rested upon his broad shoulders. He was thicker then. How do I remember this? Perhaps it was the look in her eyes. A yearning. A momentary joy, bordering on passion. She never looked at Renatus that way. She was always callous and stiff. But at that moment, her heart seemed open. Dare I say she was actually happy?

I decide to be honest and finally answer him. "I haven't spoken to her in years."

He seems lost in thought, perhaps in the same memory. He then smiles as he relives it. Did he love her? And her him? Perhaps they were secret lovers, or maybe it was just that one night—one of those fleeting moments that you never forget.

He glances at me. "I spoke to her last night."

"What?" I respond, shocked.

"Yes. She called me."

"Called you?"

"She asked me to free you, Sarai."

"Free me? How... how did she even know I was here?"

"She has her people, her spies, just like your father does, I presume."

Throughout my entire life, I cannot ever remember my mother sticking up for me. She sat back and allowed the abuse and injustices my father dished out on me, and never said a word. It never seemed to bother her either; her emotions were always hidden behind an impervious wall.

"You are willing to risk your life, your high standing within this government, for me?" I ask him.

His eyes narrow as he rubs his slender chin. "Maybe."

"So, did you love her? My mother?"

"Maybe." He is still enraptured by her memory.

I can tell he is conflicted. "What are you doing here?"

"You know, I was married once. We had a daughter. She died of leukemia at eight. After that, we just grew apart. Our marriage couldn't survive such tragedy; few marriages do."

I can't help but think about Asher and me. How our relationship has begun to erode since Silas was taken.

"I have kept her body in Cryo. In hopes that one day I can bring her back."

"I wish I could help you, but I can't. I wasn't lying when I told Percival we no longer have the technology."

He grabs my hands. "Hands like your mother." He peers into my eyes. "And the eyes of your father." He squeezes my hands even tighter. "But you have an endowment of virtue that is all your own." He drops my hands and grabs the bars of the cell instead. "This Asher of yours—you are in love with him, yes?"

I take longer than I should to answer; maybe it's because I'm still angry with him. "Yes. Yes, I am."

"And you have a child, yes?"

"We do. Silas. He is ten. In fact, he is missing right now."

"So you know what it is like to lose your offspring. You know how unnatural it is."

"He isn't dead. At least, I don't think he is." I blink away tears.

"And you would do anything for Silas? Yes?"

"Yes."

He turns to me, his eyes also moist. "If I let you go, promise me you will talk to your mother; tell her about my daughter. Ask her if they will share protocol."

"If I get that chance, I will," I tell him, not wanting to lie.

"And tell your mother... " he pauses.

"Anything."

"Never mind. Just tell her about my daughter."

"I will."

That must be good enough for him. He opens my cell door. "Then go find your son. And go make right with your husband."

What is he? A mind reader? "What of my guards? And my pilot?"

"Percival freed them yesterday. They left on your plane."

"They left me?" My face can't hide my shock.

"They didn't want to, Sarai. Percival forced them. Told them he would get rid of you if they didn't."

"Where am I to go?"

"You must go to the top of the Eiffel Tower. From there, I have arranged for a HeliDrone to pick you up and take you to an airport east of there. Your mother has a plane waiting for you there."

I still can't believe my mother is rescuing me. "Thank you," I tell him sincerely.

"Be sure to thank your mother." Marcus hands me my scourge. "You may need this; the streets of Paris can be a bit rough these days, especially at night."

I hug him and exit my cell. "You are too good for my mother, Marcus."

He shrugs. "Well, in a dyad, someone has to be better than the other. That is how we are lifted up. Inspired." He points me in the right direction. "Now go, Sarai."

"Come with me. Percival will surely punish you if he finds out you let me go."

He shakes his head. "I'm too old for this sort of thing." He looks almost as if he's contently resigned to his fate. "You see, Sarai, I made a promise to my daughter at her gravesite that before I died, I would do one more good deed. And there isn't a lot of opportunity for that around here anymore. You are my deed, Sarai. Live on. Free your son. Forgive your mother."

I hug him again. He is the father I had always wanted but never had. "Thank you, Marcus."

As I head towards downtown Paris, I wonder what life would have been like if my mother had married someone like him instead of my father.

Twenty minutes later, I hear gunshots behind me, back where I was imprisoned. His army still uses conventional weapons as opposed to plasma. Marcus must be at the receiving end. I pick up my pace while fighting back tears. How many times has someone sacrificed themselves for me? Am I worth it?

I think of my mother and how I am not the only one who has lost so much.

Asher

I am slowly suffocating. If I were to guess, I am probably buried ten feet under the heavy snow. I only hope my Tracker is still working. It's a strange feeling, like I'm drowning but can't move at the same time. Has it been thirty seconds? Ten minutes? I have lost all sense of time. I try to calm my nerves and slow down my heart rate. Tiny, easy breaths. It is cold, condensed, and claustrophobic. But somehow quiet and peaceful.

But only for a moment.

Then I start to get dizzy and lightheaded. My oxygen is waning, and I'm beginning to think this is a terrible idea. I close my eyes and try not to think about it. But then claustrophobia sets in. I start to panic. Peaceful no longer. I am now using more oxygen than necessary. I need to settle down. I feel like I might pass out. Small breaths.

Great move, Asher. In an attempt to save my son, I killed myself in an avalanche of my own making. Maybe I am a buckethead.

Then I hear something. Muffled voices. Metal clinking. Must be the shovels! I hear them calling my name. I try to answer back, but I can't open my mouth without getting a mouthful of snow. I might as well be underwater. After another minute, I can see the tip of the shovels. One of them hits my arm.

"Ow!" I manage to say while reeling in deep breaths of fresh oxygen.

"Found him!" Legion yells.

He grabs my arm and yanks me out of my frozen tomb. My lungs are still playing catchup.

"You are crazy," Aspis tells me.

"He's not crazy; he's stupid. There is a difference," Legion smirks.

"Did it—did it work?" I ask, still gasping for air.

"The entire convoy is buried," Legion informs me, wrapping a blanket around me. I didn't realize how badly I was shivering.

"You hit my arm with your shovel."

Legion taps my forehead. "You said don't hit your head, but you didn't say anything about your arm."

I take a minute before I can finally stand and see our handiwork for myself. "Well, gimme a shovel."

"Sure thing, Frosty." Aspis slams a shovel into my chest.

After two hours of digging where we believe the covered truck to be, we finally hit something metallic.

"That's it," I tell them. "Dig around it."

We heave heavy clumps of snow until the army truck starts to take shape. It is on its side. I pray again that Eleazar's Cryo capsule has not broken or been compromised in any way. If so, I will have a whole other set of problems on my hands.

We expose the back gate of the truck and clear enough snow to open it. Apprehensive, I search the back with my flashlight.

It's empty.

No Eleazar. Nothing.

"I... I don't understand," I say out loud.

"Maybe this is the wrong convoy?" Legion asks.

"No, this was it. This location at this time." I slam the truck with my fists in frustration. Without this, I have no idea how I will get my son back. This was my trump card.

"Maybe your agent's intelligence was wrong?" Aspis chimes in.

I shake my head. "That would be a first."

"What now?" Aspis inquires.

I pace, still reeling from the situation, "I don't know yet."

"We can't just hang out here. We have to do something," she presses.

"Will you stop asking me? I don't know! Okay, I don't know." Not the words they want to hear from their leader, their so-called general. But at the moment, it's the truth.

"Or maybe your agent set you up or they hacked his SatPhone," Legion states, pointing his stubby finger toward the ridge.

Above us are about fifty Lazurite elites. Twenty more flank us on our left and right. I wonder how much Renatus paid my spy to turn. He was a Dreck who had been with us from the beginning. Was friends with Cephas personally. I guess loyalty has an expiration date. I can't believe Renatus anticipated this move. And I thought I was being clever. Now, I have put my men and my friends in danger. We have walked right into a trap.

"It's an ambush!" Aspis howls. "Get behind the Jeeps!"

We scatter behind the piles of snow where the Jeeps are buried to give us partial cover. Plasma blasts explode around us. Aspis throws her dazzlers and temporarily blinds the first wave of elites coming our way. She fires her crossbow at them, penetrating their exoarmor. They don all white and blend in with the landscape like a massive snow flurry.

There are seven more to my left. I scan them with my wrist strap. My ricochet turns green, telling me it's ready. I fling it towards them. It hits all seven before returning to me. They flail on the ground like worms that have just been hooked.

There are a dozen more coming up the hill from behind us. We are practically surrounded. Legion and Aspis grab each side of the army truck that was supposed to hold Eleazar's body, and push it down the hill. It steamrolls half of them. Six scampers up just in time to meet Legion's colossal club. For him, it's like batting practice. I am glad to see ten years of sipping tea and stroking his dog Buttons haven't deprived him of his killer instinct.

I take out five more with my ricochet, while firing my plasma gun simultaneously. More emerge from the snow, almost like they were spawned from snowflakes, as their white bodies crawl up the hill. Aspis and Legion grab a pine tree that was felled by the avalanche, and manage to roll that down the mountain as well.

We are sitting ducks in our current position. "We have to move!"

Aspis barks back and tosses a few more dazzlers. "So now you want to leave? There is nowhere to go!"

Plasma blasts take out three of my men in front of me. Then I hear a scream I think I recognize. It's primordial. Prehistoric. I turn to my left, but it isn't Legion. It is coming from the top of the hill. I stand to take a closer look. Is it a tank? No, it's moving too fast.

My heart skips a beat. Maybe two.

He is at least a foot taller than Legion.

He is something out of a nightmare. His skin can barely contain his bulging and pulsating muscles. He moves with savage grace. His gait leaves behind vapors from hell. His slate-black eyes appear glossed over, like a snake hypnotized by demons. Long, sharp fingernails protrude from his beastly hands. He wears only gray pants and black boots. Snow melts when it hits his bare skin. The cold fears him.

He is Legion's brother.

He is Apex.

CHAPTER TEN

Cephas

THE SEA HAS FINALLY calmed. After two days of rough seas, Cephas can keep his food down at last. He is eating lunch in the mess hall with Jude, when the captain announces their arrival. Jude races onto the deck. Stuffing the last of his ham sandwich into his red cheeks, Cephas follows.

Jude stares at the chain of islands. "It's splendid."

"Yes, it is," Cephas agrees, licking mustard off his stubby fingers.

"First time in Alaska!" Jude announces. His smile is that of a kid who just traded in his OatBar for a chocolate bar.

"Your first time anywhere," Cephas corrects him.

"Have you been here before?"

"Are you kidding me? When would I have gone to Alaska?"

Jude nods, seeing his point.

When The Wall went up and America was split in two, Alaska became the forgotten stepchild. So did Hawaii. Alaska was much too far out to deal with, due to the country's now limited resources. Besides, they were dealing with a civil war. They became unfunded and unprotected. Now Alaska is sort of a no man's land—a new, ungoverned Wild West. Or, a Wild North, more aptly, and consists of warring clans.

Jude imbibes the fresh, crisp air and turns to Cephas. "You think Eden actually exists?"

"Won't matter if you don't figure out the cipher."

"I will; just get me there. Let's find it. Inspiration will do the rest."

Cephas snorts while shaking his head, not sharing his certainty. "I hope so, my friend."

Three hours later, they are docked and already deep in the forest.

"Let's stop and take a break," Boaz suggests, shivering from the bitter cold while sucking air.

"No time for breaks," Cephas answers coldly. "Besides, you'll get colder once your blood stops pumping."

Jude leads with the map in hand. He stops and peers around. He hears a crack, puts his hand up, and freezes.

"What?" Cephas whispers.

"I think we are being followed."

"Right you are." A bulky man with a long red beard and ragged clothes emerges from the forest. He is holding up a shotgun. "Drop your weapons."

Before they can fight back, about fifteen more ragged men emerge from the trees, all with shotguns.

"I said drop them, Inlanders," Red Beard orders them again.

"Sitkans, Red Clan," Boaz informs them nervously. "And they got gunpowder."

Cephas, Jude, and company comply, and lie down their weapons.

"What are you Inlanders doing here?"

Jude slowly rolls up the map and tucks it in his back pocket. "Having trouble with our ship."

Red Beard marches closer. "Don't lie to me. You are here for Eden. Ain't that right, Lazurite? We saw your boat come into port."

Cephas steps forward. "We're not Lazurites, we're Drecks. And yes, we are here for Eden."

Red Beard laughs. "Many have tried; many have died. Doesn't exist. Don't much matter what that map of yours says. And how do I know you're not Lazurites?"

Cephas scoffs, "Look around. We look like CellPirates to you?"

Red Beard points at Boaz. "The plump one does."

"You're partially right there. He's our intel."

"I'm gonna need more than that," says Red Beard.

Cephas slowly approaches with his hands up. He pulls his sweater over his shoulder to reveal his Pelican tattoo.

"Ahh, you're Defiance."

Cephas nods.

"Well, seeing you are Drecks and not Cell Poachers, we'll let you return to your ship without incident."

"And if we don't?" Cephas asks.

"Then you will be with the many who never return from this island."

"How about a deal?" Jude suggests.

"What deal?"

"You let us go about our business, and if we find Eden, we pay you with more gold than you can carry."

Red Beard spits a brown tobacco spray from the side of his lip. "And how do I know you're not lying to me?"

Jude looks to Cephas, then makes an executive decision. "Then take our boat. You saw us dock. If we don't return with gold, do what you want with it."

Cephas squints at Jude like he wants to slap him. Red Beard contemplates. "Okay, Inlanders. You have a deal. We'll be waiting for you at your ship. If you return with no gold, then the ship is ours."

An hour later, they continue to follow Jude and his map.

"What were you thinking?" Cephas snaps at him. "If we don't find Eden, we have no way home."

"I didn't see anyone else coming up with a better idea. Besides, they looked like they wanted to eat my spleen." Jude stops for a moment and inspects the area, then glances at the map. "This should be it."

"You sure? There's nothing here except for trees and rock," Cephas remarks.

"I'm sure, unless the map is wrong."

Cephas, lacking sleep and coming off days of being seasick, is in quite a surly mood. He grabs Boaz by his collar and slams him up against the craggy rocks at the base of a small hill.

"It's fake, isn't it? You sold us a fake, didn't you?! Eden doesn't exist, does it?!"

Boaz raises his hands in surrender. His voice cracks. "No! As far as I know, it's real! Why would I be here if I thought the map was fake?"

Jude pulls Cephas off of him. "He has a point."

Cephas shakes his head and takes a seat on a fallen log. "Fine, I'm gonna put myself on a timeout for a few. Make sure Boaz stays away from me."

Jude then notices something about the rock wall that Cephas pushed Boaz into. Some of it chipped off and is lying on the ground. Jude picks up a chunk of it and studies it. He lets his fingers strum over the wall where the pieces separated.

"Hey, I don't think this is real."

"What do you mean?" Boaz asks him.

"This looks man-made. I think this might be cement."

Cephas's knees creak as he gets up and lumbers over. Boaz gives him a wide berth. Cephas picks up a chunk and scratches it with his hardened, cracked fingernails.

"I think you're right. Pickaxes and shovels!"

They spend a good four hours chipping away at the "cement" until it finally reveals a massive, thick steel door.

"That's it!" Jude does a little dance, accompanied by a loud whistle.

To the left of the door is a small keypad with a digital readout, complete with eleven boxes.

"Cipher must be eleven letters," Cephas announces, starting to perk up.

"Answer won't be 'God' then," Jude retorts.

"Not in the English language anyway," Cephas bites back.

"You're the expert."

Cephas thinks for a moment. "Yahweh. Jehovah. Elohim."

"None of which are eleven letters," Jude points out.

Cephas holds up his bible. "From the Old Testament. Yahweh-jireh. Yahweh-rapha. Yahweh-nissi. All eleven characters."

"Could be. What I still don't understand is the Fat and the Little." Jude turns to Boaz. "What do you think? You've had this map for a while. Any ideas?"

"I don't know. I mean, they named this place Eden, right? I, too, think it's something biblical."

Jude paces. Before he turns around, he does a little subconscious hop, reserved for when he is in deep thought. "Maybe we are looking at this all wrong."

"What do you mean?" Cephas asks.

Instead of answering, Jude continues the riddle to himself over and over. "Father of the Sun. Was neither Fat nor Little. Could see and divide the invisible."

"Inspired yet?" Cephas says tongue in cheek.

"Maybe we should be thinking about what's inside Eden?" Jude suggests.

"Gold. Nukes. Art work. Supposedly, anyway," Boaz adds.

Jude is counting on his fingers.

Cephas squints at him. "What are you doing?"

Jude smiles. "Can't be."

"You figure it out?"

"Nukes," Jude states, hopping around.

"What about them? Just spit it out, brother!" Cephas growls.

Jude speaks—as if thinking out loud. "Nukes. Atom bombs. What is invisible? Atoms. What happens when you divide one?"

"An atomic explosion," Cephas answers.

"Exactly. That harnesses the power of the Sun. Fat Man and Little Boy were the names of the two atomic bombs dropped on Japan. And who was the father of the atomic bomb? That harnessed the power of the Sun?"

"Oppenheimer!" Boaz yells.

"Yes, Robert Oppenheimer!" Jude exclaims.

"Eleven letters," Cephas tallies. "You think that's it?"

"Has to be."

"We only have one shot at it," Boaz explains. "Otherwise, you'll be locked out for good."

"One way to find out." Jude types in O-P-P-E-N-H-E-I-M-E-R and pushes "Enter."

With bated breath, they wait. Then, with a moan and a squeak, the heavy door slides open.

"Good job, my friend." Cephas pats Jude on the back.

Finally, some good luck.

"Let's just hope it's not empty inside."

As they file inside one by one, no one sees Boaz stick a Tracker against the wall.

Sarai

As I navigate my way through the slums of Paris, it is evident how terrible their economy has become. Before the fall of the United States and France being taken over by a dictator, they were a thriving metropolitan mecca of art, culture, and tourism. Good wine and fancy cuisine.

Now trash, drugs, and homeless litter the streets. And from the smattering of gunshots I hear, so have street gangs, I'm guessing.

That is the problem with dictators; as long as they are fat and happy, they couldn't care less about the populace. The people here no longer have freedom, other than the freedom to create chaos—the freedom to be a criminal.

To my left, I can see the Eiffel Tower. I am operating under the assumption that the elevators are not working, and that I must climb all 1665 steps to the top. I remember learning about the number of stairs in a fancy Lazurite prep school before I escaped to The Middle. I never thought I would one day climb all 1665 of them to save my life. Assuming I make it there.

I hear another gunshot in the distance.

I check my watch; it's 3:30 a.m. The drone is supposed to pick me up at the top of the tower at 6:00 a.m. I have two and a half hours. I need to get moving.

I turn the corner into another alleyway while pulling a protein bar from the backpack that Marcus graciously gave me. My legs are stiff, and my back is sore from sleeping on concrete the last three nights. When this is all over, I think I'm going to return with Legion and pay Percival a visit.

Just as I'm about to take another bite of my bar, I hear something. A shadow ducks behind a dumpster. I freeze. Is my mind playing tricks on me? I have barely slept in three days, and when I have, my sleep has been fitful and full of nightmares. I blink and see the shadow again.

Then, footsteps behind me.

I swing around. A man with no teeth and a long beard is pointing a gun at me.

"Hello there, Mademoiselle. What's in the bag?"

I toss him the backpack. "Here, take it."

He rifles through it, disappointed there are only a few snacks and bottled water. "What else you got for me?"

"Nothing." My voice turns stern. I fire a warning shot. "Nothing that you want anyway."

He eyes me up and down with a slimy, toothless grin. There are scabs on his face and on the tip of his pointy nose. "I'll decide that, Mademoiselle."

Behind me, two more street thugs carrying knives emerge from behind the dumpster.

I turn so my sides face them and take a wide stance. "Whatever you think you want, you are not going to get it."

He licks his dry, cracked lips. "We will see about that."

I assume the other two don't have guns; otherwise, they would be wielding them instead of knives. I grip my scourge, which is hiding under my coat. I click it on, and it lights up. In the dark, it looks like a glowing, coiled snake wrapped around my waist. The three of them pause their advance for a moment.

"You want it? Come and get it!" I growl, unfurling my scourge. Before he can pull the trigger, I snap my weapon. It wraps around his wrist, and I pull him towards me. The shock causes him to drop the gun instantly. As he stumbles toward me, I step forward and boot him in the groin as hard as I can. With his knees buckling, he folds to the ground, writhing in pain, calling me every nasty name in the book. In French.

Yes, I also learned French at my fancy schools.

I quickly turn. One of the other street thugs is already upon me, slicing his knife back and forth. Before I can move, he slashes my shoulder. I step back as he pushes forward, and at the last second, I step back into him and shatter his nose with my forearm. Asher taught me that one. At the same time, I whip my scourge towards the third thug; it wraps around his neck, and I yank him towards me. He comes barreling into his counterpart, and they knock heads so loudly I can hear their skulls fracture.

It's not a bad way to shake the rust off.

"I hope you got what you wanted, monsieur," I spit, picking up my backpack and hurrying from the alley.

As I turn the corner, I have to stop. My headache is coming on strong as I realize I enjoyed that a bit too much. Sure, they deserved it. But the old me never relished hurting anybody. Never enjoyed the fight. How much have I changed? What has protocol done to me? Or have I simply become hardened from years of burden and turmoil? I don't have time to think about this now, as the clock is ticking.

It takes me fifteen minutes to reach the Eiffel Tower's base. There is an encampment directly underneath the massive citadel, full of drug dealers and more thugs. From my vantage point, it looks like the Tower has given birth to the worst of humanity.

I take a deep breath, sip water, and steel myself for the climb.

Forty-five minutes later, I am halfway up. It's another forty-five until my drone is supposed to arrive. I stop for more water and stretch my now-burning hamstrings. Being a politician has turned me soft—at least, softer than I used to be. Years of wielding a pen rather than a sword will do that to you. That or it's the years. I make a mental note to spend more time training with Hagar when I return.

But the higher I go, the more peaceful I feel. There's something about having a God's eye view of things: looking down on a once beautiful city now full of crime, filth, and drugs, you can see just how dreadful the human condition has become. Some people can't see it when it's always in their faces, close up and invading. It becomes normal. But from up here, it all seems so ridiculous. The city looks even more stunning as the rising sun burns off the decay of night and the street rats go back into hiding. The serene view makes me think of Silas.

Then my thoughts drift strangely to Neriah and the loss of her own son. As angry as I am with her, I don't completely blame her. As a parent, you will do anything for your child. My father has seduced her with the promise of bringing back the one she loves so dearly. Isn't that the way evil operates? It makes an appeal to your most vulnerable emotions. Your most profound and deeply rooted devotions. Then, we sometimes act on those emotions instead of our principles. I have been there. Sometimes, I am still there. I have to believe that deep down, Neriah is a good person. Perhaps even an ally one day.

Then I hear the whoosh of rotors. To my left, the HeliDrone is coming in hot. I have a hundred more steps to go. I take them two at a time, at a fast clip. By the time I reach the top, I am gasping for air.

As the drone hovers above me, I peer down and see four of Percival's army Jeeps pulling up to the tower's base. His soldiers jump out, carrying rocket-propelled grenades (RPGs). They are going to shoot the drone down!

A rope ladder emerges from the belly of the flying beast. I jump onto the rope and grab a rung. I am terrified of heights; this is more Asher's thing. As the ladder rolls back up into the drone, one of the men fires their RPG. The rocket blasts right past me, just barely missing the drone. I wonder if the drone is remote-controlled or on autopilot.

It feels like forever for the drone to reclaim the ladder with me on it. My heart thumps. My sweaty hands white-knuckle grip the swinging ladder, as my surge of adrenaline begins to mingle with fear. Another rocket whizzes by me as the bottom of the drone opens up and swallows me. Not a moment too soon, as two more rockets streak towards us. I am shoved backward as the drone successfully evades the rockets and disappears toward this so-called secret airport.

Ironically, we usually do everything in our power to avoid these flying menaces. But today, it has saved me.

And apparently, so has my mother.

Asher

I don't think I have ever seen Legion afraid before. Aspis laughs in the face of danger, but I can tell it's feigned.

"Seems your brother wants to join the party," Aspis says, smiling at Legion.

But I see her legs shake. So do Legion's.

So do mine.

It is bitterly cold out, yet I am starting to sweat. My men fire their plasma rifles at him. But he moves so fast. The shots that do come close, he blocks with plasma-absorbing material attached to his forearms. He moves like a nimble tornado. Unlike Legion's long hair, he is bald, like Renatus. His eyes look like they are solid black. I notice his knuckles are the size of walnuts; I wouldn't want to be struck by them.

He suddenly stops, about fifty yards from us.

"Cease fire!" Apex booms.

His voice reverberates off the trees. It is so commanding that even my men stop firing. That, or they are afraid of what he might do if they piss him off. He slowly marches towards us, leaving giant, deep footprints in the snow. His breath produces so much steam it's like smoke from a chimney.

"Brother," Apex says to Legion. "Where have you been, brother? I have been looking for you. For ten long years, you have been lost. Have you been consorting with Drecks this entire time?"

"What is it that you want, Apex?"

"You." He then points to me. "And you. The rest of you are free to leave. Free to live." He motions to Aspis. "Even you, cousin."

"You mean I'm free to castrate you?" Aspis replies with less bravado and confidence than usual.

Apex laughs, pulls a severed head from his satchel and tosses it. It rolls to a stop at my feet. It is my spy. I hide the fact that I am horrified. I knew he wouldn't have willingly betrayed me.

"He held out for quite a while," Apex tells me. "But eventually, he gave you up and did what he was told. They all do."

It's an odd sight, watching Legion summon the courage just to converse with someone. "You taking us to Renatus?"

"Doesn't matter, brother. You are a traitor to Zion. We can play nice, but if not, I get to have some fun."

Legion stomps a foot. "Renatus is just using you as he did me. You don't have to do this, brother. There is another way, a better way to live. I have learned much since being under his thumb. There is another path to freedom, and it's not him."

Apex sighs and flashes his yellow teeth. "Oh, older brother, you have always been weak. An idealistic fool. You think these people aren't using you? You won a war for them, and what did you get out of it? Come with me now, and Renatus will forgive you. I will forgive you. You can play for the winning team once more."

"You are Renatus's tool, an apparatus of Zion. How can you not see that? Listen to me, younger brother. I have been around. I have been down your path."

"Everyone is a tool in some capacity. If you are of no use, you might as well be dead. You belong in Zion. You belong with family."

Legion grunts in thought. Is he thinking about it?

"C'mon, my brother. Zion will rise once again. We will bring back the Canonization. Just imagine you and me dominating the arena. You will be loved by all, like days gone past. Victorious and triumphant. You will never again be bested by a Dreck with a boomerang. We will fix your eye."

Legion rubs his chin, still contemplating.

"Renatus's return to power is inevitable. You can be with us or against us. I don't want to hurt you, brother." Apex gives Aspis a sideways glance. "Or you, cousin."

"Bring it!" Aspis yells, full of false boldness.

"Always the loudmouth cousin. Don't make me quiet you."

Legion releases a sigh full of regret. He slowly marches towards his big brother. They are face-to-face, and the size difference is almost shocking. Legion is to Apex what I am to Legion.

"And you will spare my friends?" Legion asks.

"Yes. Of course. Now kneel, my brother."

Legion kneels. This isn't happening. If I lose Legion, I'm finished. Silas will have no chance. I can't do it without him.

Aspis grits her teeth. It looks as if she is fighting back tears. Apex holds out his mighty hand. His massive callouses look like yellow cauliflower sprouting from his palms.

"Kiss my hand and swear allegiance to Zion and Renatus once again. Then, all will be forgiven."

My brain starts computing all the different scenarios of how we will get out of this. How can we fend off both Apex and Legion? I am pretty sure Aspis is still with me. The only choice will be to run. Then what is next for Silas? How will I rescue him without Legion? I don't believe I can win this war without him.

Legion grabs his brother's hand. But, instead of kissing it, he pulls Apex towards him, while delivering a mighty uppercut to Apex's jaw. A blow like that would have killed any ordinary man. And even though Apex's head is whiplashed towards his spine, he barely seems fazed. He pulls a tooth from his wide mouth and holds it up. It looks like a chipped yellow piano key. He spits out blood, defiling the pure snow with his crimson Lazurite blood, then drops his tooth as if to say: "Game Over."

"Not a good idea, brother," Apex states quietly, as he swings his hammer-like fist into Legion's side.

I can hear Legion's ribs crack. The impact sends him rolling on the ground towards me.

I immediately fling my ricochet at Apex. He reaches out and catches it in midair. The electric pulses don't seem to bother him. This is not good. He hurls my ricochet, jamming it into a tree. It won't return to me.

All chaos breaks loose. Plasma blasts everywhere. Apex and his men charge us. We back up. I fire my plasma gun. Legion swings his club at Lazurite elites as they swarm us. Aspis tosses dazzlers at Apex. He swats them away as if they are mosquitoes.

"Retreat!" I yell. "Back to the hills."

As the supreme commander of all of our forces, I am not proud of the fact that I have probably yelled the word retreat more than I have ordered an attack. Yet we are still alive. In my defense, we are usually outgunned and undermanned, as we are now.

We fall back into the valley, heading towards the hills behind us. Apex blocks plasma with one hand, while smashing my men underneath him with the steel plate on his other. He is an absolute wrecking ball. Half of my men, out of pure fear or because they didn't hear me, head further down the ravine.

Apex pulls one of the buried Jeeps from the snow and tosses it down the hill. It mows down more of my men.

We finally make our way over the first hill. Legion is to my right. Aspis is to my... she was to my left.

"Where's Aspis?" I yell.

We edge back up the hill under a canopy of trees. She's there below us, battling with Apex. She is as nimble as she is mean. She slides in between his legs, kicking his knee to the side. Apex falls. She shoots her crossbow, sticking him in the arm while kicking him in the head.

"Aspis!" Legion wails, galloping towards her.

I follow him, hoping the three of us can take him. But it's too late.

Apex has Aspis by the neck. Her kicking feet are off the ground. His colossal hand clasps onto her head like a vice. He squeezes. I cannot watch. I close my eyes as he crushes her skull.

"No!" Legion screams, barreling towards him.

Apex tosses her lifeless body aside, as though she is a bag of trash. Then, as if things couldn't get any worse, two HeliDrones emerge from over the ridge and dart our way.

"Legion! Come back!"

With Apex and those drones, we don't stand a chance. We need to retreat. But Legion, tears streaming down his face, is at full speed. Apex grins and begins to pick up speed himself. I can't imagine the collision that is about to take place—like a semi-truck smashing into a tank.

But it doesn't.

One of the drones drops an ElectroNet on top of Legion. The volts bring him down instantly, so much so that he is unconscious. I see the disappointed look on Apex's face—he is miffed that the net got to do what he wanted to. Before I can cry for Aspis or think to run, another net is falling from the sky above me.

Amos

Amos was a student of history. It was his favorite subject growing up. Especially military history. Sun Tzu. Napoleon. Patton. Rommel. These were just a few he studied. One of his favorite wartime deceptions of all time was Operation Fortitude.

Operation Fortitude was the code name employed by the Allied forces in World War Two to mislead Nazi forces as to the timing and location of the invasion of Normandy. It was multifaceted, but using rubber tanks and dummy landing craft caught General Amos's attention. Everything was faked and staged to make it look like the invasion was happening somewhere other than Normandy, so that Hitler would have to spread out his defenses.

Amos watches his armies implement his version of it. He is delighted that Neriah chose him to lead this deception. Or is she simply obeying Renatus's commands? Doesn't matter. He is here. In a valley of what used to be Reservation 13 in Colorado. It's right where you wouldn't want your army to be—the perfect place to trap an opposing enemy. He plans to lure what was left of Sarai's army for a final annihilation.

He had fake tanks made of rubber. He had blowup HeliDrones, which were nothing more than giant balloons. There were thousands of tents and campfires constructed. The only thing that wasn't fake were his men. Five hundred, to be exact. They were to stay here as sacrificial lambs. No LifePacks for them, containing second chances. These are not elites; Life-Cells are not to be wasted on them. Amos does not have second thoughts about their upcoming extermination. They are a means to an end, to win the war. But more importantly, to give him glory. His aspirations, those set in motion with the kidnapping of Silas have come to fruition thus far.

If only his father could see him now—no longer a simple patrolman. He is a general of Zion. A leader of men. Although, if pressed, he is not sure his men would agree. He leads with an iron fist. Many cowards do. It's much easier to force subordinates to comply than to have them willingly follow, based on your actions and virtue.

Castigation is easier than inspiration.

He may look exactly like Asher, but they are polar opposites. But Amos doesn't care. As far as he is concerned, there is only room in this world for one of them. He still suffers the humiliation of Asher stealing his identity. The disgrace and ignominy are because he allowed Asher to be sculpted to look like him, and Zion lost the first war. Worst of all, he made Renatus look like a fool.

Amos longs for the day that he will face Asher on the battlefield, where he will let all of Zion celebrate his triumph. And if he were to lose? No matter. Renatus will simply bring him back to life. He can live on and on, long after Asher is gone.

But when he really thinks about it, he realizes the only way for redemption, the only way to restore his pride, is to take Asher down once and for all. To end this war and end The Defiance.

He surveys his counterfeit armory and is quite pleased with himself. The only thing he loves more than being clever is others thinking he is clever. Maybe it is because his grades were always mediocre or because his father called him stupid.

Not anymore. If this worked, it will go down in history as one of the cleverer wartime deceptions.

Don't congratulate yourself too early, Amos.

He turns and spots one of his men perched on a log, sipping water. He kicks the water out of the soldier's hand.

"Who gave you permission to take a break?"

"Sorry, General."

To his left is a loud hissing noise. It's like air being forced out of a balloon too fast. Amos turns, and that is precisely what is happening. One of his men is lying on his back while a rubber blowup drone is oozing air. The pressure causes it to bump off the ground, until it is finally deflated.

Amos marches towards him; the look on the Lazurite's face is also deflated.

"What happened here, soldier?"

The Lazurite stands at attention. "Sorry, sir. I was trying to tie it down so it wouldn't blow away in the wind, and when I cut the rope, my knife accidentally hit it."

"These were not cheap."

"Yes, sir."

Amos starts to undo his belt. "Turn around and take off your shirt, soldier."

The Lazurite obeys. Amos reaches back and whips him with his belt. Ten, maybe more, times. He stops when blood begins to seep from the man's back. The rest of his men watch and shake their heads.

Amos slips his belt back on—the same belt his father used to beat him with at the slightest infraction. Now he has the power. "Put your shirt back on."

"Yes, sir."

"And don't bleed so easily next time."

Amos clears his throat and marches towards his small army. He has yet to give any kind of speech to the men he now leads. *Might as well practice on the soon-to-be departed. If it bombs, who cares?*

Amos clears his throat. "Men. Soldiers. Friends."

A few silently scoff; they know he is not their friend.

Amos continues, "You all know why you're here. What you are doing is necessary. Necessary for the victory of Zion. And even though most of you won't come home, you will be remembered. You will be celebrated as heroes. What you did here today will be taught in schools. You are the tip of the spear. You represent the best in what we believe, in what makes Zion great. Now be brave and make Zion proud!"

A few cheers, but not the response Amos is hoping for. Oh well. To him, he is being inspirational, a leader. To the dead men walking, he is just another lying Lazurite spewing cliches of war. Amos doesn't understand that respect is earned. Yes, one can also garner it through instilling fear, though that is temporary.

His men watch with disdain as Amos boards the only real drone in the area and is flown away to safety.

Poet Ralph Waldo Emerson once said, *Every great institution is the lengthened shadow of one man.*

When the sun shines on Amos, you can see the shadow of Renatus.

Renatus

Renatus stands in the middle of his new battle arena, wearing nothing but black athletic pants and a short-sleeved gray shirt. He dons a LifePack on his back, containing multiple LifeCells. His veins are so pronounced they look like they are trying to escape his long, wiry arms. It is a new condition and most likely a side effect of protocol. One of his scientists inspects the LifePack and ensures it is properly connected to him.

His new Canonization coordinator and arena designer, Jokim, approaches him with a small vial of blue liquid.

"This will help with the pain," Jokim tells him.

Renatus scowls at Jokim's corpulent frame and smooth hands. The man's golden hair is shiny and perfectly combed. His ears are pierced, and jutting from his lobes are oversized diamonds. His nose is also freckled with tiny emeralds. When the light hits him right, his face lights up like a Christmas tree.

Renatus doesn't particularly like him. Except for all the piercings, he is too clean-cut. A bore. *An indoor man.* Never seeing the sun or feeling the invigorating chill of a cold rain. But he is clever and diabolical.

Renatus knocks the blue vile from his hand.

"What? And feel nothing?" Renatus snarls. He enjoys the pain of death as well as rebirth. For him, it is cathartic. He slaps Jokim's cheek. "Coming back to life wouldn't be nearly as extraordinary if there were no pain in death."

"Of course, my Sultan."

Renatus studies him. "Perhaps you should give it a try?"

"I prefer not, my Sultan." Jokim was born devious. Before becoming Renatus's architect of his death games, he came up with various punishments for disobedient, disloyal Lazurite soldiers. As a child, Jokim's favorite pastime was torturing and killing small animals, including his neighbor's pets. He was creative and loved to experiment. Always wanting to push the boundaries of what a human could take mentally and physically.

Of course, he never experimented on himself. In Renatus's mind, he is the perfect choice.

On Renatus's hip are two Tomahawk axes. In each hand, he holds a mace—a handle with a chain attached to it. Attached to the chain is a spiked metal ball. Renatus has an affinity for medieval weapons and an obsession with Roman Gladiators. This is his Colosseum. His Rome. He is Caesar.

"Let's see how you did," Renatus barks at Jokim, his tone threatening. Jokim understands the subtext of the statement: *You better have designed me an arena worthy of a looming and new Canonization. And the populace better love it.*

Jokim shuffles out of the arena as fast as his tiny feet will take him. The lights go dim as fake crowd noise is pumped in. The lights then flicker back on as the arena begins to simultaneously rotate side to side, and in a circle.

Two separate doors open, and four Lazurite elites enter the arena. They don swords and clubs. They know better than to inflict any actual harm on their Sultan. They know they are the chosen sheep for the day, marching towards their slaughter. What choice do they have? Their family's lives depend on it. They know full well that Renatus will not waste a LifeCell on them. Some are even deranged enough to call it an honor to die at Renatus's hand.

Jokim watches nervously from his luxury suite. He knows his life is on the line today as well. Two elites charge Renatus, making a show of wildly swinging their weapons. Just as they are about five feet away, Renatus swings both of his maces, burying the spikes in one's forehead and in the other's ribs. One falls with a thud. The other collapses on his knees, reeling and squealing in pain. Renatus swings the mace around until the spikes impale the back of the elite's skull.

A third elite swings his club and intentionally misses Renatus's bright, bald head. Renatus swings down and smashes his kneecap. The man rolls on the ground, writhing in agony.

"Get up!" Renatus growls. "You are no elite! You are an embarrassment to Zion. Stand up!"

The Lazurite uses everything he can muster to stand on one leg, his other leg dangling backward from the knee. Renatus finishes him off with a hit to the chest. The last elite wants no part of this, and turns and runs towards the exit. Jokim presses a button and quickly closes the door.

Renatus grabs his Tomahawk and flings it at the fleeing elite. The ax digs into the man's spine and sends him flailing to the ground. Jokim shakes his head, knowing that Renatus will now kill that man's family, for what he calls *desertion*.

"Is that all you got?" Renatus yells up to Jokim, his hands held triumphantly in the air.

Jittery, Jokim presses a few more buttons on his tablet, and a tiger jumps out of one of the doors. Renatus drops his maces and now holds both axes. He bares his teeth, as if trying to intimidate the giant cat. He even growls.

The tiger immediately pounces towards Renatus, who swings but misses. The tiger swipes his mighty paw, and his claws rip into Renatus's chest. Blood streams down his belly. Renatus falls onto his back as the tiger vaults on top of him, going for his jugular. Renatus quickly swings both Tomahawks and lops the animal's head clean off.

He stands, wipes some blood from his chest, and tastes it. He spits it out in disgust, "Is that all you got, Jokim?! Is that all you got? A little pussycat?"

Jokim is now drenched in sweat. If he wasn't so frightened, he might ponder the irony that if he doesn't kill Renatus, Renatus will kill him. He scrolls through a few menus and presses a few more buttons.

The ground underneath Renatus's feet suddenly opens, sending him falling twenty feet below. Seconds after he hits the ground, the walls start closing in on him. He patiently and calmly waits until the concrete walls are about three feet apart, seconds away from crushing him. Then he quickly places his Tomahawks horizontally between the closing walls, essentially making two steps. He is able to pull himself up and out of the closing hole just as the walls snap his Tomahawks in half.

He peers up at his arena master. "What else you got?"

Jokim's fingers are now sweating, making it challenging to use his tablet. He is running out of death traps. He finally finds another one of his insidious creations and presses the button.

The arena moves from left to right and spins faster and faster. Large rocks fall from the ceiling. Renatus dodges them, while also sidestepping the newly formed holes of boiling oil now opening on the arena floor. The swaying of the arena sends him backpedaling towards the wall, where six twelve-inch steel spikes suddenly emanate from the concrete.

His body is slammed into them. One of the spikes goes through his heart. His body slowly slides off the spike and thuds to the ground.

Before Renatus stops breathing, a slight grin cracks the side of his face. Jokim watches as the LifeCell travels from his pack through the tube and into Renatus's body. A minute later, Renatus is jolted awake, as if he had just put his hand into a light socket. He bounces up and grabs his weapons.

"Again!"

Sarai

I am tired from the long flight home, but there is no time to waste. I am escorted down the dirt steps of the underground compound, one of many that used to belong to the Defiance. We gather around a round stone table, where two small fires light the dark room. Electricity is out in this sector.

Kenan and three of my generals stand.

"My Prime," Kenan nods.

"Please be seated," I tell them.

Our setting looks medieval. I feel like we are the Knights of the Round Table.

"We are working to restore power. An EMP went off nearby," Kenan informs me.

"Then Neriah knows we are close by."

"She has been systematically setting off EMPs on all known past Defiance hideouts," says one of my generals, a man with a long beard, through gritted teeth. His glasses are missing a lens. If my generals aren't even afforded proper eyesight, I hate to think how ill-equipped my remaining army might be.

I am afraid to ask, but I do. "And what is left of my army?"

Kenan thumbs through a folder full of papers. "My best estimates are twenty-five percent still loyal to us. But we lose more every day. Neriah is offering them better pay and rations. She has also threatened those who don't initially accept."

"Did you speak to them, my army?"

Kenan stares at the floor for a moment. "Yes, I did. I did my best. I think some of them actually believe Neriah's rhetoric."

I lean across the table, my tone solemn. "Are we going to have to fight on two fronts?"

"You mean Neriah's army as well as Renatus's?"

"Yes."

"Tough to say. We have seen no indication of Neriah's army mobilizing. But that could be intentional, to throw us off track." Kenan scratches his head.

"And what of my father's army?"

"My scouts have spotted them staging at Reservation 13, old Colorado."

Another general, whose uniform is too tight, studies the map while pursing his narrow lips. "This ravine is massive. If his army stays there, we could have the high ground on both flanks."

I look at the map. "Then we should move immediately."

"Yes, Prime."

"Please call me Sarai. I am no one's Prime anymore."

"Of course."

"Any word from Cephas?" I am wondering if they found Eden. If it actually exists.

Kenan shuffles through his papers; he really needs to be more prepared, but he didn't ask for this position, so I will give him grace. "Last communication had them making it to the island they believe Eden is on. Since then, nothing."

If the nukes are there, that will give us some leverage. And we could use the gold. We are running out of weapons and provisions for what is left of our army. I can't match Neriah's three squares a day and higher pay.

I take a deep breath, hesitant to ask, again afraid of the answer. "Any word from my husband?"

Kenan shakes his head. "No, ma'am, nothing."

I stand; they do also. "Assemble what army is left. We leave for Reservation 13 at first light. And be on the lookout for any soldiers loyal to Neriah, but pretending to be with us."

"How can we tell?" Kenan asks me.

"Watch for any unwarranted communications. And also watch for those who ask too many questions."

Kenan scoffs, "That isn't going to be easy."

I don't answer. I can usually spot the difference between a Lazurite and a Dreck from a mile away. That elitist gait, that snobbish vernacular. Unless, of course, it's my Dreck husband imitating a Lazurite.

Sensing my anxiety, Kenan approaches me and whispers, "Not to worry, ma'am; Asher always comes through."

I force a smile. "Thank you, Kenan, and yes, he always does. And Kenan, you can lose the 'ma'am.'"

Now, he looks troubled. "No, ma'am, or Prime? What should I call you?"

"Sarai, Kenan. Just Sarai."

"Yes ma'am... I mean Sarai."

As they file out, I am having trouble concentrating on war planning. My mind continually drifts to Silas. And Asher. I close my eyes and think about the good ten years we did have, and I wonder if I am asking too much. To live in peace with my husband and my child. But the scars on my chest remind me that I shouldn't be here, and neither should Asher. We cheated fate; now fate is against us. Are we so naive to think that we wouldn't have to pay the price for immortality? Perhaps we are lucky to have those ten years, and should be happy with that. I close my eyes.

What happens next is the last thing in the world I ever expected.

A sentry enters. "You have a visitor, ma'am."

"Who?"

He clears his throat and brings her in.

My jaw drops. It's Joanna.

My mother.

"Sarai... I... " Joanna stutters. Her hands shake. She looks me up and down and places her palms on her heart. "My darling Sarai. My dearest daughter."

Darling? Dearest? Who is this person, and what have they done with my mother?

"What are you doing here, Mother?" I say coldly. Anger wells up in me.

"I... I want to apologize. For... for everything, my sweet daughter. For the Canonization. For the way I let your father treat you. For the way I treated you."

"Are you alone?"

"Why, yes, dear. I came alone." She looks confused by my question.

"You didn't bring my son with you? *Your* grandson?" My tone is accusatory.

She drops to her knees. "If I could, I would have. You have to believe me, Sarai. I barely got here myself."

"Is he... is he alive?"

"Yes. I would have brought him if at all possible. I understand your anger and will leave if that's what you want."

"Why are you here?" My inflection is still lukewarm. Distant.

"Your father, he... he has gotten worse. I don't recognize him anymore. The more times he dies, the worse he gets. Maybe I was in denial before, but I see it now. I see his evil. I see what protocol has done to him." She clasps her hands together; tears rain down her bruised face. "Please, Sarai. Please forgive me. I was evil, too."

I want to, but there is something inside me that wants to see her suffer. That wants revenge. I didn't used to have these thoughts. My eyes burn as I stare into the fire. I shake it from my head. I don't want my soul to burn, either. I turn to her, grab her hands, and lift her off of her knees.

"Thank you, Mom, thank you for calling Marcus. You saved me."

I can see she is lost in a memory. "Ah, Marcus. He was a good man. How is he?"

I will eventually tell her the truth, but not today. We are having a bit of a moment I don't want to ruin. "He is good, Mother. He sends his regards."

She stares at me and must realize I know at least a little of their history. "Sarai, your father wasn't always like this. We were young and in love once. He was an idealistic young man. Overly so. When he conceived second-life protocol, he wanted it to benefit all of society. He wanted to help people; he really did. He had such grandiose and noble plans."

"What happened?"

She shakes her head in sorrow. "Like most, he couldn't handle the power. Something like that isn't meant to be handled by mere men. I think part of the problem was that the idea's genesis came from a place of pain and loss. His parents, his sister. Then, our son. And, of course, power leads to corruption. But there is something else. Something about protocol has warped his mind. His spirit. His soul. The goodness has emptied out of him and replaced with something heinous. Something hateful. I think he is beyond saving."

I touch her bruised and swollen face. "Did he do that to you?"

Her head droops towards the floor. "Yes. And this isn't the first time."

"That must be hard, watching your husband transform like that." I think of Asher, and I worry for us. Is this our future? Will protocol do that to us?

"It was so subtle, so slow, I didn't notice it. I... I was like a frog slowly being boiled. And before I knew it, everything had changed."

"But you jumped out in time." I smile, trying to make a joke to lighten the mood a little.

"I would be remiss if I didn't tell you how proud of you I am. You, my daughter, Prime Servant. Giving your all to put a fractured country back together."

"I'm Prime Servant no longer, mother."

She manages a slight and modest smile. "I knew you had it within you to be a leader when you were very little. The way you were with your brother, with your friends. You knew how to serve and tell people what to do all at the same time. Strong yet yielding. Your father never saw it, unfortunately."

"If only I were Eleazar," I manage to reply, thinking about my father's *wounded* prince. *Wounded* family is more like it.

She grabs both of my hands and squeezes them, pulling them towards her heart. For the first time, I see affection in her emerald green eyes.

"Oh Sarai, your dear brother, you must know it wasn't your fault."

Now I start to tear up.

"You did everything you could; you must stop blaming yourself."

I'm not quite ready to talk about it, especially not with her. At least not yet. "I know, Mother."

"There's more." Her head slumps towards the ground. Her shoulders follow. "Asher. Your father has him."

CHAPTER ELEVEN

Cephas

EDEN IS EVERYTHING IT was advertised to be and more. There are pallets and pallets of gold bullion.

"We are going to need a forklift," Cephas says in awe.

Jude can't help himself; he dances on top of a stack of gold while holding up two bars. Cephas shakes his head.

"Get off of there, buckethead! You look like a leprechaun!"

"I feel like one!"

Boaz shifts his greedy eyes from left to right, then tries to slide a gold bar into his coat pocket.

"Don't even think about it," Cephas growls at him.

"But I was promised." Boaz sounds like a spoiled child whose mother just took away his candy.

"We will divvy and disperse it when we return."

"I can't believe it's real!" Jude dances on, still amped.

"I told you, didn't I?" Boaz boasts. "You didn't trust me, but did I deliver, or what?"

Jude breaks his bubble. "We still don't trust you, hoss."

"Tally it up." Cephas points to the gold, thinking about the weapons and provisions he can now provide for their army. Food for their people. Education for their children. More rehab centers. Parks and playgrounds.

But he is getting ahead of himself; first, they must win the war and take back power.

They march through another tunnel, where they find twenty massive lead crates. One of the engineers with red hair and long sideburns waves a radiation/uranium detector over the boxes.

"These must be the nukes," he informs Cephas.

"Deactivate them and prepare them for shipment," Cephas orders him. "Last thing we need is an accidental detonation or radiation leak on our way home."

Cephas ensured they brought two nuclear scientists and two engineers with them, just for this reason.

"Now Renatus and Neriah aren't the only ones with nukes," Cephas states, his tone relieved.

Jude, who disappeared momentarily, struts back in. "Come check this out."

Cephas follows him through another tunnel, which leads to a heavily insulated room. On the shelves are freeze-dried bags of seeds. Jude reads them off.

"Apple, pear, corn, tomato, watermelon."

Just about every seed imaginable is stored and cataloged here.

"This is like the doomsday global seed vault in Norway," Jude explains.

"You're just 'a little known fact' guy, aren't ya?" Cephas smirks.

They enter another room, which is full of books and technical documents. Jude finds a cabinet full of CDs with different labels:

- History of the world: 1800-1989.

- The study of nuclear physics.

- The history of farming.

- The origins of computer science and the computer revolution.

- The Industrial Revolution.

- Military history and strategy.

- NASA and the moon mission.

And on and on.

Jude shakes his head. "If humanity needed to start over, there is just about everything here, including enough gold and weapons to be an instant superpower, assuming everything else was destroyed."

Cephas thumbs through the CDs. "This must have been built in the 1980s and last updated in 1989." He is referring to the history one that only goes up to 1989. "I hope those nukes are still viable. They're over a hundred years old."

"It's like déjá-vu, with the rusty guns at the Fort Worth Armory," Jude adds.

"Let's hope the outcome is the same."

"Let's see what's in the next one."

Cephas follows Jude into another cement room. It is full of art, paintings, and sculptures. Cephas stares at Norman Rockwell's *Freedom From Want*. He studies the happy smiles of the children at the dinner table while the massive turkey is being served and thinks about a simpler time, back when the American dream was alive and real.

"We have gone backward," Cephas states quietly, to no one in particular.

"Technology has replaced humanity." Jude's tone is heartfelt.

"Technology has replaced God, is more like it," Cephas asserts.

"Hey, check this out!"

The next room is a micro-museum of sorts. A wax sculpture of Hank Aaron in mid-swing. Another one of Joe Montana about to throw the pigskin. A family on green grass behind a white picket fence, the dad manning the BBQ, his wife beside him sporting big fluffy hair. Michael Jackson moonwalking. Mary Lou Retton in her American Flag gymnastics outfit. A miniature space shuttle. A teenager break-dancing. An Atari game system. A Rubik's Cube, which Jude quickly pilfers. A snapshot of America in the 1980's.

As they exit the room, Cephas spots a portion of concrete littered with graffiti. It is a piece of The Berlin Wall. Underneath it is a picture of

Ronald Reagan and a quote from his famous speech, "Tear down this wall." Cephas thinks about the irony of it all: *Here we are, a hundred years later, with another wall that needs to be torn down.*

The room beside it is full of music CDs and VHS movies. Jude browses through the VHS tapes.

"Yep, definitely 1980s."

Cephas picks up a VHS and reads it. "The Karate Kid."

"Ever seen it?"

"No."

"You'd like it," Jude smiles. "You're kinda like Mr. Miyagi."

Cephas grabs another labeled: *Top Gun.* Jude snatches it from his hand and pockets it.

"Hey!"

"I'm taking this one," Jude announces. "For Asher, he will appreciate it. Besides, I feel the need for speed!"

Boaz enters. "Cephas, sir, your engineers need to speak with you." He then eyeballs the vintage items before him. "Wow, look at all this Americana!"

Minutes later, Cephas and Jude arrive. An engineer named Daniel has one of the lead crates open. The nuclear warhead is inside.

"These are already deactivated," Daniel explains, adjusting his thin rectangle-shaped glasses as he points to the nuke.

"That's a good thing, isn't it?" Jude asks, thinking that it will save them time, and they can now head back home.

Daniel rubs his hands through his oily hair, then motions to a spot near the bottom of the warhead, where there is a small hole. "Look here. The detonators are gone."

"What do you mean, gone?" Cephas inquires, concern creeping into his weathered face.

Daniel clears his throat and scratches his crooked nose; he is intimidated by Cephas's gruff manner. "The detonators are small, hand-held devices that screw in here. Without them, you are looking at a heavy piece of worthless metal."

"That is loaded with uranium," the other engineer adds.

"And you searched the entire crate? Everyone in this room?" Jude asks.

"Yes."

"Unbelievable." Cephas totters his head. "It's like finding a Ferrari without an engine." He turns to Boaz, "Is there anything on that map suggesting anything about the detonators?"

"No. I don't believe so."

Jude taps his nose. "Can they be hacked?"

Daniel squints. "Activation without the detonators would be extremely unlikely but not impossible, I suppose. The problem is that this technology is a hundred years old. The programming language used here is archaic at best. It would take months, maybe years, to decipher, if we could at all."

Cephas stomps his foot and knocks his head with his knobby knuckles. He then realizes everyone is watching his tantrum. He is supposed to be their leader. Their rock. He smiles and takes a deep breath. "They have to be around here somewhere. Why else would the nukes be here if they were rendered useless? Doesn't make sense otherwise. I want every room in this place searched top to bottom."

"Maybe it's a safety protocol," Jude speculates. "Perhaps the detonators are at another EDEN somewhere; you know, two people need to turn the keys instead of one, type of thing?"

Cephas is having a hard time keeping his optimism. "Can't be."

"Why not?"

"Because if that is true, we have lost."

Asher

I watch as Legion is placed into a WallBox and wheeled into the back of a massive truck. A WallBox is essentially a giant steel crate, the top and all four sides of which are made from the same translucent material as The Wall. Legion is awake now, but the volts will kill him instantly if he touches anything inside the box except his seat.

It saddens me to see such a powerful man of honor and integrity caged like an animal.

"Where are you taking him?" I ask Renatus.

"You will see shortly." He smiles. "Now come, have you ever been to The White House?"

Before I know it, I am being escorted inside The White House by Renatus and his elites.

"No need to follow," Renatus tells his guards.

He is not worried for his safety, as my hands are cuffed behind me. I have a GuillotineRing around my neck, and Renatus has the remote. All he needs to do is press a button, and I'm decapitated. Besides, if I did manage to take him out, they would just perform protocol on him again. The man is living a no-risk existence.

But, without the threat of danger, you become complacent and eventually slip up. Just because you don't feel pain doesn't mean you can put your hand in the fire. I'm waiting for him to do so.

As we stroll down the West Wing, I eye the portraits of the different presidents that have served throughout history. Renatus points to the drawings.

"Who was your favorite?"

"Does it matter?" I ask him. "You think that you compare to those men? They were elected."

"So was I," he corrects me.

"Yeah, but they had term limits. It was a democracy, not a dictatorship."

"You speak as if that was a good thing," Renatus replies.

"It isn't?"

"Don't you think it would have behooved the country to have presidents like Washington and Lincoln serve more than two terms?"

I scoff. "Is that who you compare yourself to? You're Lincoln now?"

"He freed the slaves. I gave people a second life, another chance."

"Yeah, for you and your rich buddies, at the expense of the poor and people like me. If anything, you have enslaved people."

He shakes his head. "Oh, Asher, if only your people hadn't started the war, things were peaceful in Zion. Before your uncle's bloody Defiance."

"People were living a lie!" I yell at him. "Your lie! The lie of protocol. You called it a gift to all. You failed to mention to them the cost. That it takes life to receive it. That you are a murderer, plain and simple."

He stares at the paintings, his tone philosophical. "Yes, the natural order of things, isn't it? There is no salvation without bloodshed. Even with all our technology, we still couldn't get around that one. Maybe someday. Besides, some lives are worth more than others, are they not?"

"Not in God's eyes," I spit. "Then again, you see yourself as a deity. How many times have you gone through protocol? Hundreds? Thousands? I bet you look forward to it now, and relish in the power of your own resurrection. I mean, what good is a person who sees himself as a God without getting to use their divine-like powers? You probably even see your death as a sport. I'm guessing every time you die, you feel a bit of a martyr. But true martyrship takes sacrifice. It also requires you to remain dead."

He laughs. "What a shame, Asher. You could have been a psychologist, instead of a warrior playing for the losing team. And let's not forget that you and my daughter have partaken in your own resurrections. So, as much as you and your people think, you aren't the martyr either." He smiles. "At least not yet."

"Enough of this. Where is my son!? And why am I here?"

He gives me a beastly grin while waving his hand in the air. "So many questions, Asher. You will find out in due time. I will tell you this, and so much more. But come, now it's time for some bloody fun."

"I'm not going anywhere until I see Silas," I demand.

His eyes blink rapidly, feigning bewilderment. "Oh, Asher, are you awake? Or have you slipped into a dream where you actually have an ounce of control of your current situation? Let's not confuse and complicate things. You have no power here. You have no choices here." He holds up the remote to the GuillotineRing. "Now come, boy, let's not lose your head."

He is right. I have no play here.

I follow him downstairs into an underground bunker. We then walk through another door into what looks like an old command center. There are monitors and screens everywhere, and the presidential seal is on the floor in the middle of the room.

"I won't lie to you; I'm enjoying my new digs, but miss my citadel on the ocean. I hope you have kept it up."

"Your puppet is there now." I am referring to Neriah. "Did you also cheat when you won your election the first time?"

"Doesn't matter how I got here, Asher. I am fated to be here."

The scary thing is that he really believes it. That this is his destiny, that he is some kind of hero, mankind's salvation; that he is a deity, anointed.

"Have a seat," he orders me.

I plop down into the soft, cushy leather chair and wonder how many secret operations have been managed from this room throughout history. How many presidents have graced this very room before Renatus defiled it with his mere presence?

He presses a button, and a massive HoloTube comes to life. On it is live footage of an arena similar to the one where I fought Legion.

"What do you think? My new arena."

I humor him. "What's it for?"

"Ten long years since we have had a proper Canonization. I am bringing it back. With some upgrades, of course," he smirks.

The arena moves on all of its axes. It also spins. There are tigers chained at the corners, and two pits of burning hot oil near the middle. And that is just for starters. He has become more deranged. Then, I spot Apex inspecting the new arena.

"Where did you find him?" I point to Apex.

"On the streets, much like his brother."

"And he, too, is under your spell."

Renatus scratches the surface of his white teeth. "I am giving him what he wants. All men of power need an avenue to express it. Showcase it. Channel it. I simply gave that to him. He is also a warrior and a man of violence. That can only be bottled up for so long. Our relationship is symbiotic."

"True men of power, virtuous men of power, abhor it. They don't wield it," I reply. "They only use it when it benefits others."

"Said the man with no power."

I am growing impatient. "Why am I here? And where is my son?!"

Again, he ignores my question. "We are getting a little preview. A test run of my arena. I assure you from personal experience that it doesn't disappoint."

He is going to make Legion fight Apex!

"You're sick!" I spit at him. "Soon, your army will be crushed. Soon, you won't be the only one with nuclear weapons. Your little ruse with Neriah will only give you so much power."

"You referring to your wife's attack on my army in Colorado? They are walking into a trap set brilliantly by the man you pretended to be. You used Amos against me; now he will be your downfall."

Dread washes over me. He knows. He is luring Sarai and Kenan exactly where he wants them. I can only hope Sarai discovers it. Kenan isn't experienced enough. I promoted him too fast. I expected too much of him too quickly. I have made so many mental and tactical errors since Silas was taken from me. I have been doing the bidding of my emotions.

"Not only would you murder your grandson, but your daughter too? What kind of monster are you?"

"The kind this world needs. Besides, she chose to fight against me, if you remember?"

"Even so, but soon you and your army will be wiped out regardless."

"Oh, you mean Eden? Trust me, no nuclear weapons are leaving that island."

He also knows about Eden. How? Boaz! I should have seen that coming. He hovers over me, and this time, he spits in my face.

"And neither is your uncle."

Sarai

It is slow going, but we have finally crossed over into Reservation 13. While passing Reservation 9, I could see our Weeping Willow in the distance. The one Asher and I were married under. I don't want to stop our entire convoy of Jeeps and trucks just so I could relive a memory of happier days. Days I may never see again. This is a silly thing to say, but our tree looks somber. As though its long strands are tears. Perhaps it is reflecting on how I feel.

Kenan, who is leading our convoy, stops his Jeep and jumps out. I am silently pleased, as I have taken as much bouncing around as I can stand. It's not helping my recurring headache.

Kenan marches towards me. I exit my Jeep. A thin layer of frozen snow crunches underneath my tan tactical boots. I forgot how tight they feel around my wide feet. The footwear donned by a politician was much more comfortable. I stretch my legs and bounce up and down, finally feeling a bit spry. Mentally and physically, I need to be war-ready. Ten years with the pen have accomplished almost nothing. It is time for the sword.

"Sarai, one of our surveillance drones just reported back."

He holds up a tablet that shows the drone's footage.

"A small contingent of Lazurite elites are staging just over that mountain. It would be wise to make our attack now."

I can't think straight at the moment. My mind wanders from Silas to Asher, and now to my mother. Her visit was a surprise. But a pleasant one. It gives me hope that no one is ever completely lost. Perhaps there is hope for my father? I can't think that way. I can't fight this war when my enemy is gray. It has to be black and white. Evil or good. How can I fight my father if there is the slightest sliver of good in him?

"Ma'am? I mean Sarai." Kenan wakes me from my fog. "Shall I order the attack?"

"How small?" I ask.

"About half of our army."

I am a leader. I need to act like one, even when it's hard. I shake my head, shimmying off the trance of self-pity and sorrow. I need to remember who my father is and what he has done. That he now has Silas.

I continue to bounce up and down. I know I must look ridiculous, but the physical movement activates my brain. "Split our army in two. I will lead a charge into their middle. You flank them. Send a small detachment ahead of us, armed with rocket launchers. Have them take out any HeliDrones before they get a chance to leave the ground. Also, charge four Rollers."

Rollers are balls about the size of a small car that are charged with explosive plasma, much like a giant rolling grenade. As our technology grows, the more destructive we become. What was meant to make a better world has destroyed us.

"Yes, we will do our best."

"Don't let your soldiers hear you speak like that. You are a general now, Kenan. There is no 'do your best' in war. It's win or lose. Live or die."

"Of course."

I want to instill more confidence in him. I want him to know it's not just my men. I want him to act like a general, not just don the stripes. He needs to own it. "How long until *your* men are ready, general?"

"We can be battle-ready in three hours. Two and a half if we don't eat."

I shake my head. "Make sure your men are well fed."

"Of course."

"And what of Renatus's main army? Are they still camped in the ravine?"

"Yes, five miles south. We should immediately push on after this battle, before they have time to move."

"One step at a time," I tell him.

I spend the next few hours re-acquainting myself with my scourge. Except for my lovely stint in Paris, it has been a while since I used it. Not quite the weapon of a politician. Truth be told, I prefer this kind of battle to political debates with dishonest bureaucrats. At least here, you know who your enemy is, and where they stand. At least here, they shoot you in the front, instead of stabbing you in the back.

Black and white.

Treading that gray area is for politicians.

Soldiers deal in the absolutes.

I slip on my exoarmor and check that my plasma gun is charged. The exoarmor is more uniform now than anything else, as both sides have exoarmor-piercing plasma. It is helpful, though, if it comes down to hand-to-hand combat. Cephas and Jude were working on a new genera-tion of armor, but it was not quite ready.

The exoarmor feels good on me; a little snug, but I'll take it.

The last time I donned this outfit and these weapons, I fought alongside Asher and Cephas. Now, we are separated, fighting our own battles on three fronts. I can't help but think it's intentional. My father's doing. He's undoubtedly diabolical enough. This isn't the first time he has divided Asher and me, physically and mentally.

"You ready?" Kenan asks.

I nod. He takes a deep breath; I can tell he's nervous. His left leg shakes. I place my hand on his shoulder. "You got this, Kenan."

"Yes, ma'am... I mean, Sarai."

"Listen to me. Your men are well-trained. They know what to do. Just don't do anything to make them doubt your orders, doubt why we are here, or doubt that we will be successful. Lead from the front. Most people will follow courage. You are a general now, hand-chosen by Asher; show them why. Prove to them you belong here."

He smiles, and his leg stops shaking. He storms off towards his men. Asher could have probably said it better, but I think that did the job.

Thirty minutes later, we are in place. Half my soldiers and I are just atop the hill facing the enemy army. Kenan and his half are to my left. Ten men with rocket launchers are perched up higher in between us. There are six enemy drones just a hundred yards behind their staging area. I motion to the unit with the rocket launchers.

"Now!"

They fire the rockets into the drones, destroying all six of them.

"Rollers!" Kenan orders.

His men push four Rollers down the hill, two on each side. The Lazurites are just finding their bearings from the drone explosions, when the Rollers bounce their way through their camps. Four large plasma explosions send men, weapons, tents, and equipment flying.

"Go!" I scream.

We race down the hill toward the Lazurites. Kenan and his contingent do the same on my left. Plasma blasts everywhere. We have them flanked and surprised. But they do have one thing going for them—trees. There are thousands of them, where they are staged. This makes for close-quartered combat. I am ready for it.

I turn on my scourge.

It comes back to me like riding a bike. I whip it towards an elite hiding behind a tree to my right. It wraps around his neck and sends a burst of electric shock through his body. He goes down. I notice he dons a backpack that holds a glass cylinder filled with pink translucent fluid. I wonder if they are kept nourished and hydrated intravenously during battle this way. Not a bad idea, actually.

I spot a foot from behind another tree—time for the training wheels to come off. I flick my wrist, and my scourge wraps around his ankle. I yank back, and the Lazurite is pulled from behind the tree. I finish him off with my plasma gun. I take out three more.

Coldly.

Maybe because I have been politicking for so long, but taking out what used to be my fellow brethren is easier than I remember. Or maybe it's what protocol has done to my brain? Or perhaps I am more like my father than I realize? I duck a couple of more plasma blasts. One grazes my left ear. But I am not fazed. There is no room in my emotional palette for fear at the moment. All it does is slow me down; it lies to me. Tells me I can't win, tells me I will never see Silas again, tells me Asher is no longer in love with me. That my father hates me. That Eleazar's drowning was my fault. I refuse to listen to it anymore.

But what I see next leaves me dumbfounded and terrified.

The elite I just killed is standing there, pointing his gun at me.

Cephas

After searching all of Eden, they find twenty-five rooms, or at least twenty-five doors they could not access. Each door is made from thick concrete. The only other room they can access was what looks like a control room. There are screens and computers in the corners.

"Maybe we can open those doors from here?" Jude suggests.

After some pondering, they determined that this place must be run by a nuclear generator somewhere within the premises; otherwise, how else would they have power?

Cephas turns on the computer screen.

"Computer is locked." Cephas turns to Jude. "Maybe the cipher is the same?"

Jude types in O-P-P-E-N-H-E-I-M-E-R.

The computer spits back a message: *Access Denied. This system can only be accessed biometrically by authorized personnel.*

Jude notices a pad next to the computer that would accept a thumbprint.

"Biometrically, but whose thumbprint?" Jude wonders.

"That's a good question. We have no other choice but to get the drill."

They brought along a giant drill about the size of a small bike that could be pushed around on three wheels. It was their contingency plan in case they couldn't guess the cipher correctly to get inside Eden. It was good that they did guess it, as the drill would have never gotten through that massive steel door. With concrete, on the other hand, they had a fighting chance.

"That's gonna take a while."

"Until we come up with something better, we have no choice. We need to find those detonators. I'm not bringing home worthless nukes."

Cephas knows that the only way to deter Renatus from using his nuclear weapons is to have some of their own. He stops for a moment to pray and thinks back to all the insane and preposterous things they have done, and the victories they led to: sculpting Asher in the hope he would win The Canonization, and then banking it all on the hopes he could convince the Lazurite army to fight with him. Then, finding weapons at The Fort Worth Army that still worked. And even after all that had transpired, they still had to defeat Renatus's army, which outnumbered them four to one. And that *still* would not have been possible if it weren't for Legion and The Sons of Levi coming to their rescue. Yet almost the entire time, Cephas was confident they would succeed. It was impossible to think they didn't have divine help along the way.

Cephas believes they still do; he has to. How else can he explain it?

Ten sweaty hours later, they are still drilling through the concrete.

"I think we're almost there," Jude states hopefully.

"This isn't working; this is taking too long," Cephas replies. "What do we have for explosives?"

"Not a lot."

Cephas furrows his brow. "I refuse to believe we came all this way for nothing."

"We're through!" Jude yelps.

"Nice. Back the drill out, slowly."

Jude reverses the drill. Then it gets jammed.

"Stop it! Stop it!" Cephas barks.

Before Jude can shut it off, there is a loud clank.

Jude shuts it down. "What was that?"

"Pull it out by hand. I think you broke it."

"Why are you blaming me?"

"You backed it out too fast. Didn't you hear me say slowly?"

"It was slow."

They pull the drill out by hand to reveal that the tip busted off. Cephas scowls.

Jude, always the optimist, puts his hands up. "At least we can get into this room."

"And if the detonators aren't in here, we're screwed."

"Time for prayers then."

"Get your scrawny butt in there!" Cephas slaps him on the back. Jude is probably the only person there skinny enough to fit through the hole they had just drilled.

Jude squeezes his body into the freshly drilled hole. The door is about ten feet thick, so he flicks on his lighter so he can see as he scuttles through.

"'Come out to the coast, have a few laughs,'" Jude quotes.

Cephas is confused. "What?"

"Die Hard! It's a line from Die Hard."

"Never seen it."

"Remind me to grab the VHS before we leave."

"Will you just hurry up?" Cephas shakes his head and whispers to himself, "Quoting movies that are over a hundred years old."

Jude reaches the other side, crawls out of the hole, and then slithers inside the pitch-black room. Using his lighter, he finds a light switch and flicks it on. What he sees jolts him.

"You're not gonna believe what's in here!" he hollers through the hole.

"What? Is it the detonators?"

It takes Jude a minute to find out how to open the door. When it slides open, Cephas sees Jude's shocked face.

"What is it?" Cephas asks impatiently.

"Look."

They slowly trudge to the middle of the room, where two eight-foot capsules are perched on an elevated stage. A man is frozen inside one of them, a woman in the other. Numerous tubes are inserted into them, and the computer monitors beep quietly.

"What is this?" Cephas wonders out loud. "Can't be for protocol. That didn't exist back then. Did it?"

"Not that we are aware of. They look like cryogenic chambers," Jude replies.

The male's chamber is labeled 'ADAM.'

The female's is labeled 'EVE.'

Jude is still awed. "Adam and Eve. Eden. I don't get this; what is it?"

"Get Boaz in here."

Minutes later, Boaz, as well as the scientists and engineers, are scrutinizing the capsules.

"You have any idea what this is and why they are here?" Cephas asks Boaz.

Boaz places his hands on his rotund belly, giving them a shelf. "These must be... they must be the Operators."

"Operators?"

"If the rumors are true, which apparently they are, not only did Eden have everything needed for a society to start over in the event of a nuclear holocaust or an extinction-level event. But they would also need to begin the process of repopulation."

"Hence, Adam and Eve," Jude adds. "What do we do with them? We can't just leave them here. We have to bring them with us."

Boaz circles the cylinders, stroking the glass. "Hard to believe they have been in here for a hundred years. Can you imagine the stories they could tell?"

Jude counters, "I'm just imagining the dread they would feel seeing what our world has become."

"It must not have been all that great if they saw the need for this place," Boaz replies.

Then Cephas has an epiphany. "Wait a minute. The biometrics must be linked to them! They can open the other doors for us. Get us the detonators."

"So we just press a button and wake them?" Jude asks, half joking, half serious.

Cephas turns to his engineer, Daniel. "Can you figure out how these contraptions work? Get them safely out of there and functioning?"

"I don't know. This is hundred-year-old technology. They have been in there so long we would be risking their lives."

Not the answer Cephas was looking for. "Can you try?"

Daniel clears his throat. "I'll see what I can do."

Jude slides up next to Cephas. "Ya know, all we need is their thumbprint."

Cephas frowns. "What are you saying?"

"I'm saying that if they don't survive coming out of cryogenic sleep, we can still use their biometrics to open the doors."

Cephas can't think about death anymore, or risking others for their own purposes. "I won't kill them for our detonators. If Daniel deems it safe, then we awaken them. If not, we find another way."

CHAPTER TWELVE

Sarai

"Didn't expect this, did you?" the elite I just took out tells me, pointing his plasma gun at me.

I go from bewildered to horrified. I still don't believe what I'm seeing. Those packs on their backs must contain LifeCells. My father has figured out a way to perform protocol almost instantaneously. It used to take two weeks, with the help of doctors and various machines. Now, he has an invincible army. Or one with many lives, at least. How can we possibly win such a war?

"Sarai, the great traitor to Zion." The elite's long hair flows in the wind, and his teeth are so white they look painted. He has a red sash on each arm, signifying he is one of the upper echelons. "Must be my lucky day. The reward for you is very high. Dead or alive. *Sultana.*"

I wonder how many LifeCells are in each pack. Luckily for me, I find out. The elite is shot from behind. He falls to the ground. Behind him is Kenan, his plasma rifle in hand. He is as confounded as I was mere seconds ago.

"What is happening? I don't understand. They are not dying!"

I point to the LifePack on his back. "They carry LifeCells with them. Instant protocol. And look for the red sashes; it seems only the elites have them."

Kenan's stutter makes an appearance. "How... how many times do we have to kill them?"

The elite is still lying on the ground, motionless. "Seems twice. Hurry, tell all your men. We still have them outnumbered. We can still do this! And if possible, have them shoot the packs off their backs first."

Kenan takes off to warn his men that the enemy must be killed twice. The ones with LifePacks, anyway. I don't want them being ambushed, as I was. I march to my right and witness a ghastly scene. A newly resurrected Lazurite comes back to life, and immediately begins to defile the body of one of my dead soldiers. The evil nature propagated by protocol seems almost as instantaneous as the resurrection itself. They are like bloodthirsty zombies. It's almost as if killing is no longer enough for them. He moves on to another dead Dreck. Before he can gouge his eyes out, I fire my plasma gun at him and move on.

The entire scene nauseates me. Instantaneous resurrection. The thought of someone else's LifeCell swimming around in their backpacks is almost too much to take. Those were people. Drecks, most likely. Mothers and fathers. Children. But in their eyes, life has less meaning when it's condensed down to a single cell. Invisible. Faceless. Even the name: Protocol. It sounds like a sterile, clinical set of benign instructions or formalities, as opposed to the murderous abomination that it is.

Then, I think I see... no, it can't be. I think I see Asher. Are my eyes playing tricks on me? Then I see the man who looks like Asher fire upon my soldiers. Am I having another nightmare? What is happening? Am I asleep? No.

Amos.

How quickly I forget my husband was sculpted to look like this man, so long ago. I think about the sacrifice Asher made to rescue me from Zion. To free the Defiance. To defeat the enemy, he had to become them. I knew about the physical, but never thought about the emotional toll it must have put on him. But Amos returned the favor in full. He stole my son, my Silas.

I experience a sudden and unbridled fury. This is the man who has taken everything from me. I can't even find the words to describe how hard it is that the man I love more than anything and the man I hate with a passion look exactly the same.

"Amos!" I scream.

I dash towards him, firing my plasma gun. He scampers towards me, dodging the blasts by sidestepping in and out of the trees. He fires back, barely missing, as I head straight towards him.

"Amos!" I howl.

He tucks behind a tree. I spin to my left, roll to the ground, and flank him. I whip my scourge; it wraps around his body. His exoarmor gives him some protection from the electrical current.

"Where is my son?! Where is Asher?!" I shriek as I pull him closer to me.

I am too enraged to see that one of his arms is free, holding a StunClub behind his back.

"Piss off, you Dreck traitor," Amos growls through his teeth. Before I can react, he swings his StunClub, hitting me in the chest and sending me flying into a tree.

My exoarmor saved my life. But I'm seeing stars for a moment. He has broken free from my scourge. He picks me up by my hair. It's an abominable feeling looking into the eyes of pure evil. Eyes that look like my husband's. How can you love and despise the same face? The difference is that the left side of Amos's face is covered in burn scars.

"You'll see your husband and your son soon enough," Amos tells me, putting his plasma gun to my temple. "Look at my face! Your husband did that to me, and for that, you will pay."

I am so close to him that he doesn't see me slip a plasma grenade between his chest and exoarmor until it is too late. Once he realizes what has happened, he momentarily releases me in shock. I boot him in the chest as hard as I can, and dive for cover just as the grenade goes off. Dirt and rock are hurled in my direction. My ears ring from the sonic ting emanating from the grenade.

I pull myself up off the ground, brush myself off, and watch Amos's life slowly fade from him. He holds his chest where the plasma grenade ripped open his exoarmor. Then I see the LifeCell travel from his LifePack into the tube connected to his heart. I'm not letting him have another chance. I'm going to pull the tube from his body before the stolen life enters his cells. He doesn't deserve another chance. He is not worth a Dreck's life.

But before I can reach him, four elites race up from behind me. They take a knee and fire at me, causing me to retreat behind the cover of trees.

They drag Amos to safety while protocol does its thing. I'm angry he got away, but I regain my composure.

I let my emotions take over and get the best of me. Through the chaos, it's difficult to monitor our progress. Kenan is leading a platoon about a hundred yards to my right. I quickly joined up with him. I will see Amos another day.

"Status?" I ask him, my chest still sore from the StunClub. I wonder if my ribs are cracked. Every breath hurts.

"The remnants are retreating towards their base camp," Kenan informs me. "We can take chase now and wipe them out."

I think about it for a moment. Something doesn't seem right. Why would Amos be here with an undersized army? And why set up such a horrible defensive posture? "Wait."

"Wait? But this is our chance!" Kenan pleads.

"Make camp here for the night."

I cough, and it's excruciating. I need to find something for the pain.

"But Prime! I mean, Sarai, we have them right where we want them. We can finish them off. They haven't moved from that ravine."

"That's what scares me," I respond. It hurts to talk.

"I don't understand. What scares you?" Kenan is as frustrated as he is perplexed. He is ready and wants to finish this. Prove himself.

"Don't you think it seems a little too easy? A little too convenient? The fact that they would set up in the worst possible place? They obviously know we are here now, and they are still there. Doesn't it smell like a trap to you?"

"It's worth the risk, Sarai. We might not have another shot at this," he argues. "They are hurting, on their heels. We can finish this today. Let's do this. My men are ready. They are hungry."

"No," I tell him, plain and simple. My father is more competent than this.

He tries to convince me by using my husband's words. "'Hesitation is the enemy to victory.' Asher told me that."

"And sometimes you need to hesitate to think. My answer still stands. Stand your men down. That is a direct order."

"Let it be noted, I disagree. *My Prime.*" Kenan adds a little insult as he wanders off to set up camp.

Being a leader doesn't make you the most popular person on the planet. In fact, if you please everyone, you probably aren't a good one. Sometimes, to do what is right, you must be uncompromising.

I guzzle some water and head straight to my tent. Due to the pain in my chest, it takes me a good two hours to fall asleep.

At three in the morning, one of my sentries shakes me awake.

"It's General Kenan!"

"What?" I ask, perturbed, holding my ribs while attempting to sit up.

"He is gone. And he has taken half your army with him!"

Cephas

"They are awake."

Cephas and Jude jump up at the news from Daniel, their engineer. It has been thirty-six hours since they figured out how to safely bring Adam and Eve out of their cryogenic sleep. And not a moment too soon, as they are running low on food, water, and patience. Besides, The Defiance is eagerly waiting for what Eden has to offer.

Cephas and Jude stroll into a recovery room of sorts. Adam and Eve are both in wheelchairs. They look to be in their late twenties. Their bodies are littered with needles and tubes.

Daniel points to them.

"Their muscles have atrophied; these are quickening the recovery process."

They slowly approach Adam and Eve. They look weak and emaciated. Their skin is pasty white; they are both hairless.

"I am Cephas. This is Jude. What are your names?"

"Who are you?" Adam asks, suspicious. The man's voice is hoarse and raspy. It takes effort for him to speak. They haven't used their vocal cords in over a century.

"We are friendly," is all Cephas offers for the moment.

Eve blinks her eyes, adjusting to the light. "What happened? Has there been an apocalyptic event?"

"Your names, please," Cephas says again.

"I am Adam. This is Eve," Adam croaks.

"Your real names," Jude asks.

They eye each other, and he repeats their names. "I told you, I am Adam; this is Eve."

"That's quite the coincidence, seeing as you're in Eden," Jude opines.

Cephas paces. "Listen, you no longer have to use code names. We know what this place is and why you are here."

"Who are you, and what do you want with us?" Eve asks.

"And why did you wake us? Has there been a nuclear war?" Adam eyes them wearily.

Cephas isn't sure how to explain this to them. "There has been a war. You see—"

"What year is it?" Eve asks.

"09," Jude tells them.

Adam peers over at Eve. "We have been under for twenty years."

"A hundred and twenty," Jude breaks it to them.

"What?"

"It's 2109, not 2009," Cephas tells them lightly.

They both take shallow breaths. It seems they are in shock.

Eve looks to Adam. "We have been under for over a century." She shivers and turns to Jude. "A blanket, please?"

"Of course." Jude rushes to get each of them one.

"Look, I know this must be hard and will take a long time to explain, but we don't have much time right now," Cephas says. "We need you to open all the doors to this facility."

"We have been frozen for a hundred and twenty years, and you're talking to me about time?" Adam scoffs.

"Who are you?" Eve asks again. "And who sent you?"

"We are from Zion; we are part of The Defiance—" Cephas stops, realizing they would have no idea what he is talking about. "We are from America. There has been a civil war of sorts. Long story short, the bad guys are winning. We need the gold and nukes that are housed here. But we need you to access the detonators. We will explain more on the way home."

"Home?" Adam's eyes narrow.

"Yes, America. Or what once was. You are coming with us, correct?"

Adam shakes his head. "Our job is here. We swore an oath to the United States to rebuild in the event of a holocaust."

"There may never be a *United* States again if you don't help us," Cephas pleads.

Adam scrutinizes Cephas. "How do we know you are who you say you are? You look Russian to me."

"Russian?"

"Yeah, tell me, who won the most SuperBowls in the 1980s?"

"I have no idea. I don't follow sports, especially from a century ago."

Jude, a student of history, breaks in, "We are not Russian. The Soviet Empire fell a long time ago. I'm guessing the Cold War ended soon after you were put under. We are Americans like you. We are trying to save our divided country and its people from slavery."

"Slavery has returned?" Eve asks, wide-eyed.

"In a manner of speaking, yes," Cephas tells them, referring to his people being harvested for their LifeCells.

Adam looks to Cephas. "What caused this second civil war?"

"We tried to play God," Cephas answers vaguely.

"What does that even mean?" Eve inquires.

Cephas is blunt, his tone hurried. "It means if you are rich and powerful, you can live forever. As long you don't mind taking the lives of others to do so."

Adam and Eve glance at each other, understandably confused still.

Cephas continues, "They built a wall and imprisoned us behind it. We—the underprivileged—are being harvested, in exchange for their immortality. Look, I know it sounds crazy, but that is the truth."

"Will you do it? Will you help us?" Jude asks.

"This is against all our protocols," Eve tells him.

Cephas is losing his patience. "Those protocols were written over a hundred years ago, for a different time, a different world, a different purpose. A lot has changed since then, trust me."

"You're here seeking weapons and gold. You are at war. The world hasn't changed that much." Adam's tone sarcastic.

"We need to think about it," Eve replies.

Jude eyes them with sincerity. "Look, I know you two have given up a lot for your country, but so have we. We are on the same side. You must believe us."

Adam's tone is resolute. "Like she said, we will think about it. Could you leave us for a moment?"

"We don't have time for this!" Cephas grabs the back of Adam's wheelchair and pushes him towards the exit.

Jude is befuddled. "Cephas, what are you doing?"

"I'm taking them to the control room, and I'm going to force his thumb onto that scanner and open that computer! Open those doors! Then we are getting outta here."

"You are KGB!" Adam barks.

"Just wait a minute!" Jude raises his voice. "We are not KGB. We are not Russian. You talked about your protocols. What is your etiquette for unfreezing? I mean, if there was a Holocaust and there was no one here to take you out of Cryo, then what?"

Eve chimes in, "It's supposed to be automatic. If a nuclear war started, we could be remotely awoken. And if that didn't happen, this place can read radiation sensors from around the globe; if the levels were high enough, the process of our melting, for lack of a better term, would start on its own."

"Exactly my point, then." Jude leans in. "If there wasn't a nuclear war with Russia or whoever, then why would the Russians come here? I mean, they have their own nukes, don't they? Besides, if we were the bad guys, we would just kill you or cut off your thumbs. You don't need to be alive for us to access your prints. Think about it."

Adam shakes his head. "None of this makes sense."

Cephas's patience is almost gone. "Nothing does anymore."

Jude is still playing good cop. "Look, I know this must be hard, but the world is different. Heck, I don't even understand it sometimes. But imagine how much the world changed from 1860 to 1980. That is how long you have been under. You have to trust us. Even if it doesn't make any sense."

"How did you even get in here?" Eve asks.

Jude responds proudly, "I figured out the cipher."

"How do we even know it's 2109?" Adam asks skeptically. "I mean, if you're not Russian, you could be terrorists or thieves here for the gold. It happened once before." Adam peers at Jude's Back to the Future shirt. "And from what you're wearing, it doesn't seem far past the 1980's."

Good point. Jude says, "That is a long story."

Adam shivers underneath the blanket. "I'm not convinced you are who you say you are, and I'm definitely not convinced it is 2109."

Cephas peers over at Jude. "Go get one."

Jude returns a minute later, holding a plasma rifle. He fires it against the wall. "Did they have these in 1989?"

Eve peers over to Adam, "I believe them."

Adam looks up at Cephas's red face. "Guess we don't have a choice in the matter."

Asher

Renatus holds my ricochet as he paces behind me. He gently taps one end of it on the back of my neck, silently projecting that he holds all the cards, has all the power, has my life in his hands—as well as Sarai's. And my uncle's. My friends'.

My son's.

When you are out-gunned and out-manned, the one thing you can't afford to be is outsmarted. But I have been outplayed. I let my emotions get the best of me. Instead of clear and rational thought, I let my feelings try to win this battle.

"You know, young Asher, I could call it all off."

"What are you talking about?"

"It's not too late to save your wife. Your uncle."

He wants something from me. I humor him. "How?"

He circles the table, tapping my ricochet as he goes. "We were so good together, weren't we? You and me. I, your commander, you leading my armies. Sarai was happy, my wife was happy. We were together, enjoying life, enjoying each other. We were prosperous. Zion was prosperous. We were a family. Don't you agree?"

I do remember a happiness swaddled in Zion's bosom. It was the only time Sarai and I could be together in peace. The only time there weren't active external forces trying to separate us. But, it was fleeting—a mirage. Having what you want the most can blind you to everything else.

"Join me again, Asher. I can re-instate you. You can once again lead my armies. I won't lie; you were good at it. They respected you. A respect that was earned, not forced. Guess that's why you got half of them to fight against me. And as much as I wanted to kill you for it, you earned my respect for pulling off such a feat. You were the perfect match for my daughter—if you were a Lazurite, and not a Dreck. What a great prince of Zion you would have made. We can end this war and finally reunite this country. Let's end the death and devastation. That would be something to be proud of, Asher."

"And what of protocol? Whose LifeCells will you plunder if not my friends'? If not, Drecks'?"

"Second-life rights were intended to be a good thing, Asher. A benefit for all humanity. Truth be told, I never intended it to go down the path it has gone. One day, perhaps we will be able to create a synthetic LifeCell.

Imagine a second chance for all, without sacrifice. But, let us not forget, it was you Drecks, you MidLanders, who abused it. That was the entire reason The Wall went up in the first place."

"You lied about it," I snarl. "You never told people the cost."

"The public wasn't ready for it. But I think their choice would have remained the same. Not all lives are created equal, Asher."

"Spoken like a man who thinks he's a God."

Renatus reaches out his hands. "Join me, son. We can create a paradise, unite this country again, and have a peaceful reign of a thousand years."

"Don't call me son."

"Side by side, we can do great things together."

"Never," I tell him. But then I have a thought. Silas. "If I do, my son. Will it save Silas?"

He rubs his hairless head and feigns deep thought. "Hmm... um... NO." He turns to me. "But, we will keep him on ice until we can find another donor who fits the profile, who is also... *wounded*."

I think about it for a moment, then realize it would cost the life of another to do so.

I shake my head. "I'd rather die than join you." I spit.

"Pity. That will happen soon enough. But first, let us be entertained."

He points to the giant HoloTube in front of us, where Apex, looking agitated, kicks up dirt and rock from the arena floor. He looks like a flustered bull readying for a charge. The four Lazurite elites are forced into the arena, donning exoarmor and holding a plethora of weapons.

"Where's the audience?" I ask in disgust.

"This is a private viewing, a test run if you will." Renatus waves his hands wildly in the air. "Trying out some new ideas."

Within seconds, Apex vanquishes the four elites as if they are mere children. Renatus licks his lips and gives a barbaric, almost homicidal smile, clearly enjoying what he just witnessed. "Apex likes to warm up before the main event."

Renatus has gotten so bad he is now willing to waste his elites in the name of entertainment. Or maybe they'll just go in for protocol? None of them look as scared as they should be. Next, Legion is wheeled into the battle arena, still inside the WallBox.

The walls on the WallBox turn off. Legion looks confused as he exits his small prison and steps onto the arena.

Apex parades around him, like a two-footed, nimble tank. Legion slouches a tad; he doesn't want to be here. Who would?

"We don't have to do this, brother," Legion pleads with him, having to step over a dead elite. "Renatus is using you for his pure leisure. Can't you see that? You are being manipulated as I was."

Apex struts towards him. "You are mistaken. I don't do anything I don't want to do. Never have, brother."

"You want to be here? You want to kill your brother for the sake of entertainment? To quench Renatus's savagery?"

"No. I want to kill my brother because he is a traitor to Zion. And because—because you are weak. And anyone who shares my blood cannot be weak."

"Weak? Weak because I chose another life? Because I didn't want to give in to primitive and murderous instincts?"

"You are weak because you tried to change who you are, Legion. We are warriors, and without a war to fight, nothing is left for us but to die. You were the older brother, Legion. You were supposed to protect us. Lead us. You shirked from your responsibilities."

Legion's eyes turn sad. "You're right, Apex. I failed you. I should have protected both you and Aspis."

"Too late."

I watch as Apex charges him. He is thunder. He is lightning. A bull uncaged. His hand furls into a stout fist, hitting Legion square in the chest. Legion wobbles back at least four or five steps before regaining his balance.

A chained tiger swipes at Apex, barely cutting into his leathery skin. Apex clamps the chain and yanks it free from where it was clasped to the ground. The tiger charges him—but Apex swings the chain in the air, the tiger still attached, and throws the beast at Legion.

The tiger goes for Legion's throat. Apex watches, amused. Renatus sticks out his tongue, drooling with blood lust.

The tiger claws at Legion's arms, leaving giant, bloody scratch marks. Legion and Apex are so big that the tiger almost looks like a cat from here. Its jaws are just inches from Legion's neck. Legion manages to grab the chain, wraps it around the tiger's neck, and pulls. It takes a minute, but he manages to squeeze the life out of the animal.

"Oh, poor kitty," Renatus howls, popping crab cakes into his mouth.

Legion pulls himself up. Apex begins his charge. His brother follows suit. Am I seeing what I think I'm seeing? Old cars start to drop from holes in the ceiling. They smash onto the ground, barely missing the dyad of destruction as they weave their way between the cars.

Renatus hoots and hollers at his new set-piece.

He is really dropping cars on them. This sadistic sickness is beyond what even I imagined. What other demented surprises does he have in store? Before they reach each other, holes open randomly on the floor. Not only that, but the entire arena teeters back and forth. Legion steps into one of the holes, and squeals in pain. I realize what they are: shallow puddles of boiling oil.

Again, barbarous and perverse. I wonder if Renatus came up with this himself? Legion pulls his leg from the puddle, some of his skin melting almost to his knee. He grimaces in pain but keeps his composure. The arena rotates and spins. Metal spikes jut from the floor, then retract. Legion loses his balance and falls backward. One of the spikes impales his left arm. He is stuck there. A portion of the ceiling opens up, and an old compact sedan falls directly toward him.

Legion closes his eyes, and so do I. Then, at the last moment, Apex barrels into the car with his shoulders, like a linebacker. The automobile lands two feet from Legion's head.

"I will not let this arena take what's mine," Apex tells him. He wants the honor of extinguishing Legion himself.

He grabs Legion's hand and peels him off the arena floor. Legion screams as his shoulder slides off the metal spike. Apex punches his injured shoulder. Legion plops back to the ground.

"Get up!"

Legion stays there.

"Get up, brother, and fight back."

"I won't fight you, " Legion says sorrowfully. He then peers up at one of the cameras and looks directly at us. At Renatus. "I won't give him the satisfaction."

"Do it! Fight back!" Renatus blurts, wanting more action.

Apex picks Legion up by the neck. "Then today, you meet the reaper."

Renatus chews on a slab of chocolate, licking his muddy lips. Apex sprints towards the side and slams Legion into a wall of metal spikes. I watch in horror as blood pools around Legion's massive bare feet, painting his nails red. His face contorts in agony.

Apex spits on him. "What a shame, brother. We could have put on quite the show."

"You, you are not... you are not my brother," Legion utters through bloody teeth.

I cover my mouth as Renatus stands to get a better look. Gawking at death.

Legion, the savior of The Defiance, warrior-poet, my friend, takes his last breath.

Sarai

It has been an hour since I was awoken to the news of Kenan's defiance. It takes me another hour to prepare the half of my army that I have left. I am angry at his insubordination. I am angry at Asher for promoting him too soon. But I know why Kenan has done it. He has consistently been underestimated and marginalized. He wants to prove to me and everyone else that he has what it takes to be a general—a leader. Unfortunately, intellect becomes buried when pride takes over. And we all know pride comes before the fall.

I only hope that Kenan is correct and that I am wrong. Either way, we have to help him.

It is dawn when we arrive at the top of the mountain overlooking the ravine that Kenan is keen on attacking. As the sun rises, the wildflowers at my feet burp steam from the cold ground. I peer through my binoculars and see Kenan and his forces fighting a small remnant of Lazurites below us.

"What do you see?" one of my commanders asks.

"A massive piece of cheese."

"And we are the mice?"

"Let's hope not," I tell him. "Get your men to go down the west side. We will meet Kenan and his army in the middle and finish them off."

"Yes, Sarai. And if it's a trap?"

"Then eat as much cheese as you possibly can."

He orders his men to be ready. Within minutes, we are charging down the hill into the ravine. I whip my scourge, taking out Lazurites on my left and right. None of them have LifePacks on. There are very few elites. That means these men are expendable. Not a good sign. And why aren't those HeliDrones taking off? A dozen of them are sitting there unused, along with their tanks. Also, why didn't Kenan think of taking them out first? Again, I feel frustration at how unprepared he is to be a general. Asher wasn't thinking clearly. Another emotion-based decision; it has become an epidemic around here.

It only takes thirty minutes for us to meet Kenan in the middle. A dozen or so Lazurites head for the hills. I don't want to take chase. I want to be out of here as soon as possible.

"Let them go!" I order my soldiers.

The dozen or so Lazurites that are left drop their arms and surrender. My army corrals them near the tents. Kenan swaggers towards me, brimming with pride and bravado.

"I told you! We have defeated them!"

I fight the urge to rebuke him, especially in front of his men. "You ever read Sun Tzu's Art of War?"

He frowns. "No, what does that have to do with—"

"It should be required reading for anyone in the military, especially for a general. Particularly the part about deception."

Kenan is still perplexed. "What are you talking about, Sarai? I know I disobeyed you, and for that, I'm sorry. But it worked. We ambushed them. This is a big win for us today. We are that much closer to winning this war!"

I remove my dagger from its sheath and march to the closest HeliDrone.

Kenan raises his hands in the air, still looking confident, still defiant. "What are you doing, Sarai?"

I stab it into the HeliDrone's belly—there is a whoosh of air. The rubber drone shrinks to the ground like a giant deflating balloon. Kenan stands with his jaw open, bewildered, along with his army.

"I... I... don't... I—"

His stutter returns.

My timbre is stern. "*We* are the ones that have been ambushed. Didn't you wonder why the drones weren't attacking? This trickery was textbook. And perhaps you would have known that if you had followed standard conventional battle protocol and taken them out first. Or even better yet, followed orders."

"I... I... am so sorry... I... I should have seen it."

"Now what? Other than eating cheese," my commander queries.

"We have to get out of here as fast as possible," I answer.

"You're not going anywhere," spits a Lazurite elite with a red sash on his chest.

I grab him by his exoarmor and shake him. "What does that mean? What is the plan? Tell me what the trap is?"

"Look," is all he says, smiling.

I look behind me. Way off in the distance, I see small pillars rise from the ground about every fifty yards. I know what this is. It can't be. Can it? Next, a semi-translucent barrier of electricity connects all the pillars. I drop to my knees.

Another Wall.

In an instant, everything we have fought for in the past ten years evaporates. That feeling of dread returns. The feeling of being trapped, physically and mentally. I can see the last remnants of hope waft from my soul and disappear into thin air. Just looking at the electric barrier makes my soul feel caged. The first Wall is what separated Asher and me ten years ago. Now, two walls are keeping us apart, one of them from within.

Kenan pulls me to my feet. I pull out my binoculars and see that The Wall has formed a giant square, encapsulating us for hundreds of miles. Like the first time, my father built it right under our noses. That is why he always sent small forces that hardly engaged us for the past ten years. This is part of what he was doing. I can't imagine what else he has been up to.

The elite smiles. "Like I said, we aren't going anywhere. *Sultana.*"

"Now... now what?" Kenan's words hang over us like a foul odor.

"We die," the elite answers, shrugging his shoulders.

I can no longer contain my rage. I throw the elite to the ground. "How?! Are reinforcements coming? HeliDrones? Or are we to be starved? Tell me!"

"I guess it doesn't matter now if I spill the beans." If the elite is afraid of dying, he doesn't show it. "We are to be nuked."

"Nuclear? He is going to drop a nuclear bomb on us?"

"That's what I'm told."

That seems overkill, even for my father. But if he's as far gone as my mother says he is, he is capable of anything. Maybe he wants to radiate the entire Middle. He hates The Middle. He always has.

At least it will be quick. At least we won't suffer.

I turn to the elite, who seems resigned to his fate. "Why? Why die for my father?"

He fights back emotion. Perhaps he is human after all. "Not for Renatus. For Zion."

"But what is Zion?" I almost whisper, asking myself more than him.

"Zion is a place where my children and my family will be fed, will be safe. That is why I die out here. Wouldn't you die for your family?"

My thoughts go to Silas and Asher. Was he able to save our son? That's all that I have the capacity for right now. It is all so overwhelming I feel paralyzed.

I stumble off into the woods.

"Sarai! Sarai! Where are you going?" Kenan yells, "What are we to do next?"

I can barely hear him; my senses are numb. I don't look back. I trudge further and further. Finally, I break down, my knees hitting the dirt. Tears fall from my eyes like never before. I close my eyes and picture myself fishing with Asher on his small tin boat, while taking in the sweet fragrances of jasmine and lavender. I blink a few times and am immediately taken to our willow tree, where we would spend lazy days, making each other laugh while eating our fresh catch. Was I so naive to think those days would last forever? That war wouldn't follow us wherever we went? Maybe Asher and I are destined to suffer. Maybe this war isn't winnable. Maybe we need to win the war against ourselves first. Maybe the reason protocol changes you, is that somewhere deep down in your subconscious, lives a guilt you cannot shed. The guilt that another was taken so you could live.

I don't hear the HarvestDrone hover above me. The rotors cause the leaves around me to scatter like scared mice—my hair whips at the wind. I don't look up. I no longer have the capacity to deal with what may be next. I just wait for it to happen.

I can barely feel it suck me up into its cold steel belly.

CHAPTER THIRTEEN

Cephas

ADAM PLACES HIS THUMB on the biometric scanner. The computer unlocks.

"Open the doors," Cephas orders.

"Patience," Adam replies. "I haven't used my fingers in a century."

Jude winks at Eve. "You guys look good for being a hundred and forty-five years old."

Cephas nudges him. "Buckethead."

Adam scrolls through a few different menus and windows until he finds what he is looking for.

"There." Adam looks up from his wheelchair. "They are opened."

"Which room has the detonators?" asks Cephas.

Adam looks at the screen. "Number eighteen."

Cephas and Jude begin to head out.

"Wait." Adam puts up his hand. "We need to go to number ten first."

"Why?"

"Let me back up a moment. How did you get here?"

"A boat," Jude replies.

"How big?" Eve inquires.

"Why?"

Adam starts to huff. "Listen, you may think you are in charge here. You may think you know everything about Eden, but you don't."

Cephas folds his arms. "Then educate us."

Eve glances at Adam. "It's better we show them."

They push Adam and Eve down the hallway until they reach the open door of room number ten. Cephas and Jude slowly march inside.

There are a hundred more, just like Adam and Eve, suspended in Cryo chambers.

Adam wheels up next to them. "We call this room the Ark. If there was an apocalypse, this is where we would start over. Fifty males. Fifty females, to repopulate the earth."

"Why aren't you here with them?" Jude asks.

Eve replies, "We are the Operators. The ones in charge." She clears her throat. "Gold and nukes aren't the only thing you're taking back. We are not leaving without them."

Cephas shakes his head. "Our ship isn't big enough."

Adam hoists himself up from his wheelchair. "I was a marine!" He staggers towards Cephas. "I still am a marine. I won't let you pillage Eden and leave them here to die. They are coming with us."

"I don't have room. Listen, we will come back for them. I promise."

Adam falls to the ground. Cephas helps him up and back into his chair. "I promise. We will return for them all."

"Rest assured, I will hold you to it."

Jude pats him on the shoulder. "He is a man of his word."

Adam leans back in his chair. "What, what is the world like now?"

Cephas grunts, "It's dark. We, as humans, went where we didn't belong. We took God out of science. The human brain doesn't have the capacity to act as a deity. We have been stripped of our morals, and what is left is the worst of human nature."

Jude holds up the VHS tapes. "There's no beating the 1980s." Jude digs his tongue in his cheek, "If I were you, I would go back in the icebox."

"Oh, it's not all that bad," Boaz says in a saucy tone, appearing out of nowhere. Next to him are six Lazurite elites holding plasma rifles.

"I knew it!" Cephas barks. "How much are they paying you, Boaz?"

Boaz pats his belly. "More than enough."

"You selfish traitor!" Jude snarls.

Boaz is taken aback. "Traitor? That hurts. How can I be a traitor? I never pledged allegiance to you or your silly Defiance."

"What's happening? What is going on here?" a bewildered Adam asks.

Boaz trudges closer. "What's happening is I am taking the nukes and the gold."

Jude shakes with anger. "Why? Why bring us? Why not just give the map to those stinking CellPirates?"

Boaz sniffs. "I tried that first, but no one could figure out the cipher. That's what we needed you for, my slender little friend."

Eve wheels in closer. "Can someone please tell us what is going on?"

Cephas motions to Boaz and the elites. "It's these people. They are the reason we are here."

"On your knees!" an armed Lazurite demands.

Jude and Cephas drop to their knees. Cephas slowly reaches for his plasma gun tucked in the back of his pants. His lips quiver in rage. All the grief, misery, and tribulation have finally fractured him. For a moment, his faith is set aside. He is brought back to his primal self, his old self.

"Don't," Jude whispers to him. "It's not worth it, he's not worth it. We live to fight another time."

"Hey Boaz." Cephas's restless eyes are like embers, "You think they'll waste a LifeCell on you?"

"What?"

Before Boaz knows what is happening, Cephas shoots him. Boaz stumbles backward, holding his burning arm. The shot wasn't fatal. The Lazurite elites fire at Cephas, but Jude leaps in front of him.

"No!" Cephas screams.

Plasma blasts ring out as Jude's small frame is riddled with them. He falls over onto his back. One elite kicks the gun out of Cephas's hand while the other kicks him in the back of the head. Cephas grabs Jude, swoops him up, and holds him in his arms.

"No! Why? Why Jude?" Tears slide down the scars, cracks, and crevices in his face.

The Lazurites aim their weapons at Cephas. "Don't even think about doing that again."

Boaz holds his burnt arm. He bounces around and whines like a child. "Medic! I need a medic."

The elites shake their heads at his feebleness. "Get yourself a Band-aid, mate."

Cephas holds Jude's limp body in his arms. "C'mon Jude, wake up, wake up Jude. Please wake up." Cephas rocks him back and forth. "Why Jude? Why did you have to go and do that? It was supposed to be me, not you. Wake up!" Cephas blinks away tears and whispers into his ear, "I should have been a better friend, Jude. I should have been a better friend."

Jude's eyes flutter open, his breathing slow and sporadic. "Spoken like a true buckethead."

Cephas strokes his hair. "There's my Jude."

"I told you not to."

"I'm sorry, Jude. I'm sorry. I should have listened."

"Stubborn Cephas. Always stubborn."

"I know, I'm sorry, I—"

"Will you shut up for a second? Make sure you do me this one favor," Jude stutters, his breathing sporadic. "Don't bring me back. Whatever you do: Do. Not. Bring. Me. Back."

"You don't have to worry about that, 'cause you're not dying."

"And one other thing, win this war. Once and for all, finish this. Make sure Asher and Sarai never give up." Jude's voice cracks. "Oh, and I almost forgot—Linda, from your rehab group. Will you stop being so daft and finally ask her out? For some silly reason, she likes you." Then his eyes roll to the back of his head. His breathing stops. A smile still on his face. It's fitting his last words were in jest.

"No, Jude! No! Wake up, will ya! Don't leave me, Jude!"

An elite spits, "He's dead, mate, and you're next if you don't quit your damn bloody blubbering."

"You two should get a room," another elite chuckles.

Adam and Eve stare at Boaz and the elites, and are physically revolted. Now they understand the evil Cephas was talking about, and what they are up against. They can only wonder what the rest of humanity is like since they have been under.

Cephas ignores the taunting and holds Jude's dead, listless body in his arms and rocks him back and forth. He was a brother to him. His sardonic friend. His only friend, really. Besides his wife, Jude was the only one he could be completely honest with. They were like brothers. Jude was the softer side of Cephas's hard edge. No one liked Jude's cooking, but everyone liked him. He could tell you the truth without making you feel bad or judged. He could also lampoon you and somehow make it feel like a compliment. He was always there when Cephas needed to unburden himself. He also took the brunt of Cephas's acid tongue.

Cephas shakes his head and wonders what he was thinking. Of course, they would shoot back. Of course, Jude would take a bullet for him—or in this case, a plasma blast. Seeing Boaz and those elites come in and take over finally busted him. Cephas finally popped.

Everyone has a breaking point.

Cephas has hit his.

Asher

I watch as they drag Legion's dead body from the arena. Apex nonchalantly peruses the bloody battlegrounds, studying its sadistic contraptions as if he is shopping for a new lawn mower. He sticks his bloody fingers in his mouth and sucks them clean, like a kid with chocolate-stained digits. He is a savage. They both are.

I turn to Renatus.

"You enjoy watching a good man die?"

"Not to worry, mate, I'm bringing him back. Like I said, this was just a preview, a warm-up. You think I would waste Apex versus Legion without an audience? When I am finished with you and my daughter's little uprising, we will have the greatest Canonization yet. Brother versus brother."

"And if he won't fight again?"

"He just needs the proper motivation."

It slightly comforts me to know that Legion will be coming back. But at what cost? Whose LifeCell? And will he be the same? Sooner or later, will he just be another Apex? Has Apex died before? Is that why he is so vile? Is it because he, too, has gone through protocol more than once? Although unlikely, who could kill Apex? Unless, of course, he is a thrill seeker, like Renatus.

"Motivation? You just had his cousin killed, his only family. You have taken everything from him that he cares about."

Renatus smiles. "Not you."

"Is that why I'm here? Is that why I'm still alive? He won't fight his own brother for me; trust me, he doesn't love me that much."

"That is where you are wrong. Legion needs a cause in his life, someone to fight for. First, it was me. Now, it's you. You will fight again, Asher. In case you have forgotten, you were a fan favorite ten years ago. Vanquisher of the once almighty Legion. Who knows? Maybe one day you will beat even Apex. Albeit unlikely, mate, but you have a way about you, a way of surviving. Brains over brawn. Or perhaps you are just lucky?"

"And why would I fight? You are about to take everything I care about as well. What motivation would I have?"

He is pacing again. I can almost smell evil wafting from his sweaty brow. "It is true, your uncle will die at Eden. Your army will be obliterated at Reservation 13. Well, all but one."

Sarai.

"So if I don't fight, you will kill your own daughter?"

Renatus suddenly loses it, like flipping a switch. He slams his fist against the table, screams, and spits in my ear, his face crimson red. I can almost see the steam rising from his glossy, smooth head. I can feel the heat from his shaved, satiny face.

"SHE IS NO LONGER MY DAUGHTER!" He swallows vast gasps of air, snot drizzling from his nose. "When she hitched her wagon to you and your bloody Defiance, she ceased being my blood. She is a simple traitor of Zion. A Dreck. She deserves a traitor's death."

"And if I decide to fight and win, then what?"

His anger switches to a rabid laugh. "Asher, oh Asher. If you defeat Apex, I will hand you the keys to my kingdom. I did that once already, didn't I?"

Perhaps I do have a bargaining chip. "My son. If I win, you can keep your kingdom. I just want my son."

"No."

"Then I won't fight," I say, hoping my gambit pays off.

"Then you and Sarai both die."

I grit my teeth. "Then we both die."

Renatus raises a bushy eyebrow, surprised. "Really? You would make that choice for her?"

"You don't know your daughter, but I know my wife. She would agree with me. We would gladly sacrifice ourselves if it meant a chance at saving

Silas. Besides, we don't fear death in the way you do, not absolute death anyway."

"You think I fear death?"

"Why else would you use protocol?"

"I don't fear death, Asher. I fear dying without having once again held my Eleazar, watching him fish on my boat, and once again swim in my ocean. You misjudge me. You misjudge my motivations. You can't beat what you don't understand. That is why you'll lose."

"What you said about Eleazar—that is exactly how I feel about your grandson. Please, don't do this to Silas. You can break this never-ending cycle of generational death right now. I beg you to spare my son."

Renatus raises his hands. "Well, too late."

"What do you mean, too late?"

Renatus presses a button, and on the giant HoloTube is my son. He is floating in the pink gel substance. Next to him is Eleazar, also suspended in the same material. He is preparing them for protocol. He is going to take Silas's LifeCell! I begin to shake in rage. My vision blurs; all I see is red.

"No, don't do this. You don't have to do this. There has to be another way."

"Oh, Asher. Remember when I told you that when you had a son of your own, you would do anything for him?"

"That is your grandson!" I scream. "How could you do that to your blood?"

"Sarai is no longer my daughter, so what does that make Silas?"

I plead with him. "Listen, you don't have to do this. You can come back from this. It's not too late, Renatus. You can still be good. This, this whole thing, the way you are, it's not your fault. It's protocol. It warps the mind. It causes evil. Your daughter and I have seen it firsthand. Our scientists have proved it changes the brain. Ask your scientists; they will tell you the truth if you let them. It's not your fault, Renatus. It's not too late."

He scoffs. "You have made the improper assumption that I don't like who I am. I think I have finally self-actualized."

"You don't realize it's happening! Please, Renatus, it's not too late; we could be family again. Like you wanted. You could have your daughter back. Your wife. Your grandson. We can help you. We could reunite this country."

Renatus gives me a sideways stare as if he is actually contemplating it. "You had your chance." Then he picks up a red phone on the desk.

"Begin the process."

His protocol engineers, in their red suits, hook the LifeCell transfer tubes between Eleazar and my son.

"No!" I bawl. "No!"

The computer systems linked to my son and Eleazar beep and chirp. I see purple fluid begin to snake its way into the tube. Renatus places his hand on the HoloTube screen.

"My *wounded* prince is coming home. Finally, after all this time."

"Stop! Please stop!" I beg. "Listen, I will fight. I will do whatever you want. Just wait, just hold off. What do you have to lose?"

He looks at me, waiting.

"You said yourself, I have no chance of defeating Apex. Please, hold off, and I will fight. And when Apex defeats me, you can do what you want."

He is either contemplating or toying with me.

I appeal to his sadistic nature, his thirst for blood. "It will be the show of the century. A Canonization no Lazurite will ever forget. It will bring Zion back to its past glory. You will be exalted once again. You won't regret it. Please."

He rolls his head and speaks in a creepy sing-song voice. "My cake and eat it too?"

"Yes, and all the frosting. It will be the spectacle people will talk about for generations to come."

"And you will give it your all? And convince Legion to do the same?"

I once again speak his language. "Yes, it will be a spectacular display of bloodshed and violence."

He rubs his chin, "Hmm... but you're getting old Asher."

"And wiser. What did you tell me? 'Brains over brawn.'"

He can't help himself. As much as he loves his son, he also loves his Canonization. He picks up the red phone. "Stop. For now."

I sigh in relief. I have bought some time. But my joy for temporarily saving my son is short-lived. Renatus picks up a blue phone.

"Prepare the nukes."

Kenan

"Where is she?" Sarai's commander asks.

Kenan shrugs. "I don't know. It's like she just vanished out of thin air."

Kenan and a group of Dreck soldiers scanned the entire area for almost a full day, searching for Sarai.

"She wouldn't just leave us."

"She... she... she was taken. She had to be," Kenan deduces.

Kenan's stomach flutters, his stubborn stutter still sticking around. His men take notice and eye him, still unsure of his leadership. They know it's because of him they are in their current predicament. With Sarai now gone, he is the top-ranking officer here. He feels like he is going to vomit. He is now responsible for the lives of these men. They are trapped behind four massive walls that can't be scaled. Nuclear annihilation is on its way, death from above.

Get it together, Kenan. I have to lead. Fear is a tool of the enemy. Time to step up and lead. What would Asher do? What would Sarai do?

"What about drones? Can we use their drones to fly over the wall?" suggests the commander.

"They're all rubber," Kenan reminds him.

"Oh, right."

"Besides, we would need a hundred of them to get us all over in time."

The Lazurite elite would not tell Kenan when they would be attacked. He claimed he did not know. All he said was that it was imminent. Kenan racks his brain. He is good with geography. And like Jude, he is a student of history. He has a realization.

"Map. I need a map."

His commander brings him one, and they unfurl it before them.

"Here." Kenan points to the map. "Forty miles southeast of us."

"What?"

"Cheyenne Mountain."

The commander looks confused.

"NORAD," Kenan tells him with a smile.

"You think it's inside the wall?"

"One way to find out."

"You think we can get there in time?"

"One way to find out." Kenan rolls up the map and jumps onto a tree stump. "We are moving out! Only take food and water, minimal weaponry. We will be marching at a fast clip."

"Where to?" one of his men yells from the back.

"NORAD."

"NORAD? That facility is no longer operational. It has been abandoned for years," declares one of his skeptical captains.

Kenan clears his throat and fights back the urge to stutter. "That is true. But all we need to do is get inside. Deep in Cheyenne Mountain is a massive underground bunker built to withstand a nuclear blast. But we must hurry."

"How do we know it's not locked?" another captain asks.

"We will deal with that when we get there. Unless you have a better idea?"

"Asher would!" one of his soldiers yells.

"Yes! What would Asher do?" another bellows.

Kenan sighs and realizes that his men still don't trust him, and would rather fight for Asher. He can't blame them after leading them into the trap they are now caught in.

"Yes, what would Asher do, indeed? Listen, I understand I am no Asher. I don't pretend to be. In fact, I never will be. All I can do is do the best I can. What would Asher do? I can't answer that. What I do know is he wouldn't just stay here. I realize we are in this current predicament because of me. I am asking you to trust me to lead you out of it. I am open to hearing other ideas. This isn't about rank anymore. This is about our survival. This is about going back to our families and living on to fight another day. The best idea wins. Anybody?"

Silence. He wonders if Asher would be proud, but doesn't have time to dwell on it. His speech seems to work for now.

"Then let's get moving."

His army hurries to gather the essentials. Kenan approaches the Lazurite elite. "You and your men are welcome to come with us. You don't have to die here. You will be treated well."

The elite spits. "I'd rather die here than huddle in a bloody bunker with a bunch of feck-witted Drecks."

"Suit yourself."

One of his captains approaches Kenan. "What if they alert Renatus of our plan? We can't just leave them here, alive."

Kenan thinks for a moment that he doesn't want to kill them, but forcing them to march with them will only slow them down; he rubs his broad chin, "Find and destroy any means of communication."

"Leaving them here is risky, General."

"What isn't? Now get moving, Captain."

Five hours into their trek, they make a quick pit stop. Kenan wonders if they will make it time. Or if Cheyenne Mountain is actually inside the wall's border. He peers ahead with his binoculars and doesn't see it yet. *Maybe coming here was a mistake?* But he can't see the other side of the wall yet, either, so there is still hope.

After another hour, they go over another mountain, and Kenan checks again. He can see Cheyenne Mountain. And it's inside the wall! He tells his men the good news, causing them to pick up their pace. Even though they are exhausted, this lifts their spirits and gives them all a jolt of much-needed energy.

Kenan is constantly checking the sky for incoming missiles or drones. *Just hold off for a few more hours.*

Two and half hours later, they stand in front of the tunnel that burrows into the mountain. Kenan peers at the iconic sign: 'CHEYENNE MOUNTAIN COMPLEX.'

"We made it; now, let's hope we can get in," his commander states.

They march into the tunnel, and the massive five-foot-thick steel door is open. At the beginning of the war between The Defiance and Zion, NORAD was among the first places to be plundered. Renatus got there first. Its nukes and other computer systems were taken and moved from The Middle. Luckily for Kenan and his army, they didn't bother to close the door on their way out.

Kenan smiles inwardly. He did it. They made it. He finally made a tactical decision that so far has panned out. He hopes that perhaps this will earn him a bit of respect with the men he has been tasked to lead. If not, at least they live on to see another day.

"This way." Kenan motions to his soldiers as they wearily march by him. Everyone, including himself, is ready for food and shuteye.

He looks out to the horizon and sees what looks like shooting stars slowly streak across the sky. But he knows what they are.

Four ballistic missiles.

Cephas

Cephas and the rest of his band watch as the elites load up all of the gold and nuclear warheads into carts and wheel them out.

"Is that all of them?" Boaz asks one of the Lazurites.

"Yes, your Highness," he responds sarcastically, patting Boaz on his injured shoulder.

Boaz winces as he approaches Cephas. "I'm sorry, Cephas. I truly am."

"Sorry? You're sorry? That's a joke, you snake."

"What is to become of us?" Eve asks.

"You are to be permanent residents of Eden," Boaz tells her.

"Wonderful." Cephas rolls his eyes.

"You should be thanking me," Boaz replies, genuinely believing it.

Cephas's face turns blood red. "Thanking you!" He grabs Boaz by the throat. "Because of you, Jude is dead!"

"Actually, it is because of you," Boaz shoots back. Cephas tightens his grip.

The elites aim their weapons at Cephas. "Release him."

Cephas ponders it momentarily, then loosens his calloused hand from Boaz's pudgy neck.

Boaz rubs his neck, choking. "Look, they wanted to kill you. I convinced them to leave you here."

Cephas shakes his head. "Locked in here? So we can slowly starve to death? Sounds like Renatus's idea, you slithering vermin!"

"There is enough protein slurry stored here to last you years. I'm sorry, Cephas, nothing personal. Just business."

"Ain't it always so with you, Boaz."

Before they leave, the Lazurites shoot up all the computers and electrical systems in the control room. Then Boaz and the elites march towards the exit.

"Hey Boaz." Cephas's words barely grind through his thick teeth. "I will see you again one day. And it will be personal, not business."

The look in Cephas's eyes sends a flutter of fear through Boaz's stomach. He doesn't respond. Instead, they march out of Eden and shut the massive steel door, locking them inside.

Adam and Eve waste no time wheeling themselves into the control room. Cephas follows.

"It's destroyed," Adam informs them, inspecting the computers still melting and smoking from the plasma blasts. "There is no way we can open the door from the inside. Eden is now a tomb."

"And what of this protein slurry?" Cephas asks, his tone surly.

Eve turns to him. "It's what keeps us alive in Cryo. Although we need twenty times that amount to stay healthy once awake than when our body is frozen."

"How much do we have?"

Adam does some quick math in his head. "Let's see, there are twelve of us total, and if we used what is left from myself and Eve... hmm... I would say about four months' worth."

Daniel, the engineer, pipes up. "A hundred times that."

Eve looks at him. "What do you mean?"

"There are a hundred more still in Cryo. What about their slurry?"

"You suggesting we take their sustenance?" Adam asks.

"Not suggesting anything, just going over our options."

Everyone is thinking about those *options*—their dilemma. Starve to death in a few months, or take what is keeping the people frozen in Cryo alive.

Well, everyone but Cephas.

"We will not kill those people," Cephas states plainly. He then slogs out of the control room.

Three hours later, Cephas is in the room where Jude had died in his arms. His lifeless body now lies on a makeshift cot.

"Why did you have to go and do that, string bean?"

Cephas drops to one knee. A lone tear emerges from his bloodshot eyes. *I should have asked him more questions. I should have asked how he was doing. He wasn't just that sarcastic, jovial fellow; there was more to him. I always took for granted that he would be that festive and cheery rock. He always put up with me. Was always there for me. I was self-centered, nothing more.*

Cephas places a blanket over his head. "Goodbye, my friend."

He sits down next to him, completely crestfallen. He thinks of protocol and how that could bring Jude back, but that Godforsaken technology is what started this whole damn war to begin with.

That is a line Cephas won't cross.

Speaking of battling demons.

Adam rolls in. In his lap is a bottle of bourbon.

"I was saving this in my personal stash for when I was awoken. Like to join me and see how well this stuff has aged?"

Cephas eyes the bottle, and the caramel-colored alcohol swirling inside it. It is calling for him—a daily battle since he quit twenty years ago.

"No, I... I uh... "

Cephas closes his eyes; his spirit is broken, his soul crippled. "Oh, what the hell."

Cephas snatches the bottle from him. His eyes squeeze shut as his throat burns. Adam watches as he guzzles it.

"Whoa, easier there, big guy. Save some for me."

He hands the half-empty bottle back to Adam. Two decades of being sober go down his throat, literally. The fight in him is gone. His faith is tested like never before. He can't figure out the point of it all anymore. Has all of this just been a test of his conviction? Or does he still have a purpose?

"I'm sorry about your friend. He seemed like a good guy," Adam offers.

Cephas manages a grunt.

Adam takes a sip. "It's ironic that we have seeds for every fruit and vegetable imaginable, but we are going to starve to death."

Cephas laughs. "Dreck life."

Adam knits his hairless eyebrows together. "What?"

"I'll explain another time."

Adam takes another sip. "Can't believe it's been a hundred and twenty years. My great-grandchild would be older than me if I had any. It boggles the mind to think about. I have been asleep for more than an entire generation."

Cephas scoffs. "You want your mind blown? Wait until you hear more about protocol. The Wall. The Canonization." His eyes grow dark. "Narcdrops."

"Tell me. I have nothing better to do."

"Later."

"I have to ask, are Chicken Nuggets still a thing? I would kill for some McDonald's French fries."

"Never heard of it, but I'm sure Jude could have told you all about it."

"I'm sorry about your friend."

Cephas clears his throat. "So Eve, is she... is she your—"

"Wife? Yes. We got married right before we went under."

"That's a helluva honeymoon you guys have had."

Adam laughs. "You know, the first time I met her was here. We were told our genetics would make the best pairing to re-populate the earth if need be. I told her that due to my faith, we would need to get married first. She agreed; then we were put on ice." Adam is now deep in thought, "Ya know, when I took this job, I knew I would never see my family or friends again. And that if I were ever to be awoken and actually experience life, it would only be because we had a holocaust of some sort. Some life, huh?"

"What on earth possessed you to take this job?"

"Good question." Adam pauses, tongue in cheek. "Maybe it's because I don't like people."

Cephas manages a smile. "I can relate to that. And what did you do before you went under?"

"I was a Marine who studied biophysics and molecular biology. Eve was a nuclear physicist."

"Quite the resumes. If we ever get out of here, I'm sure we could use you one day."

Adam takes another swig. "What about you? You married?"

"Was once."

"Want to talk about it?"

"No."

Another tear tumbles down Cephas's weather-beaten face and splashes onto the frigid, callous concrete. His despondency stifles any guilt he might be feeling. Has everything really been for naught? He turns to Adam.

"You have any more?"

CHAPTER FOURTEEN

Kenan

K ENAN LEADS THEM INSIDE NORAD's command center. The massive video screens and computers have either been smashed or stolen. The place looks like it has been ransacked.

"This way!" his commander tells him.

Kenan and what's left of his army hurry down another concrete hallway. There seem to be hundreds of them.

"Hurry everyone!" Kenan yells out as he lets his men pass. He will be the last in the bunker. Asher's words dance in his head: *First on the battlefield, last to leave. To lead your men is to serve your men.*

His commander holds a map of the facility that he found inside one of the offices.

"Down these stairs."

They trudge down a long, narrow set of concrete stairs until they reach another hallway. At the end of that is another massive steel door. One of his men peers up at the lights.

"How do we have power?"

"Must be nuclear powered," Kenan assumes.

The commander pulls a lever next to the entrance. The steel door slowly slides open.

"Everyone in!" Kenan waves his hand. "Hurry now."

His depleted army takes a few minutes to file through the door. Kenan follows them inside and pulls another lever. The door slides shut with a definitive thud. One of the men flicks on the lights. The fluorescent tubes buzz awake. Hundreds of cots line the room, thin bedding still neatly folded on top of them. There are also numerous storage closets as well as a massive communal bathroom.

Then they hear it.

Muffled but massive explosions. Four of them. The bunker shakes—flakes of cement rattle from the ceilings. The lights above them sway back and forth, like they are at the epicenter of a strong earthquake. Dust dances on the floor.

Kenan sweats, hoping that the bunker will hold. Hoping that he didn't just lead his men into an underground tomb.

"How old is this place?" a soldier wonders.

Kenan doesn't answer. He peers up at the ceiling, as if staring at it will hold it in place. He takes a wide stance as if his feet will steady the foundation. His arms are up, his palms facing the walls, as though to prevent them from crashing. The thundering rumble descends upon them, as the decibel count surges. The shock wave must be right above them now. It sounds as if a train is running directly above them.

"It's not gonna hold," a young soldier whispers and heads for the door.

"No. Just wait," Kenan orders him. He then closes his eyes and says a prayer.

The lights flicker as the tremors continue.

They finally stop. There is an eerie silence for a long minute. Then, a collective exhale.

"I think that's it. I think we survived it," Kenan whispers.

After a few subdued cheers, one of his men asks, "Now what? What do we do now, sir?"

"Take inventory," Kenan orders them.

They spend the next three hours perusing the giant bunker and all of its storage closets. They find dried food, canned food, and MREs. There are several sinks and filters linked to several underground wells. Along with that are vitamins, especially Vitamin D, for their lack of sunlight. Another room contains games, books, televisions, and VHS movies.

"We should be good on water," his commander informs him.

"And food?" Kenan's tone is hopeful.

"For the number of us down here, maybe six months. Perhaps more if we are strict on rations."

"Then we will be strict."

Kenan thinks of Cephas and Jude and wonders if they found Eden. Ironically, his predicament was very similar to Cephas's, thousands of miles north of him. He wondered if Asher and Legion were successful and if he was the only one that failed. And what of Sarai? Was she really taken or just lost? Did he leave her there in The Middle to die? Should he have looked for her longer than they did?

His guilt dissipates as he realizes if they had, he would not have gotten his men here in time. For once, he has made the right decision.

Kenan's mind shifts from their current situation to the thousands living in all the towns, small and large, near where the bombs went off. How could Renatus do this to so many innocents? He never dreamed that he would take it to this level. To nuke his own country, his own people.

His commander sits beside him and whispers, "What do we do when we run out of food?"

Kenan shakes his head. "We can't just walk out of here. The radiation levels will still be too high. Did you find any radiation suits?"

"No. Maybe we will be rescued?"

"Maybe."

"But no one knows we are here."

"See what kind of communications this place still has, if any," Kenan tells him.

"And if we find some, who do we even call?" the commander asks skeptically.

An avalanche of uncertainty and doubt suddenly overwhelms Kenan. *I shouldn't be here. Asher should have never made me a general. I can't lead these men.*

"I don't know." Kenan then looks around and realizes the seeds of his doubts are now permeating the room. To survive, he must convince them that they will make it through this. He must convince himself.

He clears his throat. "We will figure this out. We won't die in here." Some of them buy it. Some of them don't.

At that moment, Kenan realizes he hasn't slept for two days. He plods to the nearest cot and lays his weary body down. It feels as if weights are attached to his eyelids. He cannot fight it anymore. His eyes close.

It only takes a moment, and he is fast asleep. He dreams that it is all a nightmare, that he will wake up soon to a world where men like Renatus do not exist. No protocol. No Zion. No Wall. Where even the idea of narcdrops seems implausible.

He will wake up to the America his great-grandfather told him about. The one he read about. A united country. A free country.

A country where you only lived and died once. And because of that, you make every minute count.

Sarai

"Good morning, Sultana."

I am awoken by a maid who opens my shades. She is dressed in red and black. She is young and slender, with fearful eyes and a timid timbre.

I am in my bed. My old bed with the purple satin sheets and the ridiculous amount of pillows. I blink in confusion as I peer around my old room, in my father's castle at Pt. Reyes. I glance out the window and see the ocean's fingers wrap around the jagged rocks. Over and over, the salty water unsuccessfully grasps the craggy earth, before retreating to try once more.

Has it all been a dream? The war? The Defiance? Asher? Silas? Am I still a Sultana, waiting to be married off at my father's Canonization? I feel like I have been asleep for a month. Then I peer into the mirror and see the lines on my face that have manifested in the past ten years, and I know they are not a dream. My nightmare is real. My eyes are bloodshot and puffy. I have been crying.

The maid pours me some tea. Her hands shake, and she won't look me in the eye. "Good day, my Sultana."

Now I remember my dreadful situation. I have been here for three months. I have hardly left my room. I feel like a teenager who is once again in trouble for escaping to The Middle. How is it that in the past decade, we have lost everything we have fought for and more? Looking around my old room, I realize my life has been one giant circle. I am back where I started—except I am a bit wiser, sadder, and jaded. I thought our sacrifice would mean something.

My maid opens another set of blinds. I stop her.

"Please, leave them closed." I am not ready for the light.

"Of course, my Sultana."

"And please, call me Sarai."

She slightly nods and has a look as if to say that would be improper, that perhaps she would be in trouble for skipping any formality.

"What is your name?" I ask her.

"I am... I am Elizabeth. I am new here," she stutters.

"Thank you, Elizabeth."

Thirty minutes later, I eat poached eggs and smoked salmon at an absurdly large table. My father sits across from me, slowly chewing his salmon.

"How did you sleep, dear?" Renatus asks me like everything is normal. As if we are one happy family. To a monster like him, forced love is still love.

"Fine," I reply coldly. He has my son. He dangles his life over my head. I have to play along.

"Spoken to your mother?"

I don't look at him. "No, I haven't."

He slurps the yoke of his egg into his mouth. "You will need to change that, my daughter. Now that you are here, surely she will come."

He is deluded, worse than before. "I will talk to her."

"Good."

"But I can't force her to come."

He stops chewing and looks at me as if I just said something stupid or ignorant. He has been forcing people to do his bidding for so long that it is now his usual mode of operation.

I quickly recover. "I will do my best."

He has been keeping Silas in the newly renovated portion of The Mountain. He has moved everything back here. His base of operations. He prefers it here in the West, over the East Coast.

"Silas, I want to see him," I ask daily.

"Not yet, dear."

"Why not?"

"Because I would be rewarding you."

"Haven't I done everything you have asked of me since coming back here?" I plead with him.

"Yes, but we must wait and see that your husband does the same."

He is talking about The Canonization. Asher has promised to fight in exchange for our son.

"Today is the big day!" My father wrings his hands until his knuckles are white.

Doesn't matter if Asher wins or dies today. I can't trust my father to keep his promise. I need to figure out another way to save my son.

And as for Asher, I am certain that, whether he wins or loses, my father will kill him.

Asher

It is so loud my eardrums throb. The arena is packed full. It seems fans of The Canonization have missed watching others spill blood for the past ten years.

I take stock of the arena. Similar to Renatus's test run, there are tigers, lions, and pits of hot oil. It is truly perverse and outlandish. If I had not seen it with my own eyes before, I would now think it is an illusion. I have a StunClub in one hand and my ricochet in the other.

The crowd chants, "Apex! Apex! Apex!"

A band of elites in the first row beat their war drums. Then, the crowd turns silent. Renatus enters into the Sultan's luxury box, half way up the arena. He wafts his hand back and forth like he is some Roman Emperor. Boaz follows and plops himself down next to Renatus. I scowl. I can't believe I trusted him. Does my faith in the ability of man to do good have no limits? I get that from my father.

The next to enter is Sarai.

I haven't seen her since I left to rescue Silas. He has kept us apart. She is dressed to the nines in full Sultana gear. A sparkling white dress with a blood-red sash down the middle. Her hair is done up into a braided mohawk. Maroon makeup flares from the corner of her eyes. I am feeling déjá-vu. Wasn't I just here ten years ago?

Sarai peers down at me, and I can tell in her eyes that whatever she is doing is forced. Like me, she is doing it for Silas. I can't help but notice the sadness in her eyes, almost as if she is saying goodbye. But I am comforted to know that she and Silas are still alive. For now.

That comfort is short-lived.

Renatus stands and speaks into a microphone. His voice echoes throughout the stadium.

"Welcome, everyone. After ten long years, I welcome you back to the Canonization!"

Raucous cheers from the crowd.

"You may remember a fan favorite." He points down at me. "Asher, Son of Silas!"

They boo me and call me a traitor to Zion. But then Renatus talks me up; he is setting the stage.

"The only man to ever defeat the mighty Legion!" Renatus pats the air with his hands, trying to silence the crowd. He loves the sound of his voice. "Well, today we have even something greater!"

The crowd has already heard the rumor. They continue to chant, "Apex! Apex!"

"That's correct, my fellow Lazurites. Legion's younger, yet bigger, brother. Apex!"

THUMP. THUMP. The war drums start up again. My heart beats in rhythm with them. A concrete wall slides open. Slower than it needs to be, adding to the tension. Smoke drifts out for effect.

After it clears, I see him. He somehow looks bigger than the last time I saw him. I was lucky to beat Legion ten years ago. I knew his weakness. I don't know what Apex's is, or if he even has one.

I peer up and see Renatus is almost drooling with blood lust. Sarai is doing her best to remain strong, but I spot a lone tear drizzling down her cheek. Boaz licks his lips. Apex holds no weapons. He doesn't need them. He casually strolls towards me as the drums get louder and louder.

THUMP. THUMP. THUMP.

I close my eyes and try to concentrate, steeling myself. When I do, all I can see is our Weeping Willow. It has been scorched black from the nuclear blasts. Most of its strands look like charred candle wicks.

But it still stands.

Any normal person would be in acute terror right now. But I'm not normal. Not anymore. I am long past fear. I have no room for it. I have no time for it. I have been through so much it no longer has a hold on me. Have I become so hardened?

I open my eyes to see Apex picking up his pace. He is charging towards me like an enraged bull. A fog of dirt forms at his heels. He is a tornado of death—hell on earth. Even if I win, I don't believe it will save Silas.

Soon, his LifeCell will be taken.

Sarai is held captive.

Cephas and Jude are dead.

Kenan and my army were annihilated.

Conventional wisdom says there is no way I can defeat Apex, much less survive.

Cephas would tell me, "When all hope is lost, what do we have left?"

Faith.

ACKNOWLEDGMENTS

First and foremost, I want to thank my readers for once again following Asher and Sarai on this journey. I know your time and money are valued, and I am humbled that you have again decided to join The Defiance. I also want to thank my crew of beta readers: Clint, Nancy, Jessalynn, and anyone else I might have forgotten. Your valuable insight and support are very much appreciated. Speaking of support, I must thank my wife, Erica, who has patiently championed and encouraged me throughout this process. On days I feel like I'm going up against Apex, she reminds me that with enough faith, the Davids of this world can beat the Goliaths.

To my children, Noah, Madelynn, and Marshall: You are my inspiration. Stay true and keep the faith. Keep that tenacious spirit and follow your calling. Lastly, I would like to thank God for giving me the creativity, confidence, and desire to write. I am not clever enough to do this on my own.

I eagerly look forward to sharing the next chapter of Asher and Sarai's odyssey with you in book three. Your continued support and enthusiasm mean the world to me, and I can't wait to see you there!

If you enjoyed this novel and are so inclined, any reviews would be greatly appreciated!

If you would like to stay informed on my upcoming novels and other news, feel free to subscribe to my mailing list:

https://www.BrianAlanPenn.com/#contact

www.ingramcontent.com/pod-product-compliance
Lightning Source LLC
Chambersburg PA
CBHW020339010826
48970CB00012B/1751